FIGHTING DOWN
INTO THE KINGDOM OF DREAMS

Fighting Down into the Kingdom of Dreams

ROBIN WYATT DUNN

Published by
JOHN OTT

San Diego

First Published 2014

© Robin Wyatt Dunn 2014

"The Dream of the Rat" first appeared in the Spring 2013 issue of *Yellow Medicine Review*, © Robin Wyatt Dunn, 2013.

There has not yet been a democracy on the face of this planet, with the possible exception of our paleolithic ancestors. May one come this century.

Cover art by Barbara Sobczyńska

ISBN 978-1-940830-02-5

Library of Congress Control Number: XXXX

Learn more about the author at www.robindunn.com

For my cousins,
Dan, Geoff, Kate, Tess, Emma, Tyler and Perry.

And for Richard Adams, just for the hell of it.

Ing wæs ærest • mid Est-Denum
Gesewen secgum, • oþ he siððan est
Ofer wæg gewat; • wæn æfter ran;
Þus heardingas • þone hæle nemdun.

Ing was at the earliest • together with the East Danes;
Beheld by warriors; • Until he later eastwards;
Upon course of action departed • ran in pursuit of a vehicle.
Thus the Hard Ones • the man named

— The Old Inglish Rune Poem

Unscrew the locks from the doors!
Unscrew the doors themselves from their jambs!
Whoever degrades another degrades me,
And whatever is done or said returns at last to me.
Through me the afflatus surging and surging, through me the
        current and index.
I speak the pass-word primeval, I give the sign of democracy,
By God! I will accept nothing which all cannot have their
        counterpart of on the same terms.

— Walt Whitman, *Leaves of Grass*.

My body carries on; it ages. This record is for myself; for you too. Be gentle with me. I've been gentle with you, though it wasn't easy. We can work together now, as though we were stars, making light.

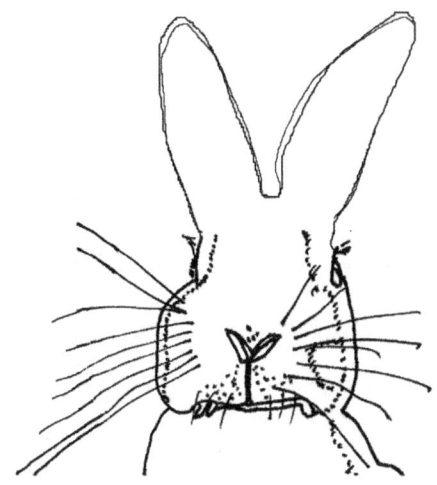

Table of Contents

n a beginning,

When you were a child, you knew only your mother's voice. You knew no words, only her sounds. You knew that all stories were part of the same story, that the knight was always the moon, that the moon was always a brave knight. You knew that Berlin was London, and that New York was the Rat City called Roth, that all cities were one and the same city.

Remember what you knew. Come with me. And with Hrothbert, down into our several Earths:

BOOK ONE
Fighting Down for Ing

he

Wight had descended into the earth. The smear of peat and duff cut down into the forest floor, a dark ramp. At its bottom Hrothbert could see a door.

Hrothbert was no longer a priest; he had left his religion behind him. As he had left his love. But now he wished for his cassock again, to take away his fear.

The door opened a crack. A *nedding* crept out, its dark limbs poised and shining. Its skin was black and its green eyes were dark as lake mud. It crawled up to Hrothbert and looked at him with wide eyes.

"Hello," said the *nedding*.

Hrothbert swallowed, then managed: "Hello."

"I'm hungry," said the being. Hroth tossed a crumb of bread at the *nedding*, who caught it in its wet mouth.

It swallowed, making a gurgling sound. "The sun's wings," it said.

"Can you show me the way in?" said Hroth.

"Yes," it said. Its voice was careful.

"Are there many of you?" he asked the *nedding*.

"Are there many of Ing's men here?" it asked back.

Hroth made the sign of Ing without thinking and realized his mistake. The *nedding* was no ally, unless he made it one.

The *nedding* smiled; it was older than it looked. Hrothbert felt weak suddenly. If he was to do this deed, a deed not unlike what Ing did long ago, he would need to sharpen his wits.

He felt a breeze, and though he had left his religion behind as Ing had left behind the Hard Ones, it seemed a sign his time was running out.

"Take me inside, *nedding*," he said, and the *nedding* smiled and went into the earth.

* * *

You may have heard this tale before. I must tell it anyway, because it was told to me, though I play a part in this version. Tales know no end; they are fire.

Hrothbert was an outcast. To the men of Ing, this was like being dead. I have been outcast too; but I return. I am returned to you. Do you remember me?

*   *   *

He stepped inside the wooden door and the *nedding* vanished. Hrothbert's breathing quickened. He saw a stone rectangle, set into the earthen wall. Below it a ditch. On the stone was the mark of Frey, and Hrothbert knelt before the rune and whispered a prayer.

Below the mark of Frey was another sigil, written in soot, one he did not recognize. Roots snaked down into the ditch. Hrothbert pulled on them; they felt strong. He began to climb down, his eyes adjusting to the dark.

*   *   *

With the last slivers of light from above, Hroth made out the earth below the roots, and hopped down. He landed in a crouch, and smelled the air. It smelled like food somehow, and lake water. He felt ready. Though all this would likely mean his death.

*   *   *

"What will you do?" she had said.

"I will come back for you," had been his words. But her eyes had doubted him.

*   *   *

Hrothbert reached into his purse for a candle but stopped when he saw the *nedding* watching him.

"Nedding!" he said. The *nedding* smiled. Hrothbert saw it was not the same one; it had different, angrier eyes.

"Human!" it said.

"I don't mean you harm."

"No?" it said.

"I'm looking for something," Hrothbert said.

The *nedding* said nothing, but wrinkled its lip slightly.

"What do you want, the maze? The enemy?" it said, in a voice like spitting.

"What would you suggest, cousin?" Hrothbert said.

"Cousin," it said.

6

"What is your name?"

"Name?" it said.

"How are you called?"

"*Nedding,*" it said, and its eyes flashed.

"But you don't call yourselves that."

The *nedding* shook its head, smiling.

"If you want the maze first, the enemy is weaker. But you won't leave the maze." It sounded as though it recited.

"Have you been in the maze? Say, do you mind if I light a candle? It's getting dark."

"No, don't do that," it hissed.

"I need light."

"I will light," it said, and it did a little dance, shaking its dark skin as though it were a wet dog, and Hrothbert saw that its skin had begun to glow.

"This way," it said, and Hrothbert followed.

*   *   *

You no longer remember the early fires, when we laid the wood and slept under savannah skies. When our word for hero was *esori*. This word meant simply: watcher.

On watch, you cannot daydream. The stories you need are quiet. With each sensation, interpretation. With each color, story.

Each fire made ten thousand stories. Back then, doom could be good: a certainty. A good doom, a strong fate, could bend favor for families, or lovers. If you were lucky; if you were right.

*   *   *

"You want the maze?" the *nedding* said, jumping along in the corridor.

"Does it go down? Or just forwards?"

"Down."

"But the enemy, you said, he's somewhere else."

"Maybe. Why should we care which is where?" The glow of its skin had begun to fade and it shook itself again, flashing the narrow space with shadows.

"I'm going deep, *nedding*."

"You are?" it said.

Hrothbert nodded.

"You have food?" it said. Hrothbert tossed it a piece of bread.

"You fed my brother," it said. "I'll take you into the maze. Can you be quiet?"

*   *   *

Hrothbert's people had come fifty generations before. To this new earth for Ing. They could not return. If a Wight had cut this path, everything his people knew was at stake; their very memories. Hrothbert could feel it, like the pull of the earth had developed a new center as he walked down. Which did Hrothbert mean to meet? The Wight, or its destination?

*   *   *

"Come in," said the *nedding*. They were at a turn in the corridor, and the *nedding* ducked under and through a hatch. Hrothbert followed. When he emerged he saw a hundred of the creatures in a large chamber. Pale fire glowed in the middle, reflecting off the earth ceiling and casting beautiful shadows.

Hrothbert knew he had been tricked; still, he wasn't sure whether the *nedding*'s admonition to keep quiet still applied. But he kept his mouth shut.

A murmur spread among the *neddinga*. The sense Hrothbert had been having that the weight of his body was pending towards the wrong center faded a bit, as though the *neddinga* were a gravity.

9

The *nedding* he'd been following spoke, glancing back at Hrothbert. The creatures nearest him gazed at Hrothbert eagerly, in a way he did not like. Running hardly seemed a sane option, though.

"Speak to us," the *nedding* said.

Hrothbert opened his mouth.

"I was cast out," he said. Some of the *neddinga* grinned. "Have my bread." He tossed it all to the black-green-brown creatures, who devoured it. "If you accept me, I will be grateful. I have a quest, from my countrymen, though they say it's insane. I'm chasing a Wight. Help me, *neddinga*."

The *nedding* he had followed continued to grin, but its eyes had changed. One of the *neddinga* made its way forward through the crowd towards Hroth, and the first *nedding* said "our king," which made many of them laugh. The approaching *nedding* wore no crown or finery, but it moved carefully. It stood before Hrothbert, its eyes dark amber, one of them bloodshot. It spoke to Hroth in its own tongue.

At length, the *nedding* nearest the "king" translated:

"You are human and so we will kill you soon. But first, do something for us."

Hrothbert nodded, and the king smiled slightly. Another look came into its eyes.

"Your kind has hunted us at times. We have hunted you. I declare a truce for two days, to find if you're telling the truth. If you are a hero, you will know many things which we do not know. You will tell us what they are."

The king paused, to spit a black gob from its mouth. When finished the king grinned, a thin strand of black saliva trailing from its mouth.

"Either way you serve us. You must be hungry. Follow this one"—and he gestured at the *nedding* Hroth had already been following—"into the maze. He will tell you what to do."

This seemed to be the end of it, though the *neddinga* did not leap back into activity. They slipped into a meditation, an open-eyed sleep. The guide *nedding* threaded his way through the crowd, Hroth following.

"You gave away all your food," it said, and made a sound remarkably like a human, *tsk tsk tsk*.

Hrothbert still had some cheese.

* * *

Often Hroth had felt that the universe was aware, like he was aware. As he walked through the motionless *neddinga*, he felt as though the walls had begun to breathe.

* * *

As he rounded a bend in the tunnel, Hrothbert heard a noise like a cat, low and rumbling, rising fast to a piercing pitch. In the next moment he saw his guide duck behind him. He heard the thumping of a thousand feet. He tried to duck back into the tunnel, to avoid the open space ahead, but the *neddinga* were behind him now, shoving him forward, and it was all he could to point his sword like a spear, and impale two small bodies on it like a spit, as he was thrust into the den ahead.

Hrothbert fought down, not only into the hole of the Wight, but into the basement of his senses, into the low ladle of his nerves. Digging for the jewel within.

He danced and thrust and grinned into the loving and murderous faces of the beings below, cutting open their throats and laughing, adrenaline a strange music, thumping in his ears, aware only of that righteous moment, the joy of killing, strange gift from his ancestors, the pleasure that is murder locked away inside his brain.

The *neddinga* who followed him screamed with joy, holding high their wooden and their copper knives, laughing at the trick they'd played, at the working of Hrothbert's sword on their enemy.

Hroth fought his way through the den to a side tunnel at the back and ducked into it. He ran, laughing as though insane, down into the earth.

* * *

He had miraculously escaped uninjured, though the glow-lit toothy faces of the *neddinga* would stay burned inside his memories all of his days.

The magnetic pull of the earth, the force that had coaxed him to conquer his fear at the Wight's door, was stronger now. He knew, quite consciously, that the man he'd been above had gone. These energies had made him quiet, and fast, without a thought. Life flowed in him, thick and rich, swayed by currents he could not identify.

He took turn after turn by instinct. Though he knew he was inside the maze he hardly cared; it was only an interim thing, like a small lake he could swim in an hour.

Hroth ...

"Yes?" he called out.

Hrothbert? ...

"Who is that?"

Your love ...

* * *

Have you seen the city in a true dark?

Hrothbert had entered Eklaihah.

Scuttling arcades of stone twined into ravaged faces along the starved avenues; their eyes glowed. Hrothbert saw ghostly midgets in procession, their mail shining, as they saluted a huge robot in violet orange raiment, its flowing cape swept back over their small bodies, spiralling together down into a throbbing sienna cocoon ...

Vanished plants ate Cyclopean cattle; vines digested bone to excrete child-sized cities, arrayed in polished calcium across the cavalcades. These bone cities glinted like chips of mica in sandstone; their lights shone over Hrothbert's face. Each sparkle lasted an eon, arcing its rainbow penumbra over Hroth's features, his eyes now an aspect of their eternal sadness. Those child vineborn cities curved skywards into three-dimensional chess games, glacially agitating for dominance.

Sounds to herniate the brain coursed through the rubble, skyscraper sins and ocean bombs, thousands of invasions murdered swept under the shrill paean of time, (Hyperion recovered), a shallow trembling echo.

Ironic handfitted granite sculpures of cannons artfully described attack upon the dripping maw of a goblin, large as a church, teeth gold-silver.

One paving stone Hrothbert stepped on filled his mind with itself, it was *this* step, it had been *that* step, that had *been* the step, *precisely* that one, and it was still going on. The mind of the paving stone examined Hrothbert's step like a theologian might examine a disputed verb, a hideous gravity of thought wherein the meaning of time itself shaded a slow and awesome hammer descending a thousand times into every second of Hrothbert's past and future lives; anonymous, final and serene, a horrifying certainty.

Eklaihah knows no trouble because it can no longer communicate except through ghosts, each ghost recursive, regression an artform, like the madness of the caddy corner avenues, launched beautiful and terrifying in spiral arcs into the sky.

Hroth entered the blue streets, frescoes and mosaics, a hundred million shades of blue, ocean wrought in stone. Fish numberless and each a different color, blue on blue, cornflower moths eating ultramarine eyes of azure frogs, flying between the cobalt anodes of a skyscraper battery; its electricity the Aegean. A turquoise army lay sleeping on a phthalocyanine beach.

Hrothbert wept and the city was a hundred billion oceans, methane oxygen hydrogen and alcohol, liquid eyes, watered bloody ink of stars and churning cement. Hrothbert knew the logic of the ocean and it morphed before his eyes into psilocybin matricies of green and yellow, spinning deep behind the fading afternoons, each a million hours long.

He did not leave there. I who am mortal have nevertheless seen eighty thousand versions of that doomed dead man, Hrothbert who *is still there*, despite what I will tell you of his adventures—

There is the Hrothbert who was a simple murderer, killing children in alleys. The Hrothbert celibate priest, worshipping an ochre statue that hummed like a refrigerator, starving in a thousandth-floor tenement, the Hrothbert who nuked Eklaihah for the billionth time, but who had found a nuke that was itself recursive, one so obcene it may have caused me to come into being, I cannot be certain ...

Hrothbert was also a woman, baleful and blue-eyed, two hundred kilos, eating only starch by a river of blood, and Hrothbert was a man who cut off all his own skin with a laser, slowly, screaming into a stereo recorder.

Eklaihah is ageless and so old that its madness is behind several of the fundamental forces of the universe, and yet Hrothbert did make it through. I promise you that. Over and besides all the deadly Hrothberts toyingly thrown into the crucible of narrative by that undead beast city, this one made it:

Still young, often unaware, but hopeful, the one we shall follow, Hrothbert of the Ingaevones.

*　　*　　*

Eklaihah drips memory, thought Hrothbert, listening to be sure he had kept to the digging path of the Wight.

He had made it through the maze. He knew he could not return that way; he would not remember the right turns. The city whispered to him, with its high chamber and pillars and dust. He munched on a bit of his cheese as he walked.

"Hello!" Hrothbert cried out. He listened to his echo.

"ello!" said Hrothbert's voice. Hrothbert smiled.

"Hrothbert!" he called out.

" ... othbert ..."

"Hello!"

" ello ..."

A bat flapped overhead. Hroth listened with his whole body. He tried to absorb what he needed. The Wight had not lain here; it had passed here.

Hrothbert sat down against a pillar that shot up into the darkness above, and put his hunk of cheese back in his purse. He sat still.

Up ahead, on the edge of hearing: water. A river. He heard the bat cry. The ghosts of the place edged up closer to him.

Who are you.

"I'm Hrothbert."

We're dead.

"I'm alive."

We're dead.

"I'm sorry."

Why are you here?

"I'm a traveler."

One of us was a man too. He's here.

The voice of the dead man slipped inside Hrothbert. It sounded like one of Hrothbert's cousins.

Do you know Earth?

"The earth above? Yes, it's where I live."

The planet. Earth is a planet.

"What is a planet?"

You must be one of my descendants. A stupid one.

"What is this city?"

This is Eklaihah.

"Tell me. Ancestor."

You acknowledge me?

"Yes."

You're a brave one, though stupid.

The bat settled on the ground, staring at Hrothbert, almost motionless but for a faint, slow stirring of its wing muscles.

"Tell me."

A city is a story. I'm part of it, even in death. Once, Eklaihah ruled. I who helped build this city ruled with my cousins, my brothers, my mother. My mother was cruel, and ambitious. She dealt with the Wigged Giants and swore we would provide them with gold, of which we had only a little. But the Giants were stupid, and helped us build.

Hroth took out his cheese again and nibbled it, tossing a small piece to the bat.

I did not age the same down here, in the earth. I lived a long time. So did my mother. She was one hundred thirty-eight years old when she died. I do not know why I stayed. I could have left. I could have been sane again …

"What happened?"

Corruption. We were not the only city here then. Our ruling circle, me among them, accepted too many gifts. I had too many women. We stopped hunting for spies.

Hroth heard what seemed a cough then from the ghost, mixed with a sob.

"It's a beautiful city."

The giants built well. Why did you come here?

"For my people."

I will never leave you now.

"We'll see."

You doubt it?

The ghost sighed. The bat flew back above, and Hrothbert stood. Sitting still had made him cold, and he rubbed his arms.

*   *   *

A city below is not like one above. Time is not the same, because a day is not a day. The light rarely changes, though it dims and brightens according to its own rhythms, moved by tectonics and spirits.

Abandoned cities work danger like a plow, funneling reality beneath them. Above, cults find them for this reason. Below, the spirits who live in them may not harm your body but might colonize your mind. The gravity of ruins repels explanation. Though many stories encounter ruins, they are usually interludes—passing fables, pictures from a forgotten world. But they are always with us. They are more real than living cities in important ways, because they know what lies after death.

I must move on past Hrothbert's time in Eklaihah, but remember that he did not leave that place. I know that he will always be in it. He knows this too.

One reason we are drawn to ruins is because of this deeper atemporal permanence. Another is that, for each city that dies, a thousand are born. Like spirals of DNA we can trace them back to a predecessor. This primordial city within whispers to us.

We exist in an interstice, in the warm happy Goldilocks zone of our star, and in the lukewarm meniscus of this iceberg, between light and dark matter. This is not to say that probing such boundaries is unwise. Our ancestors threw themselves from ocean onto dry land. I say only that leaving the ocean is painful, and, even if you later return to it, an irreversible decision.

*   *   *

Hrothbert had begun to hurt.

Hurting, is it? whispered his ancestor.

Whit ("thing") and wight ("being") have the same ancient root, which is only to say that things and beings were less distinct to our ancestors: what is alive, and what is not? Even viruses have little viruses feeding on them ...

Is the air alive by your arm? Or only arm within the air? When we eat the air, transforming its nitrogen into ammonia inside our chemists' drums, does the atmosphere mind? Viruses mind being eaten ... Hrothbert's arms pulsed now. He sheathed his sword, clenched his arms across his body, and massaged his muscles with his hands, which were suddenly stiff.

At the base of his spine, every step pounded a gentle drum, like a chemist's twisting atmosphere to food, like a wolf skull pounded with a stick, like a heartbeat. His spine thrummed with an *ahhh, ahhh, ahhh,* a pain that was almost pleasure.

"I am a man I am a man I am a weapon for my people, for my woman I am walking I walk below I walk this city I follow Wight, I seek its heart, I am a man, a man, I am a man ..."

He talked to keep the pain away. He talked for many hours. It did little good.

*   *   *

Then Hrothbert met Wallru. And everything was different.
At the edges of his vision, vision that no longer seemed real through
the mad firing of his nerves and occasional half-conscious screams,
Hrothbert saw a man, a biped. The man waited for him, huge, with a
strange head. It seemed like a fish's head with many teeth, or a fleshy,
curved bowl. Its eyes, on the bowl's lip, were wise, yellowish, dripping
fluid. The man's grey skin shone. In a rich and resonant voice he
shouted:

"You're almost out!"

Hrothbert, holding the grey stinking flesh of the man Wallru,
passed through the magic circle of Eklaihah. A place that never ends.
Often our heroes return to us broken. Unable to walk, speak, sleep,
dream, make love. Do we love our heroes for this? Or more hate
them?

Hrothbert had aged in passing through the city of Eklaihah. The
fish-man with many teeth spoke. When he did, his head resounded like
a bell.

"You're through now. Let's eat."

They ate, scraping flesh from shells there at the edge of the city,
scooping it into their mouths. Companions.

*   *   *

You no longer remember Ing. Far back in memory, Ing did something. Most of us say that he went East, following a vehicle. Long ago. So too did he go here, to this world. That is why we are, you see that? For our tongue is Inglish. We are all of us sons and daughters of that madman Ing.

*   *   *

"You ate my food," said Wallru. He laughed, a loud and squishy sound in the echo-filled dark.

Hrothbert managed a smile and a small sound, like: *enngh*. But it was a happy sound, and Wallru laughed a little.

"Come, walk now," said Wallru.

*   *   *

Behind them, Hrothbert's ancestor followed. The shade stepped closely in the shadows, each pace matched to Hrothbert's footprints in the dust.

*   *   *

"What gods do you worship?" asked Wallru.

"*Unnnh*," said Hrothbert.

They walked through a cavern lit with yellow, the paving stones beneath their feet shattered and cold. The columns that had populated Eklaihah's center were now very few, mostly pulverized. One remaining one fell just as they walked by, filling the air with sparkling dust.

"Where I'm from, the *Shhhbitsgishipnip*, I'm sometimes thought a god!" said Wallru, and he laughed again. Somewhere in the distance they heard another collapse.

"*Unnh*, oh?" said Hrothbert.

Wallru smiled. Long moments later, he added: "Please, do not worship me." Hrothbert nodded.

They walked for a long time, without stopping. They were far into the huge cavern. The paving stones had turned to dust. Eventually, Hrothbert said:

"What are you?"

"I'm Wallru," said Wallru. "I am outcast."

"So am I," said Hrothbert.

"That makes sense," said Wallru.

"Who are your people?" said Hrothbert. Wallru said nothing.

"How long have you been outcast?" asked Hrothbert.

"Long," said Wallru.

"It hasn't been long for me, but it feels long," said Hrothbert.

"It's been long," said Wallru. "It's been long." And Hrothbert knew he was speaking the truth. Hroth looked at his hands and saw they were the hands of a man much older than he remembered.

"How long was I in that city?" said Hrothbert.

"I don't know," said Wallru. "But you're not in it now. You're going below?"

Wallru stopped walking and looked at Hrothbert. His skin shone in the yellow light. How did it stay so moist?

"Yes," said Hrothbert. "I'm following the path of the Wight."

"This isn't the path of the Wight," said Wallru.

"Where are we?" exclaimed Hrothbert.

"We're going the same way. Do you believe me?"

Hrothbert looked in his eyes for a long moment.

"Yes."

*   *   *

BOOK TWO
The World Beneath the World

Ol' Joe Hannah from Louisiana,
A hoodoo king in every manner
But I found out with out a doubt,
The tables had turned on him.

He ain't got a tooth in his head,
Poor Ol' Joe is almost dead
Somebody done hoodoo'd the hoodoo man

—Louis Jordan, 1939.

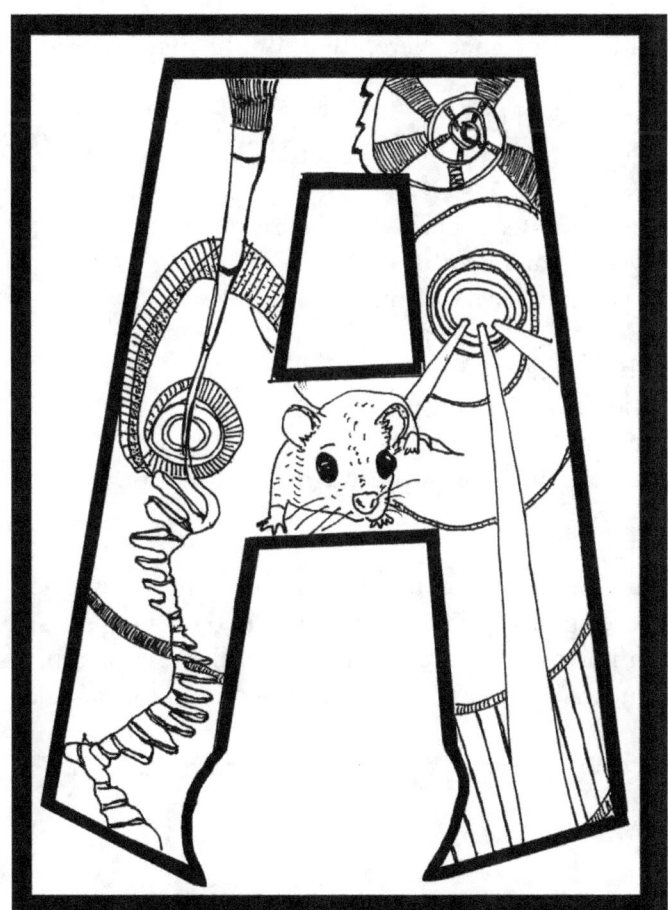

s there are stars above, so below, of a different order.

In the orbit of the sunlit realms under the world, it was to become routine for Hrothbert that all sense of direction familiar to him would change in a thousand steps, like the passing of a season, and he learned not to let it bother him. Wallru felt like a brother to him; the fish-man had saved his life.

Hrothbert and Wallru traversed a staircase over a huge void, one barely wide enough for the two of them, spiraling slowly down. In the near distance, two stars orbited one another. The void was so huge Hrothbert could not tell the scale of the stars—whether it was wizardry or nature. But it reminded him of looking at the heavens. In the nearer distance, they could make out other staircases, also winding down into the dark.

"We're going to Fall Country," said Wallru.

"What's that?"

"Another land. I knew a prince there, Ren. But he may be dead now."

"How old are you?" asked Hroth.

But Wallru only grinned one of his impenetrable fish-grins at Hroth.

"Do you believe you're dreaming?" said Wallru.

"I believe I'm awake," said Hroth.

"Do you believe you may be a dream?"

"No."

"I believe I may be a dream, often enough."

"Not always?" said Hroth, smiling.

"No," said Wallru, smiling wider.

"I feel we are far from the path of the Wight," said Hroth.

"We are. But we'll find it again."

"Yes," said Hroth.

The stairs went on forever. He could hear music from below, and they could make out the lights of distant cities. The two orbiting stars, dancing around the infinite black center of this dimensionless cavern, seemed further away now. They cast their light down onto the lands of Fall Country.

"How does your skin stay wet?" said Hroth. "Forgive me if that's a rude question."

"I'm curious like you, I'm not offended. My ancestors were ocean dwellers. I extract moisture from the air. When the air is too dry, I metabolize some of my interior organs, to moisten my epidermis. I am a fish out of water, this is true. But I can live a long time." And Wallru smiled.

"Will there be water below?"

"Yes, there should be."

Hrothbert concentrated on the steps in front of him. It did feel a bit like he was in a dream. Around they went, a hundred steps to each full round, and thousands, and thousands still to go.

* * *

It filled with him awe as they approached: the cities below swelled up around him, compendia of rich tangled desire, red blue green love, and he and his companion sunk down, down into the Fall, the season of color and the season of regret.

"What will we do here, Wallru?"

"We'll find out."

"I don't want to be a mercenary."

"What other work?"

"Do you think Ren lives?" asked Hroth.

At the top of one of the pinnacles in the half-light of the city below, Hroth noticed that a light blinking, in a rhythm he felt he understood.

"He was a devil." A small fish chuckle, gurgling. "He was a hungry man."

Hrothbert imagined entering the city to have its denizens sweep out from their many doors to make him welcome. A dangerous fantasy. As they neared the surface, Hrothbert could smell the air, somehow fresher, and he watched the light play over the buildings. Bats nestled on the wires strung overhead.

"Is it never night here?" said Hrothbert.

"Almost never."

"Sometimes?"

"Sometimes, yes. But it is impolite to speak of here."

"All right."

When they reached the bottom, Hroth hopped onto the paving stones below and let out a whoop, bouncing from foot to foot. Wallru grinned. Hrothbert realized he was starving.

"Here we are, man," said Wallru. "Here we separate for a time. I have business. But go to the Wailing Door, customary for new arrivals. We'll meet tomorrow."

His companion was gone around the corner before Hroth could think of anything to say.He walked into the city.

A woman smiled at Hroth, and he smiled back. He realized it was the smile for an older man. His age would take getting used to. He stopped then and called after her: "How can I find the Wailing Door?" She called back, "You're going the right way!"

At one door he saw a man in armor, with dark hair and eyes. This man did not smile. Hrothbert nodded to him. The man seemed to nod with his eyes but not his head. As Hroth passed, the man called above to the window, in his own tongue.

Hroth's eyes were wet with the beauty of the place.

Bunting coursed along the stone buildings, violet and yellow with curled, delicate markings. Hrothbert's stomach growled. Was the Wailing Door a hostel of some kind? Should he beg a meal?

He let his legs carry him forward on their own; they seemed to know which way to go, as did the avenue, sloping gently down, toward a main hub.

Strangely, he did not miss the sky. The suns above were beautiful, and the half-light they cast like a romance. The women were beautiful and the men mysterious, the children and their chiaroscuro faces, covered in mischief and joy. One of them stopped to stare at Hrothbert.

"You!" said the child.

"Hi," said Hrothbert.

"Who are you?" said the child.

"My name's Hrothbert."

"I'm Orkai."

"Hi Orkai. I'm pleased to know you."

The child followed after him.

"Who's your sword?" said Orkai.

"Are you fond of swords?"

"Yes."

"What do you want to be when you're grown?"

"I don't know."

"Is the Wailing Door far ahead?"

"Not far."

"Is there food there?"

"I have food! Would you like some?"

"No, that's okay. I'll wait."

"Goodbye!" said the child, and ran off. For some reason Hrothbert felt chills.

Ahead, a small plaza was visible, where two avenues met. Above it crowded balconies, and within it stalls. On the far side of it, a large circular door in a round building.

Hrothbert had no coin. He smiled at the grocers and meat sellers, and strode purposefully to the circular door.

It occurred to Hrothbert his entrance into the city had been too easy; there had been no gate, no challenge. The magic of the place had lulled him half-asleep as it had no doubt others. Suddenly he was afraid.

He knocked three times on the door. One or two of the market sellers eyed him with interest. Hroth saw a blue light wink in the darkness above. This was not a light atop a building; it hovered in the sky. Then it was gone. The door opened. A thin woman with pale face and brown hair gestured him inside with her fingertips. He went in.

Hrothbert looked around in what seemed to him a religious chamber, though the mood seemed more a lesson in a classroom. Some sat on benches and others stood, and as Hroth's eyes adjusted to the bluer light inside, he saw a young man raise his hand and ask a question. The thin woman, having let him inside, shut the door behind him and proceeded to ignore him. Hroth was very hungry. He whispered to the woman:

"Is this the Wailing Door?"

She looked at him and a faint smile touched her lips. Her eyes seemed kind. But she only went back to listening to the instructor. The instructor was saying:

"Because we all came here wanting something. And what is it to want something? Is your want a right? Is your want a hunger? Is your want a need? What can we say about our patience?"

Hroth stepped between two onlookers and moved around to the side of the gathering. The walls were polished wood, though it had worn away in places to the stone beneath. High windows let in the stars' light, and blue sconces glowed. What had Wallru expected him to do here? Perhaps this was a welcoming ceremony for newcomers, though that seemed wrong.

Suddenly weary, Hrothbert sat down next to an old woman in dark robes, who turned to him with a mischievous smile and offered him garlic. He accepted gladly, and crunched down on one of the cloves, listening to the man who spoke. He was dressed plainly, in dull white, with a yellow insignia on one shoulder, like the markings on the bunting Hroth had seen.

The garlic filled Hroth's head with fire; he was grateful for the sensation, it helped keep him awake. Hrothbert noticed, in the dimness towards the back of the chamber, a man touching the wall. The man caressed it slowly, moving to his left, as though in worship. Perhaps they intended to convert him? Hrothbert did his best to listen. The instructor was saying:

" ... war is necessary, and though it is long our lives are short. They are only sparks in the fire of our city, which will burn forever. To be beautiful, to love our city, we must learn our jobs. We must work. Tradition changes, but it remains our delivery. Even as we threw off slavery, so may we throw off ignorance, and enlighten our neighbors as our stars enlighten our faces."

The crowed shuffled. Hrothbert raised his hand. The man looked at him, and nodded.

"Your words are beautiful, magister," said Hrothbert. "Tell me, I'm a foreigner here. What job might be suitable for me? I am glad to help."

The instructor regarded Hrothbert for a moment, expressionless. Then he spoke:

"Each man is given a duty. Our wars know no interruptions and neither should we. In labor we find our weaknesses, and those of our enemies. We grow, and strengthen, and deify ..."

Hrothbert said nothing. He remembered now why he had left the priesthood. He munched on the garlic, let the words flow over him, amused as the old woman turned to look at him, winking, chewing. Hours later Hrothbert awoke; the angle of the stars had moved, and the blue sconces were dim. He felt weak. He sat up and cleared his throat, just to hear his own voice. Gratefully, he saw a short woman bearing a plate of food and she set it down in front of Hrothbert.

"Thank you!" he said. "I will try to be worthy of this food!" He set about eating, looking at the woman from time to time as he chewed, for she did not move but watched him.

Hrothbert was too hungry to make conversation, and she did not seem to require any, only waited for him to finish eating. The food was delicious, though he could hardly tell what it was. Some kind of meat, and a papery starch. The grease stuck to his hands and he licked his fingers.

"Thank you!" he said again, and stood, offering her back the plate. She accepted it, and beckoned for him to follow. Now he would perhaps be indentured, thought Hrothbert. He knew he could not stay long; he sensed the path of the Wight, further than it had been. His brain buzzed, and the food in his stomach and the dim light made him sleepy; he worked at keeping his eyes open as he followed the woman.

At a door, she stopped and whispered to him: "Leave your sword."

"I can't," he said. "But I will not harm your lord."

She looked at him, then opened the door, and gestured for him to wait. She slammed the door shut behind her. Hrothbert wiped the grease from his hands and smoothed his hair.

Some time passed. The door opened and Hrothbert stepped into a narrow hallway. The woman stood still, head bowed. He paused, watching her, but she did not move, and Hroth loosened his sword in its sheath as he walked past her.

In a room at the end he heard a man humming. Hrothbert paused, and knocked on the half-open door. He heard the man clear his throat, and stand, and then Hroth was looking at the instructor again, who now wore spectacles.

"You're late," he said.

"I'm sorry."

"Come in."

Hrothbert took a seat. He sat very straight.

"Your name is Hrothbert." Hroth nodded. "I am Paxe," said the man.

"I'm glad to know you," said Hrothbert.

"Yes," said Paxe, impatiently. "What is your training?"

"I was never formally trained," said Hrothbert. "But I was a priest, for many years. Now I am an outcast, with a duty to fulfill. I want to thank you for welcoming me here, to the Fall Country—"

"I can't welcome you to the Fall Country, sir. Only to our city, Wessalim."

"Forgive me. Thank you." Hrothbert bit back the urge to say more.

"How old are you?" asked Paxe.

"If you will forgive me, magister, how old do I appear? My travels have been strange …"

"It's no matter, you're young enough." The man hesitated, then reached into his desk and removed a thin scroll tied with yellow ribbon. "Take this." Hroth took it and stared at it. The parchment was poor, and thin. He felt it would crumble in his hand.

"Deliver it to Mr. Grames, who you will find at the Adjutant's Office. Deliver it now."

Hrothbert stood, knowing he should obey at once, but found himself unable to leave. He opened his mouth.

"Yes sir."

He turned and exited. You damned fool, he thought. He put the scroll in his purse. He had never been good at politics. He longed to be alone and traveling again with Wallru, where there was only the time before him, no duties other than the one grave duty given to him by his people, a duty so impossible that it might as well barely exist. Exile was bitter, but sweet in some ways.

*   *   *

Suddenly it came to Hroth that he was very thirsty. He followed the sound of the river—now that he had listened for it, it could never be out of his hearing. He followed the sound until he reached a black cliff, stretching into darkness and rocks below. A huge stone pipe stuck out of the cliffside, gushing cold water.

Below the water, a weir turned, its paddles silky grey-black. Hroth thrust his hands into the stream to suck the droplets off his fingers. It tasted wonderful. Hroth could hear music. Under the water's roar, there was song. He lay on his chest and extended his head over the edge of the cliff. He could see a man there, singing.

"Hello!" said Hroth.

The man stopped singing, and looked up at Hroth. Then he turned, and walked out of Hroth's sight.

"Wait!" shouted Hroth, and began to climb down the rocks.

When he reached the mouth of the cavern below the stone pipe, he jumped down, onto the silty earth.

"You could have taken the stairs," said the man. He was very thin.

"I didn't know there were any."

"They're marked. Can't you read?"

"Only my own tongue."

"You speak like me."

"What is this place?" said Hroth. The wet air was chilly; he clutched his arms.

"Cold? You need a coat. Winter is coming."

"Winter in the Fall Country?"

"I thought you were a foreigner. Yes, winter will be here. I have an extra in my workshop. Come."

"Thank you," said Hroth. "I really ought to go, though, I just came for a drink ..."

"I myself came for that reason years ago," said the man. "And I never wanted to leave."

Hrothbert laughed.

"Yes, it sounds a joke but it's true. In here," and the man stepped into an alcove cut into the rock, where tools were spread on a wooden table and a cap and clothing hung from pins attached to the wall.

"I don't wear this much," said the man. "You take it." Hrothbert put on the coat. It was animal skin, soft and warm, treated at the outside to keep dry.

"Thank you," Hroth said.

The man nodded, smiling a little.

"You're a queer sort," he said. "You look like a brave soul, but you act like a fey dancer."

"What work do you do down here?" Hroth asked.

"I listen to the walls," the man said.

"Are there spirits?"

"Of course, but that's not what I listen for."

"*Neddinga?* Do they live here in the Fall Country?"

"I listen for a song," said the man. "For the song of Amikah."

"Oh," said Hroth. "Forgive me if I interrupted you. What is this song?"

"Amikah lives below. When he comes, our city will turn to dust."

"I see. I hope for your sake then that Amikah delays."

"I hope he comes soon," said the man.

"I see. What are your tools for? Repairs?"

"You should go, I suppose. Too needy for my thinking. You may come back, though. Go now, shoo." The man waved Hrothbert off as he might a pesky cat.

Backing away, Hroth managed: "Thank you for the coat ... good night ..."

Emerging from the alcove, Hroth saw the stairs, and started up them. As he climbed, he saw sigils scratched into the walls. Hundreds of them, sigils similar to the ones he knew, but different too, cousins. But he had no time to examine them. At the top of the stairs, he raised a porthole, and saw as he emerged that it was cunningly fitted into the rock, nearly invisible save for another sigil, scratched faintly into its surface. Hroth saw with a start that it looked like the one written in soot by the mark of Frey he had seen at the beginning of his journey. When he looked up, he saw the boy Orkai running towards him.

"Hrothbert! Hrothbert!" the boy shouted. "What are you doing with Mr. Signalman?"

"Just visiting," said Hroth. "Tell me, Orkai, how do I find the Adjutant's Office?"

"I've just come from there," said the boy. "The Adjutant is sick! He wants you at once!"

*   *   *

Often in history the rulers of cities have appointed foreigners to high posts. Such rulers hope that the foreigner will, in his gratitude for the honor, devote himself to serving his adopted city. A foreigner is both expendable and unknown: if killed, fewer grieve. If the foreigner is successful, it is harder for a king's rivals to cry nepotism.

Thus, the Adjutant, on learning of Hrothbert's arrival, found it the perfect time to prepare to die.

*   *   *

"You can follow the water, you know," the Signalman said to Hroth later. "If you want to find Amikah." He huddled in his workshop, shivering, his lips blue and his eyes far away. "But I never have."

*   *   *

As Hrothbert ran after Orkai towards the ailing Adjutant, the air filled with a keening. A hundred, a thousand mouths, grieving.

"Is it a funeral?" shouted Hrothbert to the boy. The boy shook his head, panting.

"What is it?"

"Music!" But it did not sound like music to Hrothbert.

*   *   *

Later, Hrothbert dreamed in his new princely bed.

"You are like Ing," said a warm, wondrous voice.

"No," said Hrothbert, "I'm only a man."

"Ing was a man," said the voice.

"A great man."

"You could be too."

"No."

"You already are. What do you think this is, this journey of yours? We watch and wait for you; we are listening. We know you are an outcast, and this fascinates us."

"Why did Ing go East? Why did he leave us?"

"You are almost *Heardingas* now, almost a Hard One. Don't you know why he did?"

*   *   *

Hrothbert looked over at the jester, who began a desultory juggle when Hroth made eye contact. Hrothbert slumped back on his velvet stool, then remembered that he needed to sit up straight; he was Adjutant, Bread Keeper.

Hrothbert's brief rule made him slow and strange; he listened to himself more and more, and understood less and less. He had taken a woman, and she added to his feeling in him.

The tedium of rule explains many cruelties of kings. After eight hours in his informal audience chamber, Hrothbert understood instinctively how a bored king might order one of his subjects eviscerated, only to relieve the boredom of the office.

Meanwhile, north of Wessalim, Tone Hadare marched jauntily with his companions of Makkina House, their symbolic armor paper-thin but gleaming bright.

The traditional donkey kidney had already been sent ahead to Wessalim to notify the city of their impending "attack."

And at Hrothbert's court, a slave gazed at Hrothbert. Underneath the feint of Hadare and his men, the real war had already begun in the streets, a war made of thought.

*   *   *

In the cave by the waterfall, Hrothbert hunched in to the wall, examining the carvings.

"What do the runes mean, Signalman?" Hrothbert asked. Hrothbert was glad that, as Bread Keeper, he was not expected to adorn himself with finery, only an iron ring on his finger and a bronze torc around his neck.

"It's poetry, lord."

"Call me Hrothbert."

"But you call me by my title."

"Let us have a toast to brotherhood then."

The skinny man looked at Hrothbert.

"You killed our prince," he said.

"Yes," said Hrothbert.

"I loved him."

"I doubt that," said Hrothbert.

"You consort with fishes," said the Signalman.

"I do," said Hrothbert.

"You don't worship my god."

"True," said Hrothbert.

"I agree," said the man. "I'll be your brother. Because I dislike you. And because you honor our city by serving us."

They drank the *uisge beatha*, the water of life.

"When is Amikah coming?" asked Hrothbert.

"Soon," said the Signalman. "I've been calling. Look at this poem." He pointed at a series of runes etched in the rock.

Ing wæs ærest • mid Est-Denum
Gesewen secgum, • oþ he siððan est
Ofer wæg gewat; • wæn æfter ran;
Þus heardingas • þone hæle nemdun.

"Will you help fight against Makkina?" asked Hrothbert.

"What do you need?"

*   *   *

The army of Old Tone Hadare the Miner's Son of Makkina House was more parade than phalanx.

"Going to visit the brothel first thing, are you, Hadare?" shouted Hadare's sergeant-at-arms, Geel.

"I love her," said Hadare, grinning.

Their tambourines and castanets glistened in the half-light of the suns.

Ahead, one of their dancers in silk spun like a dervish and cried into the dark:

"Wendet world, a wild of a wild of a wild of a wild of a wild of a wild ..."

Their resplendent colors shone in the dim sun's light, flickering and casting red and orange reflections as Hadare's troupe came within shouting distance of the gate. They set about scooping up pebbles, laughing.

Hadare shouted at the battlements, where Wallru watched.

"I claim this city! Ha ha ha!" Hadare tossed a tiny pebble at the gate. His men did the same, making little *plonks*.

"Go dig up and eat your mother's corpse!" Wallru shouted, laughing.

*   *   *

Later, inside the city, the fish-man Wallru groaned, a sound like an ocean vessel snapping in two inside a storm, his wet gums vibrating, his teeth shining. One of Hadare's men had thrust his lance through Wallru's side, and Hrothbert knelt to thrust his sword through the partisan's mail and into his heart. The blood fountained out of the man's mouth and Hrothbert jerked his blade back.

Ahead in the street, five more soldiers hesitated, their paper armor still shining. It was unlike any war that Hrothbert had ever fought, often it struck him more as a priestly exercise than an armed conflict; he was grateful for the Signalman's advice—how else was he to know who was on who's side? The dance of Wendet, vendetta, was too elaborate for strangers.

*   *   *

How would you draw a thought, even the simplest kind?

Were we to draw Ing, to map the thoughts he had the day he ran East, away from the Hard Ones, what would we put inside his brain? We could try to describe thought war by linking the thoughts within the skulls of the combatants, describing their relative positions and their vectors of attack. However, we arrive immediately at the problem of time. Who can recall the ordering of thought, and counter-thought, or agree which was which and where and when?

Hrothbert knew such wars had been forbidden among his people, and for good reason. But the heretic within him longed to see such a war. And he did.

*   *   *

Hrothbert sits in his bedchamber, staring at the polished glass and his bearded face. He is wearing the Signalman's coat.

I'm hungry, he thinks.

Half a city away, Leyne, his mistress, sits in her room.

I'm hungry too, she thinks.

I see a man, thinks Hrothbert.

Leyne sees him too, vivid in her mind.

*   *   *

The man Hrothbert and Leyne saw sought food, and knew that he was food. He wore blue. He was on a road, beneath a blue sky.

What is that great blue above? Leyne asked.

That is the sky, said Hrothbert.

It's terrifying, she said.

Yes.

The man walked. After a time, he came to a cottage, resting alone in a field, abandoned, its paint long gone, its roof sagging, its wood decayed. Yet the door still stood in its frame, and its knob still shone faintly in the sun.

Around the cottage was only grass; grass for a thousand miles.

What is the green, all around? It makes me weep, she said.

Grass, said Hrothbert. The flesh of the earth.

But water is the flesh of the earth, she said.

Here, that's true. But not above. But I suppose both could easily be true.

I want to know what's true, she said.

And I want to go inside, Hrothbert said, and that is what the man did, he turned the knob.

*   *   *

In his chambers, Hrothbert knelt beside his bed, muttering to himself, the Signalman bent and whispered in his ear:

"Adjutant, you must be careful of doors!"

*   *   *

The man in the field of grass turned the knob, and moved through the door.

In his bedroom, Hrothbert jerked erect. He lurched toward the door to his room.

Inside her rooming house, Leyne flew to her feet and out her door, down and past her neighbors to the front of her building.

Hrothbert stepped through his door, Leyne stepped through hers, at the same moment, caught in a shared web.

*   *   *

"Who am I?" asked the man inside the cottage. He stared at the ruined walls.

You are a thought, said Leyne.

Hrothbert made him go to the walls, to examine the pictures hanging there.

The Signalman perched beside Hrothbert's body.

"Who is Leyne fighting for?" cried the Signalman. "Who is Leyne fighting for?" he whispered in Hrothbert's ear.

"For me ..." Hroth whispered. The Signalman knew this was a lie.

"Tell the lord who!" the Signalman cried into the street. No one spoke.

Inside the cottage, the man tapped the frame of a picture on the wall, and the image within righted itself. As he tapped the frame, Hrothbert groaned. Outside the rooming house, Leyne in her white and in her slippers stumbled, catching herself against the building's wall. "Who is this?" insisted the man in the cottage. He saw Hrothbert holding Leyne's hand.

Why does he see us, said Hrothbert.

You are Ing, said Leyne to Hrothbert. She began to cry.

"Who is Ing?" said the man in the cottage staring at the image.

You are, said Hrothbert.

No, it is you, Hrothbert, you are Ing!, said Leyne. Don't you see? You came to us, to me! Hrothbert remembered now why he had left religion behind him. He made the man in the cottage step back from the image.

You are food, said Hrothbert, inside the man's head, and you must run. Flee!

And the man fled the cottage.

"Don't go back through the door!" shouted the Signalman into Hrothbert's ear.

They already had.

*   *   *

In the streets of Wessalim, the people leaned in doorways or sat on the cobble stones, hands pressed against temples. Sounds came out of their mouths, fluting moans animals deep inside them, grieving from the terror.

Hrothbert's ancestor from the city Eklaihah watched. He knew these wars did not end well for either side. The shade threw himself into it, into the tale that was a thought there in Fall Country between Wessalim and Makkina.

In the middle of the street, a stone's throw from Hrothbert's kneeling body, the shade swirled out of the wind, his grey skin and glowing eyes terrifying. The citizens screamed and ran, while some knelt and muttered the names of their gods.

"I am Ash, come to you!" pronounced the shade. "Your gods are afraid!" He strode towards Hrothbert, the son of his son of his son of his son ...

* * *

Under the dark sky over the green grass the man ran from the cottage. He ran, looking over his shoulder. The stars had begun to come out.

Yes, run! urged Hrothbert in his ear. Find your vehicle! Hrothbert laughed.

Don't be blasphemous, whispered Leyne. He must do it!

"Get out of my head!" said the man.

You are only our thought, said Hrothbert.

"I'm more than that," said the man.

He may be right, Hrothbert, whispered Leyne. Hroth's eyes filled with tears.

* * *

In the street the shade spoke in a horrible voice:

"I am Ash! I'm from Eklaihah, the dead city. I'm dead but need company. Will you come join us in the shade? Why did you perform the same evils again? Thought war is an evil that you do not understand. Your vendettas are nothing compared to the horror you will spill in your skulls if you continue!

"I speak as I know! Leave your avatar in the street; give him no food. I'm here to help."

The people listened, and watched as the shade walked to Hrothbert, then stood beside him, motionless. Hrothbert stared ahead, muttering. The Signalman dripped water into Hroth's mouth.

* * *

At the gates, Tone Hadare threw his bullets, which were pebbles. Wallru, who knew some of these rituals, answered from the battlement:

* * *

It had been a long time since Hrothbert slept with a woman when the city appointed him Adjutant. Perhaps this was why he fell instantly for Leyne. A more experienced courtier might simply have bedded her and gotten what he needed.

As they in bed, Leyne told him:

"I miscarried years ago. I haven't been pregnant since."

"I'm sorry," said Hrothbert.

"It leaves me free to love you."

She straddled him and curled herself over his face with her dark eyes, and whispered: "With all that I am ..."

*   *   *

In the street, under the half-light, the shade named Ash spoke to Hroth:

"This dream of yours is not a love story for you and your mistress to play with. On one level, she only wants to sink her claws into your brain, to prove that she is ruler."

"I know that," muttered Hroth.

"While on another level, both of you have now summoned through the mirror of your thought a doom that you have no idea how to pay for. Will you, having asked for your doom, refuse to pay?"

"No ..."

"You have no cattle. No gold. You have your sword, your body, your mind. Will you serve me, son of my grandson's grandson's grandson's grandson? Will you pay for the vision you have bid your Bread Keeper give you?"

"Who is the Bread Keeper?"

"Pretend that I am, for now. And I will keep you safe."

"Yes ... all right ... I'll pay," whispered Hroth, and closed his eyes, though he could not sleep.

*   *   *

Let us toss the bones.

*   *   *

Toss and it is so: Hroth, or part of him, went away, into the lighted world of the man he thought was only in his mind, but who was much more.

In the street the shade, snarling slow and gentle, said:

"What is loneliness but a desire to be alone? You isolate yourselves here, in the dark."

One of the townspeople opened his mouth to speak, but he could not. The suns turned above, and the shade started to sing, as Hrothbert's eyelids flickered, and as Leyne's did too, a short distance away.

*   *   *

When will you come, Manhattan?
When will you come?
Bleed for me, Manhattan,
Bleed for me and suck my tears out of my skies—
I was a boy who was a deed,
Made short and fast,
Slipped into the street
To claim the lands the breeze the murdered winter's pleasure—
I shot the star within its soul,
Manhattan,
I shot its soul into a spark,
I wear it on my face,
For Amikah—

*   *   *

In the land of grass and sun and wind, the man who was more than just a thought looked back:

> and both Hrothbert and Leyne
> snapped open their eyes.

On the street, the shade laughed.
"You ignore my advice," he said to Hrothbert.
The shade jabbed Hrothbert in the chest with its dead arm, and when it touched him Hrothbert screamed.

*   *   *

Hot white agony poured down Hrothbert's spine as his ancestor beat him in the corner of the city, whacking his dead fists into the living bone of Hrothbert's face and chest, and spiking his narrow bony feet into the muscles of Hroth's legs. Hrothbert screamed, and some of the townspeople screamed too but it was as though they made no sound, as though each was in his own small world, where each was tortured in turn, by the coming of the shade and his message for the Fall Country: their heavy borrowing over a century of thought wars was at an end. Now, payback.

Wallru shouted as he saw the huge metal mammal shape loom over the city: it had ears. It was a rabbit.

"I can't protect you now!" screamed the shade at Hrothbert, and it ceased its punishment for a moment and looked at the rabbit who was higher than the city's gates.

"I'm the Hrudu Man," the rabbit said, in a voice like scraped metal.

"Hrudu Man," called the shade out to the metal rabbit, "So soon?"

"Yes, dead man," said the rabbit, and it smiled, with a horrid squeaking sound.

Wallru ran beneath the metal rabbit's legs, back through the city to Hrothbert. The rabbit itself was in no hurry. It stepped over the city gate easily, and then squatted on its haunches in the plaza, its multicolored eyes shining.

"You've been thinking," said the Hrudu Man. "A lot." The people of Wessalim gazed with mouths open. They were not frozen as they had been at the voice of the shade; some trembled. But they still felt unable to move.

"All this thinking makes me think of taxes," said the Hrudu Man. "Taxes must be paid."

"The hero will pay them," said the shade. Across the city, Leyne screamed, and Hrothbert vomited blood.

The shade lifted the tortured body of Hrothbert as he would a sack of wheat and carried him towards the metal rabbit.

"Hrudu Man," the shade said. "Whatever taxes have been incurred by Wessalim, this hero shall pay them. Do you accept this?"

"What is his name?" said the Hrudu Man, its eyes circling and twinkling.

"His name is ..." The shade hesitated.

"Yes?"

"Ing," said the shade, and closed its eyes as the Hrudu Man took Hrothbert in its rabbit hands. Then the giant metal being strode away from Wessalim, stepping over its gates and hopping swift away, each movement an echo from another world.

The shade knelt, and rotted away like dust. He sighed, and blew away.

Standing in the street, Leyne laughed insane, her peals of sound a strange music. The butcher came and slapped her, hard, and she fell to the street. The town went about its business. The boy, Orkai, was crying.

"Mother?" he said.

"Shh," said his mother. "It's okay now. It's okay." Orkai cried for a long time, and wouldn't eat his soup that night.

*   *   *

"You are a man?" said the rabbit.

Hrothbert felt the metal hand of the rabbit against his back; it was warm. He nodded.

"You men don't understand thinking," the rabbit said, hopping through the Fall County, under the half-light of its twin suns. Shining cities were like meadows under its feet.
Hrothbert blinked.

"If only you understood thinking, I wouldn't have to work so hard. But you don't, and so I do. Do you see?"

Hrothbert nodded, and the nod hurt.

"We will go to the warren. I have not been there for many years. Though you may see me as a rabbit, I am both much more and much less. In the warren I can speak with my brother, and, you might say, relax." The Hrudu Man snickered with its teeth then, a sound that penetrated Hrothbert's skull like a knife.

The Hrudu Man stopped atop a hill, whose grass was amber and red, and squatted on brown metal haunches.

"You call yourself Ing?" said the Hrudu Man, and it opened its hand and lay Hrothbert on the grass. It knelt its huge head beside Hrothbert and began to munch on the grass. Its teeth sounded like millstones.

"Yes," said Hrothbert.

"Why Ing?" said the Hrudu Man.

Hrothbert shook his head faintly.

"Did you think about it?"

"Yes," said Hrothbert.

"I see," said the Hrudu Man, and it passed droppings that landed with a bang. "Wessalim is lucky to have you," it continued. "Do you know that?"

Hrothbert watched the enormous rabbit. Its eyes were hypnotic; he found it difficult to concentrate.

"What can I do?" he said.

"Pay," said the rabbit, and it scooped Hrothbert up again into its hand, and Hrothbert had the presence of mind to hold tight onto one of its fingers as it hopped away, faster this time, creating a wind behind it, blowing the amber red seeds of the hill into the air.

*   *   *

He awoke what seemed days later, though it was impossible to tell. The Hrudu Man spoke to him as Hrothbert clung to its finger:

"Tell me what you did, Ing."

"I followed the Wight into this hole. I fought *neddinga*, and found a city. It aged me ..."

"Cities can do that," said the Hrudu Man.

"I met Wallru, a fish-man, and he gave me food. And we climbed down the long stairs to the Fall Country."

"I have heard this part before," said the Hrudu Man, with a smile in its voice.

"Oh," said Hrothbert. He swallowed, staring at the polished brown metal finger, warm and smooth, that he clung to. It did not smell like metal, though it felt like metal. "I came to Wessalim. They needed a new Adjutant, and chose me, and I met Leyne ... "

"Yes."

"I fought a war ..."

"Yes?"

"No ... yes ... I did ..."

"Didn't you betray someone? Abandon them to their fate?"

"No, no I didn't!"

"We'll see," said the Hrudu man.

He heard no more from the rabbit until they reached the warren, except for once when it muttered: "I do so much, so much ..."

This tale is not what I expected. I am obligated to tell it; but what of what it is doing to me?

*   *   *

Hrothbert lay in a pile of chewed straw, soft to the touch. Near him, in a cave, lay the Hrudu Man, breathing deeply, asleep. Then it opened an eye.

"Awake?" it said.

"Yes."

"Welcome to our warren."

"Thank you."

"Are you hungry?" The Hrudu Man said, turning its head slightly, so both shining eyes could see Hroth.

Hroth hesitated, but let his stomach speak: "Yes."

"Don't be afraid, not yet," said Hrudu. "The food is fine, it's good."

The Hrudu Man pushed across the floor to Hroth a pile of what seemed alfalfa, and grinned. Its teeth shone silver.

"It's better than you might think," said the Hrudu Man. Hrothbert took a bite. "You've been traveling along the Wight's path," said Hrudu. "The Wight is difficult to follow. In fact, the Wight is simply difficult. I hate the Wight. It is so difficult."

Hrothbert watched with wide eyes.

"Why are you following it?" asked Hrudu.

"It can take away our memories. I'm sworn to come to it, no matter what."

"Take away your memories?" The Hrudu man laughed, a huge laugh, shaking the air and the cave and even the straw Hrothbert sat in. "Why would it do that? Ridiculous."

"Wights have been known to do it," said Hrothbert, a little defensively.

"Have you known a Wight to do that? Eh?"

"Even if it is a lie, I must do this anyway. I've sworn to it."

"That is well enough," said Hrudu, settling back onto its haunches. "That's well enough. But how will you do it?"

Hrothbert did not like being interrogated, and he stood up, about to say something he might regret, then he thought better of it. Instead he stooped, took another handful of the alfalfa-like grain, and munched some of it, staring narrowly at the metal beast.

"You will meet my brother soon," said the Hrudu Man then, and it smiled again.

46

"My name is not Ing," said Hrothbert.

"It might as well be," said Hrudu. "Come, this way," and the beast stood, and beckoned for Hrothbert to follow it through the tunnel.

"After you," said Hrothbert, which made the rabbit chuckle, and then it began to move, scraping its huge feet against the stone, and Hrothbert followed what seemed a safe distance behind.

* * *

The rabbit took a huge breath, and said to Hrothbert: "What do you believe the world is?"

"How can we know?" said Hrothbert.

"That is a different question," said the Hrudu Man. "Answer mine first," it said, as its scales scraped along the stone passageway.

"Why does it matter what I believe?"

"It matters, man not called Ing, because what you believe about this place affects our environment. The decisions you make affect what it is I have to deal with down here. So tell me: what do you believe?"

"I don't know any more," said Hrothbert.

"Don't you?" said Hrudu.

"No."

The Hrudu Man sighed, a sound like a slow firecracker. After a time, it said:

"My brother is up ahead."

"What is your brother's name?" asked Hrothbert.

"And what is yours?" asked the Hrudu.

Hrothbert kept silent.

They entered a cavern with polished walls, and vestibules set into it with carvings of rabbits, dull gems for eyes. Lying by the wall was another beast like Hrudu. Metal, with huge glowing eyes, rabbit-shaped, somehow even more terrifying than Hrudu, though smaller.

"I'm Wright," it said.

And Hrothbert bowed, watching it.

"Brother," said Hrudu.

"Brother," said Wright, and it did something like smiling.

"You've been fed?" asked Wright.

"Yes. Thank you."

"My brother is generous," said Wright. "Do you know why you are here?"

"I must pay."

"Yes."

"Here, sit," said Hrudu. He pulled up a chair of hand-carved wood for Hrothbert.

Hrothbert sat.

"It's more than one's sat in that chair," said Wright.

"Sometimes we eat them," said Hrudu, and laughed.

Hrothbert said nothing. Wright shifted his weight, watching.

"Well, let's begin. I'm already tired," said Hrudu. "Your name is Hrothbert. We know. You came from above. You found Eklaihah and survived. You made a friend who you have since abandoned."

"I have not abandoned—" began Hroth.

"Shhh," said Wright.

"It's your aggression that interests us. You aided your adopted city in a thought war, with no consideration of the consequences, or for my time, or my brother's time, or the way and the weave of this realm—do you understand?"

Hrothbert shivered.

Wright watched with his golden eyes.

"We are sending you below, since that is where you want to go anyway. You may get there faster than you would have liked. And you will pay. So. What do you believe this world is? And what do you believe I am? Do you believe I'm real?"

"Yes."

"All right. I'm real then. And the world? It's real, but what kind of real?"

"I don't know," said Hrothbert.

"Weren't you a priest? Wasn't it your business to know these things?"

"Some might say so. My business was helping people. But I agree with you, Hrudu Man. The world is of our making. It is not divine, it is made, made by men, and rabbits, grass and rocks. All of us hungry."

"Do grass and men want the same world?"

"We both want the sun. We both want to die, and to live, and to have children."

"Are our dreams the same?"

"I've no idea."

"Do you dream of grass?"

And then, Hrothbert felt the man, the man who seemed the true Ing, running in the grass.

"Don't we eat grass?" said Hrudu.

"Indirectly. Cows eat it, deer eat it, you eat it."

"But you ate my grass. You slept in my grass, Hrothbert. Didn't you?"

"True."

"Walk now, and we will continue to talk."

Hrothbert stood, and the smaller rabbit Wright gestured with its head to a hole by it, a cut hole, with steep stone steps. Hrothbert began to walk down the steps. Echoing from the walls he heard the deep, inhuman voices of the rabbits, even louder now that they were more distant.

"Why did you fight the thought war?" asked Hrudu.

"To earn the loyalty of Wessalim."

"Did they adopt you?"

"Provisionally."

"They accepted you?"

"Yes."

"Why?"

"I agreed to serve. The Adjutant requested me as his replacement..."

*   *   *

The boy Orkai ran to him.

"Orkai!" said Hrothbert.

"The Adjutant is calling for you!" said the boy. They went and waited outside a huge door with gold inlay, intricately carved with interlocking pipes, long flutes that grew as vines.

Hrothbert felt a coldness inside.

The door opened.

The man was old, with kind eyes and a frail body, a rich and subtle voice.

"You're like me when young," said the old man, and Hrothbert had smiled. "I anoint you."

Hroth knelt and the old man poured oil on his head. And Hroth drank the blood. And Leyne was waiting for him.

*   *   *

In mountain regions, ones so remote that visitors may not come twice in seven years, it is the custom for the men to invite all foreign travelers to bed their wives, to keep their mountain region strong. As we hate the stranger so we love him, seeing in his face the memory of who we might become.

I am The Hrudu Man. I have decided to reveal myself, for better or worse. Although in my present aspect I hardly resemble the form I've been describing, I am still much the same in my mind. Part of why I am telling you this is I was never innocent in Hrothbert's descent beneath the realm I usually called home there beneath his world. I envied him, you see, his blind faith in the ways of his people, his determination, his single-mindedness.

So often we remember bravery only after the hero is dead. Is it too dangerous to speak of alive? Too dangerous for the hero, or for his people?

*   *   *

Hrothbert continued his descent. Unlike the spiral stairs he had gone down with Wallru, which had felt wondrous, elegant, these here were murderous dark, and they chilled him, not with temperature so much as menace. Whispering in his ear:

"Tell us why you betrayed your woman."

"I am so far away ..." Hrothbert's voice sounded like a broken instrument, sent down as food for what awaited him deeper in the earth.

"Tell us why you slew the rightful king of Wessalim ..."

"He was a prince ..."

"Sophistry ..." Wright laughed, scraping his voice into the stones.

"I worked. I served. I sat my place, I did not indulge. I waited my turn. I escorted the people who had chosen me into the place they wanted to go. Battle. I held their hand, I led them there."

"Yes." A whisper.

"I doubted my gods. I did not want them to be real. I envied the certainty of the believers. Their joy. I saw the power a thought war could bring me ..."

"Yes?" it whispered.

"I don't know!" Hrothbert wanted to weep but he could not. Inside, he saw the shadowed face of Ing, running in the grass. And in a flicker of the dark rock were the contours of Ing's face ...

"What did you do with the power?"

"I used it."

And the rabbits' laughter was a bludgeon. Hroth felt he walked through blood.

*   *   *

Hrothbert stopped then. The voices stopped. He sat on the freezing stone step. The thick darkness rested over him. Whatever light had guided him was gone.

Hrothbert hummed to himself, a tune he had known as a child.

Laugh,
Hruddabara laugh,
We're not what you thought we were ...
Laugh,
Hruddabara laugh,

You're bound for the mountain o'er ...

Hrothbert heard a whisper, one near him.

"You," it said. "You."

Hrothbert saw it poke its head out of the wall, bone white, with black eyes. A rat.

"You're a man," it said.

"Yes.

"Why here?"

Hrothbert said nothing.

"Why did you stop here?"

"What do you want?" said Hrothbert.

"My name is Murphy," the rat said. "I'm a rat, but once I was a god. They put me here out of spite. I live here now. Though I told my name was Murphy that was a lie. Do you like lies? Do lies please you?"

"No."

"You find my lies offensive?"

"Yes."

"How offensive do you find my lies?"

The rat edged further out of its hole then.

"Why is lying offensive? Here in prison."

"Do you know if there's water?" asked Hrothbert.

"Did those evil rabbit gods give you water?" said Murphy. It laughed, hideous and deformed, a twisted sound that twitched its body.

"No. You know of water?" said Hrothbert.

"Yes," said the rat.

"Where?"

"Below."

The rat backed up, closer to its hole.

"You're tall," said the rat.

"I must go," said Hrothbert, and took a step down.

"Wait!"

"I must go." He did not move, only stood, watching the rat.

"What will you give me if I show you the water?" it said.

"I have a coin," said Hrothbert.

"Money? What do I want with money?"

"Goodbye," said Hrothbert, and he began to descend. The rat scurried after.

"You are stubborn. I may show you where the water is. If you promise to give me what I want!"

Hrothbert made no sign that he had heard, but after some moments said, "What would you want?"

"Money!"

Hrothbert laughed, and kept going. Somehow he could see again, though he had not lit a candle.

"You will give me money!" said the rat, and it laughed some more, its body twitching.

Hrothbert went down, falling into the rhythm, feeling the cold, hearing his footsteps and the scurrying of the rat's claws.

"You are stupid. Rats are smart. We work hard. The rat laughed a little again, sounding sick.

"Once I had wives. They waited for me to return to the nest. Once I loved. Sang. I am dying. You will die too."

"Yes," said Hrothbert.

"Give me some food," said the rat.

"Shut up."

*　　*　　*

The rat had not been lying: it had once been a god. The desire for an avatar, the visitation of the divine, is not confined to the great apes. Many desire that one of their own might be cast into the aether above, or below, and feel the flights of stairs that course through minds awakened to their fatal floors—

*　　*　　*

"Will you love me?" said Murphy. They had been walking for some hours, Hrothbert descending steadily, the rat jumping down several steps and then pausing, then jumping down again. Complaining in its hissing voice.

"You aren't very loveable," said Hrothbert.

"I'll remember that," said the rat.

"Where is the water, Murphy?" Hrothbert stopped and looked at the rat, almost at eye level several steps back.

"It's ahead. Further down."

"Where?"

"Go, I'll tell you where."

But there was no sign of it. Hrothbert tried to fall back into the rhythm, but his body complained.

"Where is it, rat?"

"Ahead."

And they went down, and down, and down, the angle of the stairway never varying much, only a degree or two, down and always dim, Hrothbert's vision thin, the cold deepening.

"Are you cold, rat?"

"No," it hissed.

Hrothbert shivered and kept going.

*　*　*

After a time that had no measurement, Hrothbert stooped by a crack in the wall, licking grimy mud from his hand, sucking out the moisture. The rat Murphy crouched by him, licking the cold and musty soil from the wall.

Barely aware at all, Hrothbert spat the mud out and continued down. The rat followed. Though we remember our friends, and the favors we pay each other over the years, we remember our enemies better, for our love for them is often greater.

*　*　*

"Where are we?' said Hrothbert. He had grown weak; they had walked for more than a day. The passage down had curved at last, and the fine stonework had grown less precise. Hroth rested against one wall, and stared at the white rat.

The rat said nothing and stared back.

Then, to Hrotherbert's surprise, the rat continued down. Now it was the rat that led the descent, Hrothbert following in silence.

*　*　*

Hrothbert heard a noise. Somewhere ahead he heard hissing rats, fighting. "Murphy ..." muttered Hroth, and he tried to go to the rat's aid aid, but found he had grown even weaker. When he tried to lunge ahead he only slumped against the rock. The fight sounded vicious, and Murphy cried out. Hroth heard the other rat screech, a horrible noise. The two rats spoke then, urgently, at a pitch below Hroth's hearing.

"Murphy!" Hroth called out.

"I've got her pinned!" hissed Murphy.

55

Hrothbert crawled down three steps. Murphy growled atop a slightly smaller brown rat. Hrothbert could smell the smaller rat's musk of fear. Blood dripped from her neck, where Murphy's claw dug in. Both rats panted heavily.

"Kill her! Stab the bitch!" hissed Murphy. "She betrayed me!"

Hrothbert, without thinking, grabbed the brown rat in his left gloved hand, and held it to his face, its body writhing and twitching, its voice alternating between pain and spite.

"Who are you?" said Hrothbert, staring at the struggling rat.

"I'm Ruth!" said the rat.

"Stop shaking," said Hrothbert. "Tell me the truth and I won't hurt you."

"Squeeze her to death!" said Murphy.

"Shut up," said Hrothbert, and the woman rat smiled at that, and stopped struggling.

"Who are you?" she said.

"Who are you?" said Hrothbert.

"I told you. Ruth. What do you want? Let me go." Her red eyes pleaded.

"Where is there food?" said Hrothbert. Then Hrothbert felt Murphy scurrying up his leg, and Hrothbert flinched backward and cried out in surprise. Murphy screeched and lunged for Ruth.

"Stop it!" hissed Hrothbert, flinging Murphy back. Murphy groaned, a strange, low sound, and the woman rat began to sing, a sound that Hrothbert had never heard and he held the singing rat in his hand and watched its lungs take in air in his hand and press out words sung in its language. Murphy's eyes burned with hate, but he did not attack. The song went on for some time.

At last, Ruth stopped singing, and caught her breath. She looked from man to rat.

"I'm hungry too," she said. "I'll show you where there's food."

"I'll hold you," said Hrothbert, managing to stand. "Tell us where to go."

"Down," said Ruth. "It's not far."

* * *

"You were singing of Hruddabara," said Ruth, after a time. "We know Hruddabara."

"I learned that song as a boy," said Hrothbert.

"Do you know who Hruddabara was?" said Ruth, watching Hroth's face as they walked down the steps. Hroth balanced on the curving wall to his right with each step, holding the rat in his left.

"A bird," said Hroth.

"Yes. A princess bird. She was greedy. We sing of her because her greed was so great it destroyed her kingdom. Murphy knows something of that, eh, Murphy?"

Murphy hissed in the darkness ahead.

"Are you greedy?" said Ruth.

"Sometimes," Hroth said. "Are you?"

"Sometimes," she said. "But not as greedy as Murphy."

"You were lovers?" said Hrothbert.

"Yes," she said. "I suppose we were."

"What did Murphy do?"

"Murphy will tell you."

"If I put you down will you run away?" said Hroth.

"Will you step on me?" said Ruth.

"No."

"Put me down." Hroth did. Ruth watched him. A few steps below, Murphy turned and looked.

"Keep going," Ruth said.

"I give the orders!" said Murphy.

"Give us an order then," she said.

"What food are you showing us?" said Murphy.

"Do you care what kind of food it is, white rat?" she said.

Murphy turned away and continued down, and the man and the brown rat followed.

*   *   *

Later, they reached a landing, a vestibule. It was six-sided and very cold, plinths marking the stairs they had come from, stairs leading further down a few steps ahead, and a corridor on each side of the landing.

In recesses, fragments of statues stood.

Ruth started down the corridor on the left, then turned back to face Hroth and Murphy. "Stay here," she said.

"Wait!" said Hrothbert.

"If you want the food, you have to wait here."

Hroth peered down the corridor. He was very hungry; he felt he might collapse.

"Go," he said. "Hurry."

Murphy watched as she disappeared into the dark. "That way is my old kingdom," he said.

There was a flash of light then and a murmuring sound, like a chorus, and Hrothbert unsheathed his blade and whirled around. He saw a series of sparks in the stairs that led further down, and then they vanished. Hrothbert felt the blood rush from his head; he staggered.

"She will betray us," muttered Murphy. Hrothbert fell asleep.

*　*　*

He dreamed of an ocean. He floated. The sun was immense, hot in the sky.

*　*　*

I am in the ocean. I'm singing. Please, hold my voice like my metal paw. Here there be monsters, but you're one of them: sing me a song, and we might defeat them.

*   *   *

"Come," said Ruth. Hrothbert did, stumbling up, and Murphy watched, saying nothing, muttering to himself, as Hrothbert followed Ruth down the corridor. There was a light. Flicking above: a hole, cut in the roof of the passage. Peering down, lit by the yellow-red phosphorescence, were the peeping faces of a hundred or more rats, watching silent, whiskers twitching, eyes wide.

Ruth spoke:

"This man says he is a hero." Hrothbert felt too tired to object. "He follows the Wight," she said.

The rats muttered.

"Lower down the food," she said, and the rats did, holding with their teeth a string to which was attached a bag made of tiny bones. Inside the bag was fruit, dark in color, smelling delicious. Hrothbert knelt beside the food and said a quiet prayer and then put the fruits, small and fragrant, in his mouth, chewing. He slumped against the wall, chewing, swallowing the juice, seeing the brown rat Ruth grinning at him, and he chewed and sucked the juice and swallowed the fruit and lay there, immobile, overcome with the flavor of his hunger.

The rats watched.

For more than a minute Hrothbert lay there, breathing, remembering the feel of the sun on his face, the ocean under his back. He looked up at the faces of the rats.

"Thank you," he said. "It is delicious."

"Yes," said a couple of the rats above.

"That is rich fruit," said Ruth, next to Hrothbert, watching him. "We save it for visitors."

"Thank you," said Hrothbert. "We must feed Murphy too."

"He will be given food," said Ruth. "Now we must talk."

Two rats, large ones, a brown and a black, scurried down the string that held the bag, and when they reached the floor the rats pulled the string up.

Hrothbert felt very calm, and he knew it was the effect of the fruit, but also his exhaustion. He hardly objected as the three rats crawled onto him, one man on each boot, and Ruth on his left hand.

"I am Ownlee," said the rat on his left foot.

"I am Reallee," said the rat on his right.

"I'm Ruth," said Ruth on his hand.

"Hrothbert," said Hrothbert.

60

"We have forgotten how to dream," said Ruth. She began to cry. The rats cried with her, a sound that made Hrothbert want to scream, but he wept with them.

Down the corridor, Murphy listened with wide eyes.

"Long ago, the rat carried a man on his back ..." said Ruth.

BOOK THREE
The Dream of a Rat

ong

ago, the rat carried the man on his back. He was burdened with the
man, but he did not complain. Over the rocks and over the dry grass
the rat carried the man on his back, never stopping, moving steadily,
sweating in the heat of the sun.

The rat knew that eventually the man would grow strong, and stand, and hate the rat, and the rat knew this would happen but he knew that they must cross the hot grass together, and that the man was weak and needed help and that the rat was strong and could help the man and so that is what the rat did.

After a time, the rat did stop for a moment under a scrap of shade, and the man asked, "where are we" and the rat answered, "we're going, you're on my back," and the rat panted, wanting water. "where are we going?" said the man, who was Ing.

"We're going to Earth," said the rat, and so they did go, through the dry grass, under the hot sun, never stopping, never halting, moving steadily for days and weeks, until at last, they reached Earth.

Long ago, the rat dreamed, he dreamed of a long night without fear, and of a starry sky, caught in a rhythm of its own, pulsating gently, scarping in its courses the face of an ancient rat, ancestor unknown but dreamt of, seen. There in the den of the rat.

Ing forgot the rat. He stood, and shouted at the hot sky:

"I am king!"

And so he was, a mighty king, a man who had Gone East, who had Followed the Mighty Vehicle of Olde, who had succeeded beyond speaking beyond knowing, who had been carried on the back of a rat and never spoke of it, because of the shame.

For what is a man who must rely on rats? Can we still say such a being is a man? Or is that being something else? What does a man learn, being with rats? Does he learn to be like them? Or does he learn to be more a man?

One day, there under the hot mighty sky coursing in its darkness, the rat spoke to Ing:

"Ing," said the rat. "Why don't you leave me alone? Go found a city or something."

"I will," said Ing. "That was my plan."

And so Ing did this. He built a city under the sky. Under the broad sky, on Earth. And in that city he dreamt, he dreamt of a thousand things. But never did he dream of a rat.

* * *

And the rats screamed. And Ruth bit Ing's left hand, and drank the blood, and Ing cried, he cried in his mighty sleep.

*   *   *

Under the mighty sky, in the stone city on the Earth, Ing screamed a great scream. He screamed to his gods, which he had named along with his priests, but they would not answer. And so he built another city, another city with another name, a name we must not speak, not even here, brother, sister, son, he put it in the sky. He threw it off into the dark, the darks beyond the world Ing had come to know.

"That is only another Earth," muttered a rat, and he was right.

*   *   *

Traveling with a message that the rats had forgotten, for even rats forget, though they have long memories, that second city of Ing went to the stars.

*   *   *

What course will Man undo? Can he ring a bell without the new run through his voice, the sound in hand for his sleep, a path he might keep closer if he knew the ghost he —

But no, that is foolishness. I who have spent time in many courts and wished, quite often, that I were elsewhere, I who am bound to serve but often enjoy my service despite my bitterness, even I do not know all there is to know of rats.

How did rats forget to dream?

*   *   *

"Who am I?" said Hrothbert, huddling in the corridor.

"You're going to die," said Ruth in his ear. "This is like dreaming. Can you remember now?"

*   *   *

And the second city of Ing's came to Earth, again, as the rat had brought Ing to the first Earth, the Earth that sheltered both Man and Rat, both King and Country, Grass and Names, Ing came again, on planetfall he spoke with a voice to conquer kingdoms and that is what he did.

65

To war, to war, my children! cried Ing, leading his sons forth to the battlefield against his cousins and their cousins, and other cousins, and they spilled their blood on this new Earth, forgetting, forgetting.

The rats slept, they slept in their nests, watching, waiting, remembering.

One day a rat came to Ing and spoke:

"Ing," said the rat. "We would like a city of our own. Will you build us one?" The rat thought to remind Ing of being carried on the old rat's back but he knew that Ing would not remember that, it was too shameful.

"Why do you not build a city yourself?" said Ing, and he laughed. Ha ha ha. And the rat frowned, and went away.

"What need do you have for a city?" said the wife of the rat.

"Ing will not build us one," said the rat.

"You are only a rat!" said his wife, and the rat laughed, and they made love in the dark of their nest.

And Ing was at war! And he slew his enemies, and one of his sons was also slain, and he wept, and he cried at the sky, and he called to his wives and they wept and they held a funeral in state for the boy, the young man killed in battle, mutilated for his father's greed.

"You are greedy, Ing," said the rat by the graveside after the funeral was done, and Ing raged at the rat, and stamped on the rat, breaking its back, and then there was more war, war between Man and Rat.

What can we sing of the years of this conflict? Is there any measurement in Man for the urging of his secret sleep? His yawning force to suffer all the brothers of his land to forever silken silence? The tongue of Ing is long and lying, says the rat.

And they fought, and died, there on Earth, the Second Earth, under the darkening sky.

*   *   *

Hrothbert stared into the dark, as though on a drug, and so it was, for the dark fruit was powerful, and hallucinogenic. In his right ear Reallee whispered:

*   *   *

For what is a city of a rat? Is it a city of a man? No, it obeys its own logic, and has its own meaning. Where the city of a man is stone, and lined with houses, the city of a rat is earth, and lined with trees.

*   *   *

"Am I dying?" asked Hrothbert.
"No, silly," said Ruth.

*   *   *

After many years, many of his wives, sons, and daughters slain in war by the rats, and countless rats fallen in that same bloody conflict, an old rat and an old Ing sat down to chat.

"Ing," said the rat. "Won't you build us that city now?"

"What do you want with a city?" whispered his wife.

And Ing did this. In the wood, under the leaves, under the stars, he built for the rats a great city, and he named it Roth.

And in Roth, City of Rats, built by Mighty Ing in the long ago time on Second Earth, there was a plaza, the mightiest plaza you ever saw. And in this plaza was a fountain with a great stone rat, a stone rat who fountained water from his mouth, where all the rats drank, and sometimes Ing drank too, with a wife or two.

One day in the city of Roth Ing was drinking that water with his wife Mercury and there were several rats there too, and they spoke of politics.

"I have noticed, if you will forgive me Ing," said a rat, "that lately your farmers have been sowing new grain near our city. I assume this grain is to be shared with us?"

"Nonsense," said Ing, and they went on like that. Crops, seasons, dedications, stones, wives, children, blood feuds, and deliverances from matter into matter that is death.

But Ing, son of Ing, son of Ing, great lord of his city, many years later, forgot that his ancestor, Ing, had given the city of Roth to the rats, and suddenly wanted it for his own, for he was greedy was Ing, and Roth was a great city.

And though Ing muscled forth next day to war, the rats in their wisdom and listening to their many spies, abandoned Roth at once long before any soldier of Ing's could so invade it, and they returned to their forest, and the city lay abandoned.

And Ing found he did not want the city that the rats no longer wanted either, and it lay abandoned.

And it crumbled, and, eventually, turned to dust. And on this second Earth, there were no archaeologists to puzzle out the logic of its corridors and stones now crumbled 'neath the Earth. There was only soil, and birds singing in the boughs above its dead stones submerged.

"And so came you there, Hrothbert," whispered Ruth. And Hrothbert shivered, there in the dark.

*   *   *

But why did the rats forget their dreaming?

*   *   *

Well, sister brother son, what is a dream? Can you tell me? Can you tell what it is, other than that it is needful? What kind of thing are you that you would deny a rat its dreams?

Just listen to their screams, Hrothbert.

"I'm listening."

"What do you hear?"

"They're screaming, the rats. Like my mother used to scream, in her cancer."

"Why do they scream, Ing? They are not in pain?"

"I am not Ing."

"Why do they scream?"

"Because they cannot dream."

"And why can't they?"

"I don't know!"

"Don't you, Ing? Don't you remember?"

"No! I don't remember!"

"Yes, you do. Let us go back to the beginning!"

*   *   *

There under the stars. For what is a rat? And what is a man? And when did they dream together? Why did they do this? And why did they forget?

68

*   *   *

Hrothbert awoke, or remembered he was awake. By his right boot, Reallee was asleep, while by his left boot, Ownlee lay awake, breathing, watching Hrothbert who was Ing. And on Ing who was Hrothbert's left shoulder, lay Ruth, who suffered much. And Hrothbert stood.

"Where must I go?" he said.

"Down," said Ruth. "To get our dreams." And Hrothbert marched back down the corridor with renewed strength and a dozen of the strongest rats followed, and behind them all, followed Murphy, the white former king. They descended the next stair.

And the next stair was darker, and Hrothbert found it difficult to breathe. He descended, as if into his death.

*   *   *

What have we forgotten? Of course, I am not part of you. I am a rabbit, or look like one, and even this shape is only temporary. I have been called a god; it is an inaccurate label. But I forget things sometimes, I whose memory is longer than the lifetime of a star.

Often I remember that even small beings like you have wisdom: are you still willing to fight for it?

*   *   *

And Hrothbert could hardly speak. He was lonely, and surrounded by rats. And it was darker now, and colder, and he felt as though he might forget he were a man.

"Where are we going, rats?" he said.

"Down," said Ruth.

"Why?" he said.

"To get our dreams."

*   *   *

What is the dream of a rat? Is it only warmth in the darkness, and food? Have men fallen so far that they can ascribe only to themselves the great dreams of these worlds? Some remember that beings dream together, unless they fall apart, and are lost, and in loneliness forget the dream that they shared. Yes, like waking, dreams are shared things. They are something that beings do together, whit and wight, rat and man, mountain and ape.

*　　*　　*

At length the man and rats reached a flat place, deep in the Earth, in the darkness and quiet, and they began to crawl, for it was narrow there. They crawled in silence, rat and man.

Hrothbert crawled, and thought nothing, only crawled, smelling the earth in his nostrils, and smelling the rats around him. Then, behind him, he heard Murphy whisper: "we're getting there. I'm hungry."

*　　*　　*

Hrothbert fell into a hole. One minute he was crawling, the next, he was pitching forward. It wasn't deep enough to kill him in falling into it, but deep enough to prevent an easy escape. He shouted, falling, and landed face down in earth.

Above, the rats looked down on him.

"Look at the human fall!" said Murphy to the other rats. The rats laughed.

"Can you help me up?" cried Hrothbert.

"What do you call a human in a hole?" said Murphy. The rats listened. "A smart human!" The rats laughed, and laughed.

"Funny, is it?" cried Hrothbert, and the rats laughed harder.

"Why do humans fall into holes?" said Murphy. The rats listened. "Because they're too big!" And the rats laughed, and laughed, and laughed.

Ruth joined in: "Why did the human go into the hole?" The rats listened closely. "It forgot where we kept the cheese!" The rats did not laugh at once this time, but then they did, even harder, leaning back and scratching their bellies helplessly, rolling in the earth, laughing and laughing.

"Can you help me out!" cried Hrothbert.

"Still want to help us, human?" said Ruth.

"Yes!"

"Why?" said Ruth.

"What choice do I have?"

"You always have choices," said Ownlee.

"Because I need to. Because I deserve to, and you deserve the help. What else?"

"Can you climb out?" asked Murphy. Hrothbert squatted down, centered himself, and then lunged upwards, grabbing for the earth, but he was still a few inches shy of the lip of the hole.

"We'll help you," said Murphy. "But we'll have to bite you."

Hrothbert said nothing, but then nodded, looking at Murphy. Then Hrothbert leaped, and five rats sank their teeth into each of his hands, dangling down into the hole, and Hrothbert held back his scream, and slowly, slowly, they dragged him to the lip of the hole, and Hrothbert dragged himself out, on his bleeding hands, and saw the rats clinging to the rock wall, anchoring their cousins, waiting for him to be on solid ground again.

He crawled free, breathing heavily. The rats licked the dirt out of the cuts in his hands, and then Ruth squatted over one hand, and pissed on it.

"Rub that in," said Ruth, grinning, and Hrothbert did, gritting his teeth, feeling the deep bone sting.

And they continued to crawl.

* * *

"Where will we find your dreams?" said Hrothbert.

"Below," said Ruth.

"Were they stolen?"

"You stole them, Ing. Your ancestor."

"How?"

"We've forgotten."

"Then where are we going?"

"Down. We know that's the way to go."

They crawled, and crawled. Then they reached another hole, within the crevice, stretching more or less straight down. A wind blew up from the hole, smelling of strange things Hrothbert had never smelled. Ruth and Murphy looked at Hrothbert with needy eyes.

"Will you come down?" asked Murphy.

"Yes," said Hrothbert. "How?"

"Jump," said Ruth.

She went over the edge. And the rats followed.

"Wait!" shouted Hrothbert. They did not, but threw themselves into the void. Hrothbert, muttering a prayer to gods he did not believe in, threw himself over the edge.

The dark cold air rushed past, and he could hear the squeaks of the rats falling below him. He felt strangely calm. His heart beat. The wind brought tears to his eyes.

"Owwwwwwww!" howled Hrothbert. He heard Murphy's answering squeak.

The shaft they fell in opened wider, and the earth and stone pitched into a blur as they accelerated, and then, with a flash, like the flash Hrothbert had seen above, they were suspended in space, in a rainbow. They could not move; like specimens pinned on paper. He could not close his eyes, and he saw men in floppy white sacks and helmets scooping out the rainbow with their white-gloved hands, and around Hroth the rats stared.

One of the men in white sacks grabbed a rat and put it on a gurney of sorts, purple and yellow, and another man hauled the rat away. They did the same with the next rat, and the next. The thick air swirled about Hrothbert's face, refracting light, and he could see he was in another huge cavern, and that there was a sky of sorts, off-blue, flicking in and out, but as he watched it seemed to steady. He sensed it was adjusting to his brain, finding the right hertz.

"We heard about your little *coup*," said one of the men, and stuck a needle in Hroth's arm, and his vision dimmed.

* * *

Hrothbert dreamed, and he saw Ing, the man in the grass. The man was angry, and shouted at Hrothbert. Hrothbert was ashamed.

* * *

And then he was jogging; a man was jogging beside him. Hrothbert wore white, like his companion.

"You've been out for a long time," said the man.

"Yes," Hrothbert found himself answering.

They jogged through a large atrium, with white pillars made of metal and plaster, and plants in profusion, damp with water, shining in the artificial sunlight.

"How are you feeling?"

"Fine," said Hrothbert, "I feel fine."

"Any nausea?" said the man.

"I don't know," said Hrothbert. "No, I don't think so."

"You're coming back to us," said the man, and he smiled, and Hrothbert saw that he was handsome.

"How old am I?" said Hrothbert.

"Genetically, you're about forty-five years old, Hroth, but you're in such good shape now, I'd say you look only in your late thirties. Lura likes you, you know," said the man, and he grinned.

"I've forgotten your name," said Hroth, and they passed out of the atrium into a wood, sparkling with dew. He remembered the rats, and stopped.

"Where are the rats?" he shouted, and the man stopped too.

"Gone away," he said. "They're gone away."

"Where?"

"Don't worry about that now, you're still recovering. You've had a bad sickness, and you've gotten better. Do you remember that?"

Hrothbert shook his head.

"Come on," said the man, gently, taking Hrothbert's elbow, and they began to jog again, side by side.

"Isn't it beautiful?" said the man.

Something that looked like the sun was coming up, and Hroth felt it burned into his brain.

"What is this place?" said Hrothbert.

"Kaliforna," said the man.

"What?"

"This is Kaliforna," said the man, and smiled.

"How do you live here?" said Hrothbert. "What happened to me?"

"We thought you'd remember more by now," said the man. "But don't worry, you're getting better!"

"Where is Ruth?" said Hroth, watching his companion.

"She left a message for you! We left it for you back at the station, we knew you'd forget it."

"Take me there!" said Hroth.

"All right," said the man, "we'll circle back around."

They ran past farmers grinding the soil, who waved.

"You're far from Earth now, you know," said the man.

"We're beneath the Earth," said Hrothbert. "Along the path of the Wight."

"Some of us have begun to believe your delusion, did you know?" said the man.

Hrothbert said nothing for a time. They wound along the narrow path, past gazebos and lamia vines and colored fruit.

"What is your name?" said Hrothbert.

"You don't remember me?"

"No."

"I'm Michael, your doctor."

"I don't need a doctor."

"If you say so. I'm glad you're feeling better."

"How long have I been here?"

"Several months."

"Months!"

"Yes, we treated your injuries you received on your arrival, which fortunately were mild. But your psychological condition has been worrying us. You keep forgetting."

Out of the corner of his eye, Hrothbert saw the sky blink to black, for a fraction of a second. He smelled ozone.

The man looked up at the sky too, but said nothing.

"You've come at an interesting time," said Michael. "Since you're a foreigner, we're very interested in your opinions. I know you don't remember now, but if you're asked later what your opinion is of the uprising, it's best to say nothing. That would be my advice, though you're free to do as you like."

They had arrived back at a series of buildings, one of which, enclosed in glass, Hrothbert could see was the atrium where they had begun their run.

"You've been getting stronger!" said Michael. "You might even beat me in a sprint!"

"I doubt that," said Hrothbert, looking at his hands. They bore dozens of small scars. "Show me the message Ruth left."

"This way," said Michael.

They walked into the building neighboring the atrium, through glass doors encased with metal, into a wide entry area, flooded with morning light, huge windows everywhere, with a broad metal staircase leading to a second floor. A woman sat behind a glass desk on the left.

"This is Sioned," said Michael. "She is fertile." And Michael grinned an animal grin, and Sioned smiled, a little shyly.

Hrothbert watched this exchange warily, then said: "Hello, lady. I'm Hrothbert."

"Oh, I've met you before!" she said. "You always forget!"

"I'm sorry. Please forgive me."

"Oh, it's nothing," she said, and smiled. "What can I do for you?"

"Hrothbert would like to take another look at his message from Ruth," said Michael. "Can you open up room three?"

"Sure!" said Sioned, and she smiled at Hrothbert. "Hope you feel better Hroth! Maybe you'll remember me next time!"

Michael led the way up the stairs and Hrothbert followed him down a hallway with flickering sconces. Michael said "open" to a door, and Hrothbert heard a lock disengage. Michael pushed it open. Hroth felt he'd been here before.

"I've been here before," said Hrothbert.

"That's right! Several times," said Michael. "We find it's easier for those healing to encounter their memories under controlled conditions, which is why we didn't like to leave Ruth's message with you in your room. You might have found it upsetting. I hope you understand." Michael sounded a little bored.

"I see," said Hrothbert. He looked around the plain room. It looked a prison cell, all grey, with two chairs, and a silvery rectangle on the wall. "Where is her message?"

"Here, I'll play it for you," said Michael. "Have a seat."

They sat in the cushioned chairs, and Michael said:

"Play. Message. Ruth, to Hrothbert. First."

The rectangle filled with light, and Hroth could see Ruth's face, still and pained.

"What's the matter with her?" said Hrothbert.

"Don't let this upset," said Michael. "You've been getting better."

"She's frozen," said Hrothbert. "What is this, what did you do to her?"

"This is a recording. You understand?"

Hrothbert looked at Michael. "Let me see the message," he said.

"You feel ready?"

"Yes," Hrothbert said, annoyed. He took a deep breath, watching Ruth's face.

The image came to life, and it seemed to Hrothbert, not for the first time, that the man had lied, that part of Ruth was trapped in there.

Ruth spoke: "We're going, Hrothbert. This man Michael promises me he will deliver this message. You fell ill ..." Ruth glanced to her left, nervously. Hrothbert felt Michael grow tense.

"Get better, Hrothbert. We've gone north, to seek help. We'll see each other again, by the moon."

The image was gone.

"There is no moon here, of course," said Michael, smiling. "I'm sure your friend was almost as confused as you were finding yourselves here. But Ruth and her party insisted on leaving at once, and we pointed the way north."

"The uprising is in the north?" said Hrothbert.

"We've had some disagreements," said Michael. "Come, it's time for a meeting."

"There are other recordings," said Hrothbert.

"You know I can't show you those," said Michael.

"How long have I been here?" demanded Hrothbert.

"Do I have to sedate you Hroth?" said Michael. His handsome face looked cruel, and stupid.

"No. The meeting. Lead the way." Hroth clenched his teeth.

They left the room. Hrothbert suddenly realized he did not have his sword. Again he felt ashamed; and lost.

*   *   *

They went down the hallway, up stairs and through another door, and entered a wide, windowless room with a long, narrow table. Men and women stood as they entered. At the far end, Hrothbert saw Wallru.

"Wallru!" cried Hrothbert.

The expression of the fish man was impossible to read, though it seemed something of a smile. He said:

"You're thinking of my brother. I am Lorash."

Hrothbert stood still and said nothing, but felt the pain of his years on Second Earth.

"You are here," said Lorash. "Thank you for your company. Please, sit."

They sat and the room went dark. Lorash pointed with a stick at a window of light on the wall.

"You can see here, energy at current usage should last Kaliforna out the decade with little difficulty, provided our birth rate remains the same at one point three children per woman. As Technician Ross just told us, generator upgrades have resulted in a seventy-five percent decrease in sky fluctuations."

The meeting applauded. Lorash's bowl-shaped head glistened in the light of the window.

"Technician Ross, do you have anything to add?"

"I don't anticipate any worsening of our sky on the horizon." Ross smiled a nervous smile.

"Physician Michael, won't you address us?" said Lorash.

"Thank you," said Michael.

"Do you want the wand?" asked Lorash.

"Yes, thank you," said Michael. He took the stick from Lorash, who sat down, and Michael rapped the stick twice against the wall. Arrows and numbers appeared on a topographical map.

"The enemy is pinned down at the moment on the lower embankment of Rice Field, holding off our drones from beneath an overhang along the north canyon wall. We have offered amnesty for all but the ringleaders, but they haven't responded. Has the committee decided whether they want to engage lethal measures?"

A blonde woman in her fifties looked at Hrothbert and said:

"Hrothbert, this concerns your rat friends. You know, if you're willing, you could address them, get them and the rebels to surrender. You would save many lives!"

"I'll go at once," said Hrothbert, standing. The committee looked startled, but Lorash smiled. "My brother told me you were a man of action," he said. "We'll go in my car. And Michael, get this man his sword!"

*　*　*

In the canyons and the plains of dreams, there is suffering like there is here, though on a different time scale, and it may have causes ludicrous to those awake: a laughing doll, a cherry pie eaten, a mountain that stood too long. Often we take our dreams for granted.

And even those of us who remember that dreams are a world of their own, akin to ours but different, are often unwilling to grant those we meet in dreams the status we would those awake.

*   *   *

Hrothbert rode in the car Lorash drove. Lorash's bowl head dripped in the wind; his eyes watched the road and Hrothbert.

"Would you be a revolutionary too?" asked Lorash. "I could let you, you know. That's how they are here, you're free. Though if you choose them, we'll kill you."

"I will try to make peace," said Hrothbert.

"You're a good man," said Lorash, but his voice sounded strange.

Hrothbert watched the strange country pass by. Men tended to machines massaging the soil; wheat and other crops grew in wide corridors of green. Above, the off-blue sky shone bright.

"Do you believe in magic?" said Hrothbert.

"Why not?" said Lorash. "Why do you ask?"

"I've always wanted to be able to shoot a fireball out of my hand," said Hrothbert, and Lorash laughed, his voice wet and raucous.

"That would take a ridiculous amount of energy," said Lorash, after he'd finished laughing.

"I'm sure," said Hrothbert. "Tell me, when did you see Wallru? He was here?"

"We communicate," said Lorash.

"I see. He hasn't been here?"

"Not since you arrived, no."

"Ah."

"He spoke highly of you. He told us of your *coup*."

"It wasn't a *coup*."

"Why have you come? You really believe this is the path of the Wight?"

"I don't know. It's likely."

"I am not a wyrd like you. I—"

"I'm not a wyrd," said Hrothbert. "Just a man. I did what I could for Wessalim. But I know I failed—"

"The woman too? You did what you could for her?"

Hrothbert said nothing. Then: "Who are the rebels?"

"They want to kill our sky."

"I see. Tell me, where is your homeland?" said Hrothbert.

"Deep," said Lorash. "Very deep. In caverns numberless to Man..." and he laughed.

"You laugh like your brother," said Hroth.

"Why do you think they exiled us?" He laughed again, a little sadly.

"Will you help me and the rats? They say their dreams were taken from them."

"Rats annoy me," said Lorash.

They drove on, approaching the edge of the green fields and striking out into bare rock along the thin curved path.

"I feel I've been here before," said Hroth.

"Humans say many strange things," said Lorash. "We're all dying here, you know. The humans are, anyway. That birthrate figure was a lie. No woman has conceived for years."

"Is it a curse?"

"As you've no doubt seen by now, the whole place is a dream. A bad one."

"Who rules it?"

"Some wights."

"Wights?"

"Yes. I don't want to talk about it. Here, we're approaching the demarcation line." Lorash slammed on the brakes, and looked at Hroth. "Well, go on and talk to them then. I don't feel like getting killed, myself."

"Won't you help?" said Hrothbert, getting out. But the fish man only shook his head, turned the car around, and drove away.

Hrothbert stood on the path under the artificial sky and longed, for the first time in a long while, for home. It was so far away.

He walked down the path and felt his skin tingle as he passed the line of demarcation painted in orange on the path and the ground. The paving stopped shortly past it, and he was on the earth again, walking towards the cliff ahead. He heard a distant hiss, and looked up, and saw metal birds circling.

"Who is it?" a voice demanded. Hroth could see a woman's face, half in shadow, under the overhang ahead.

* * *

I who was born so far away, and who must serve ten thousand of your lifetimes or more; I've seen it all. The wash to war and the burn to be anew, the fatal rush to glory; but only in the aftermath, after the blood.

It is easier for me to be disinterested, though the nature of my work insists I do not take that easy road. You're part of me, after all. Your every struggle is my own, and I hate you so much for that. Why must your longing be like my own?

* * *

"You've come," the woman said. Her hair was red and shining. Her eyes were dark.

"My name's Hrothbert. What's yours?"

"Isolde. Here, we have to look." She took him to a keyhole in the rock. On seeing it Hrothbert stumbled, and chills shot through his body.

"Oh," he said.

"Come and look," she said, and he did. They saw:

* * *

Held lonely in the mausoleum, the light strained gold, the horrifying emptiness of the universe was for Ing the finest consolation. Ing trained his eyes like rifles at the horizon, extending out from the copper lips of the broad building where he crouched, as Hrothbert and Isolde watched him; they felt themselves slip in.

There, at the edges, was music. Where Ing knew he must go.

"Are you ready?" he asked the woman, Yseult.

"Yes," she said.

All around them the doors of the mausoleum beckoned, insisting they remain, reminding them there were more corpses to study, more knowledge to extract from bones.

"This wasn't supposed to happen," said Ing. *I wasn't supposed to do this.*

"I know," said Yseult. "But it happened anyway."

"We'll need food," said Ing.

"I've brought the serpent," she said, and Ing saw that it had already lumbered over, its grey-green skin darker than everything else, darker than the lapis and amber walls, darker than the sand and sky. It was as tall as a man.

"The desert waits for us," said Yseult.

"For you, maybe," said Ing. The serpent snorted.

"The building will miss us," she said.

"It will find new caretakers."

Ing looked around at the crimson rocks and battered carvings. Then he looked back out to the dunes, deceptively near. "We may not find what we're looking for," he said.

"Well, we'll see about that," she said.

They walked out of the mausoleum, leading the serpent. The stone walls of the building shut behind them.

And they walked into the setting sun, chasing the key. A key ...

And behind the serpent, another serpent, and behind the lock, a room, and inside the room, music, played by a wizard or a king, or both ... and behind them an evil god. But how can we know?

"We should sleep early tonight," said Ing.

"No, silly," said the woman, hopping onto the serpent's back. "We sleep late, right before dawn. That's how you travel in a desert."

Desert time is slow and dreamy, each step deeper into it confounds the mind, which is why a serpent is needful. A serpent does not think as we do, and so is not confused. It moves, or not, both are much the same for a serpent. Its eyes are on other matters inscrutable to man.

They coursed into the sand under the darkening sky atop the serpent and the stars came out.

"Which one is that?" she asked, pointing.

"That is Ezekiel."

"And that?"

"Winder Real."

"And that?"

"Heaven After."

"And that?"

"Loja."

"And that?"

"Remerim."

"And those?"

"The Milky Way, woman, the Milky Way."

And she laughed.

"We'll die out here," she said. Her eyes were bright.

"No," he said, solemn. "We won't."

Before dawn they pitched their tent by a rock and bid the serpent hunt its food, which it did, dashing off with horrible speed to hunt insects. They made love quickly, intensely, and then fell asleep, their eyelids yellowed by the fast rising sun, waiting for the peace of afternoon, sweating.

"We are on a great journey," Ing said, when they woke.

"Yes," she said, yawning.

"Shall we pray?" he said.

"To whom?" she asked.

"Whomever you like," he said. "A desert god."

"If you like," she said.

"No need to pray aloud, I suppose. Let's get going."

The serpent gazed at them with its inscrutable eyes, blue and yellow and black. They folded their tent and lashed it to the serpent's back, sucked down water from their weeping canteens, and headed towards the westering sun.

"I can feel myself slipping away, back there," muttered Ing.

"Don't think of it," said the woman. "You made your decision. Now we're here. We can't go back. Even if we wanted to. And even if we could, and did, it wouldn't be the same, not any more. This is what we chose."

"Yes," he said. "Are you glad?"

"Yes," she said, and held onto his back, atop the serpent.

When the sun set again the serpent opened its side, quivering in rhythm to the moving stones of that region, its organs shimmering grey blue green gold silver, and Yngvi cut its wet flesh, a strip, two strips, and he and his woman ate them raw, chewing hard, sucking down the juice, the serpent watching with its inscrutable eyes, and then the serpent, with a jerk, closed itself, folding up its body like an angular piano, and it ran off, hunting.

"We can't do this too often," said Ing.

"It tastes delicious."

"It's slightly psychotropic."

If you get a dream, if you slip into its shores, be ever so careful. It is like courtship: gentleness preserves, it brings life, in its long slow patience.

"Yseult!"

What long slow slope must we endure, we below? Sisyphus, come to our aid!

"Yseult?"

"I'm here."

"Yseult?"

"I'm here."

"Who am I?"

"You are Ing. You are so strong."

"Where have we gone?"

"We are in the desert, on the serpent's back."

"I love you."

"Take a deep breath. We've been here before. Don't waste it ..."

"Don't waste what?"
"Shhhh ..."

*   *   *

Hrothbert watched, in some time out of time through the keyhole, the woman Isolde by his side. It is not every day you get to watch the road you might have taken. To dream it, a separate future, but part of you.

*   *   *

"I am Ing!" he cried, waving his arms at the sky, and Yseult laughed.
"Shhh!" she said, turning back to Ing, taunting. "Hold me."
He embraced her, nestled atop the serpent. Into the night.

*   *   *

"What am I seeing?" asked Hrothbert.
"It's us. This is a temple, you know. A powerful place."
"I've gone insane," said Hrothbert.
"No."
"Who are you?"
"I'm Isolde," she said, and kissed him.

*   *   *

How many Ings have their been? Each age has a new hero, new Achilles for a war we can hardly dream of. As there have been many Ings, Ingrids, Ingmars and Yngvars among the Ingavones of Old Earth, so too there were a growing number of Hrothberts: the man who stood before the hole of the Wight, the man who walked through the dead city, the man who walked out of it, the man who went through the door to dream with Yseult, and the man who did not.

Of course we must not indulge too long these "what ifs," but as I write this it becomes clear I need more and more of your patience. This tale frightens me a bit for what it does to me. Someone has Hrudu-ed the Hrudu Man indeed, and I must integrate my two Hrothberts now, if I can, if I am to hold on to the life I hold here.

* * *

From the cavern beneath the overhang the rats emerged, walking towards Hrothbert.

"Staying?" asked Ruth.

"Yes," said Hrothbert.

"I'm glad," she said.

Isolde's people came out of the cavern. The men lingered, appraising Hrothbert, and the women went closer, to see his eyes, and look in his face.

"How do you plan to fight them?" Hrothbert asked Isolde.

"We can't decide," said Isolde. "We've been arguing."

One of the men patted Hrothbert on the shoulder and they all went back in to shelter, leaving some guards. Above, the silver drones circled.

"The industrial lasers we stole have been invaluable for digging," said Isolde to Hrothbert, as they walked the cavern. "But we lack lumber to support our tunnels. We did scavenge some scrap, but these five caverns are the best we can do for now. It's a bit crowded; there are eighty-three of us. Including seven children. And the rats, of course."

"Children?"

"Yes."

"How old?"

"The youngest is three months. The oldest fourteen."

"Why didn't you leave them with your enemy? Wouldn't they keep them safe?"

"Would you leave your son?"

"I just might," he said.

"Do you want water? Ale?"

"Water," said Hrothbert, and they sat.

"Do you know that this place is not quite real?"

Chills ran down Hrothbert's spine. "What do you mean?" he said.

A man stood, thick-armed with a black beard.

"I am Andrei," he said. "You were a priest?"

"Yes."

"You understand the Wights?"

"No better than you. We can ask them for explanations, which is dangerous. Their will is great, and we are often caught in it, as I have been."

"It may be they've come to amend the justice," said Andrei. "They've taken your friends the rats' side, and now punish men. Whatever their reason, they are making our cousins to the south forget. They're feeding them lies. You know this?"

"I did see the sky flicker."

"Of course, we've all seen this," said Isolde. "The question is: are we ready to live in the dark? To cast aside this false sun? Or escape to the surface?"

"There are other suns above you, more honest ones," said Hrothbert. "Don't you know about them?"

"More lies," said Andrei, and he spat on the earth.

"It's not a lie," said Hrothbert.

"Those suns are lies too, lies told by Wights," said Andrei. "I'm tired of it. Once men lived free, with the gods far away, but now they come close, and harry us. I want out."

"I know we're not quite ready to leave," said Isolde. "But whether we do or not, we must kill this sun. And the engines that drive it."

"Why not just leave?" said Hrothbert.

"You would have us abandon our cousins?" said Andrei.

"You are forgetting about us ..." rasped Ownlee.

"I haven't forgotten," said Hrothbert, turning to look at the grizzled grey-brown rat.

"You owe us our dreams," said Ownlee. "How will you get them?"

"The Wights must have them," said Hrothbert.

"No, it is you who took them from us, Hrothbert. You and your ancestors. You are forgetting."

"Tell us then, rat named Ownlee," said Andrei.

"We are cousins," said Ownlee, licking his lips. "We always have been. We like the same food. We take care of our children. We love to sleep. Sleep, the gift given to dreamers, the gift of rest and travel.

"When you began your wars in the long ago time you took our dreams from us," said the rat. "Those ancient dreams are irrecoverable. But now we have grown used to your foolish ways, which are, after all, not that different from ours. So now it may actually be that we depend on your wars for our dreams. So you must fight deeper in, if you are to recover that first dreaming, and free us from our dependence. If you achieve glory in battle against your cousins to the south, that may be the first step in our replenishment."

"This is ridiculous nonsense," said Andrei.

"Not all believe as Ownlee does," said Ruth in her bright, clear rat voice. "Though there is truth in what he says. I believe it is the Wights who can restore our dreaming. When you humans petition them for us, we can correct your ancient wrongs."

"I've already sworn to help you, Ruth," said Hrothbert, "and I will. Will you help too, Isolde?"

He looked at her, her red hair glowing in the torchlight.

"If the rats help turn off the sun," Isolde said, watching Ruth.

"We will," said Ruth.

*   *   *

In the desert, Yseult and Ing slept atop the back of the serpent, and they dreamed. Yseult flew in the air, her hair streaming behind her, and she felt as she hadn't since she was a little girl, freer than anything, drunk on the mystery of the world. Ing wandered in a bright wood, listening to the birds. A bird flew down on his shoulder, a bird he knew was Yseult. The bird whispered terrible secrets, ones that he forgot upon waking.

The sun was rising and they made their camp in the shelter of the rock, huddled in their tent. The day and the night seemed to merge, the woman and the lizard, the light and the cold, and Ing felt that he had betrayed someone, perhaps himself, because he had found a kind of happiness.

"Where are we going?" he asked.

"West," she said.

West, a word whose root meant downwards.

*   *   *

87

Hrothbert lay beside Isolde, sweating.

"You left your wife above?" Isolde whispered to him in the dark, her elbow against his collarbone, peering down into his face.

"I hope she's found another man. I know I will die down here, in this hole in the earth. But first I must find the Wight."

"I'll die with you," she whispered.

*   *   *

"How do we disable the generators?" asked Hrothbert the next morning.

"The lasers should work fine," said Andrei. "Our first concern is the drones. They haven't fired on us yet, but they will, and soon. We'll have to stay out of the line of fire while the laser recharges. It should be powerful enough; it's effective up to two hundred meters."

"And once they start attacking?" Hroth asked.

"Then we take shelter in the cave," said Isolde. "It's a battle to the death."

"That sounds like suicide. Glory instead of brains," said Hroth. "Think again."

"What causes them to attack?" asked Ruth. "Crossing the border?"

"Yes," said Isolde. "They'll fire warning shots, and then fire to kill, once you're across the line."

"It would be better to charge," said Hroth. "If we fire and then retreat we won't get a second chance at close range. If we're in the open and there are enough of us, we can keep firing your laser, even when one of us falls."

"And we can run ahead, to draw fire," said Reallee, his teeth and eyes shining. Hrothbert smiled.

*   *   *

The serpent groaned. The sun looked queer in the sky.

"What is happening?" said Yseult.

"I don't know," said Ing. "What is it, serpent?"

The serpent rolled its massive, scaled head back, to regard them with one of its huge multi-colored eyes. It made a deep sound in its throat.

Something shot across the sky, thin hot color, an arrow of light. The serpent made its noise again, complaining. Yseult bent to its side, putting her cheek next to its ear. "Shh, shh," she said. "It's okay ..." It complained, shuffling its feet.

The sun was the wrong color. No, that wasn't it. Was it twisting? Or vibrating ...

The serpent groaned louder.

"Keep going, serpent," said Ing, patting its side. It complained bitterly, but then it took a step, and then another, and they continued west, into the huge orange sun.

When night came they still rode. The sky seemed strange, the stars close.

"Will we die in this desert?" whispered Yseult.

"No," said Ing. "No."

*   *   *

This record is a part of me. We who sing are sung in the song, made new. I write Ing. And though I am larger, am written by him too. I Rabbit. I Ox. I Woe. I soar in his diaries! Let me tell you of his cousin. Let me tell you of Red.

Not for long, I promise. But the singer can decide, can't he?

Red hated Hrothbert. He hated him for his beliefs, but more than that, for his spirit. What is the spirit of a man? Why does one descend into the earth and another scoff? We say, "who are we to judge?" but it is a rhetorical question. Because we do not know, though we judge. I who am larger than, and older, I do not know either, and I judge, just like you men do.

Red hated Hrothbert, but he gave him something needful, before Hroth was banished. He gave him a book.

*   *   *

A book!

*   *   *

Gods of the Earths, help me to deliver this tale.

*   *   *

Later:

Under the fading light of the Wights, Hrothbert took out that book remembering his cousin Red and showed it to love Isolde.

He read aloud:

"Cousin, you are going away. It is my hope that you will record your journey."

Wright stopped then, his metal paws half-buried in the earth. He twisted his head to watch Hrothbert, and so did the rats.

Hrothbert continued, "I hate you, because of Elizabeth. Because of your arrogance. But I love you too, because you are brave, braver than me. You should know that we have summoned the gods, cousin, the gods you no longer believe in. If you decide to join us, I have written their names here."

And Hrothbert read aloud the names. Shall I record them here? It is dangerous. But one of them was:

Train

*   *   *

Hurr burr, give us a light on a whir.
Brother! You have my permission to die.

*   *   *

The train hurtled into the night, making its steam music. What is a loom in Massachusetts in the hands of virgins? Light. You read of the Enlightenment, didn't you? What did you think it was! Did you think it was only a fashion! What do you think light is!

The lights of the train are glorious and dull, in the rain.

They could hear it in caverns under Second Earth.

"Train," said Hrothbert.

Isolde listened and a chill inside her heart. And the lizard moved its head. The sun glimmered.

What do you think light is! A message? Only a tool? Grant it the right to speak!

*   *   *

(I am the White Light, transmitted pure and undreamt, awake in episodes uncountable. I fly in ecstasy; I become myself; I accept limits; I diminish and I burn. I am the White Light, and in my coming to you, in my diminishment, in my glories, we are whole.

This story is for you.

Wild inside, thick in his skull and terrified in his brain, Hrothbert slew the Hard Ones, there in the plain of the Red Mass. Sounds escaped his lips like music, like sex, like memory. He looked into the eyes of every warrior who faced him, and he was the man that he killed, each one, his parry the other's thrust; the death dance an unbelievable agreement of matter. His flesh a serpent insistent.

He screamed and though there was no echo of the sound, it echoed in his skull, and he cut and stabbed and opened arteries for the field, for the field like Flanders. To let Earth drink.

"Akkchhh!" and he cut. "Ackkgh!" and he cut. Three warriors, their beards bright with blood, charged him. Their voices merged like trumpets, pounding at Hrothbert, and Hrothbert crossed left and parried, ducked, kicked, tripped, scrambled and rolled, his voice soon joining his enemies' in their bloodlust.

*   *   *

Launch:

Red is a hurt to him: her hair. By now he has subdued any arrogance of doubt, for the warrior is a music, weaponized for the ears of those nearest, and furthest too: a shout from God.

Will you wail too, to have found the glory of your cities revealed as the opening of organs to the air and the skies of your world? It is the work of men to open them so, a thousand fountains of artery and vein.

No one well else will tell you so, for it is not catechism they can bear: we cut for you, and wail for you, and slice for you, and will the world to our agony.

Hrothbert dances past her red hair with his men about him, and brings down fire on the land.

* * *

And Hrothbert is screaming.

Each man carries this inside, of course, even as I carry that dance, in my own way, the unanswerable and irrefutable logic of violence. Though civilized peoples try to refrain from acknowledging that killing is the mark of a man, it is likely to remain so for some time. And in the ancient knowledge of combat, there is the deeper love of community, the terrible duty of nature, to test, to harden, to dance under the sun and scream.

"Aaaaaaaaaaaaaaaaaaaaaaaaaaaaaaaaaaaa!" he shouts and runs, berserker, lopping another head, blood in his mouth and on his face, senseless and somehow serene, without time or memory, in love and in pain.

* * *

The dance light fury, noble savage Man, Ing, the numberless Ings who came before, Y chromosome its long arc of sadness etched in killing, the legacy of men, work, rotundity, and fat that comes after war, limning down to death and night:

Hrothbert slew, and slew, his teeth clenched, his eyes on automatic, pivoting, swerving, wrenching his bones through the weight of the land below the Earth.

Around him, his brothers slew as well, cutting, and cutting, taking life away from their enemies in celebration of their own.

In the distance a mutant arose, the hero of the enemy, a man terrible to behold, swinging axes through Ing's men like scythes through grain, groaning with each stroke, an *unnh unnnnh*, fountaining blood. Hrothbert felt the hearts of the men near him quail. Some backed up a step, in awe of the huge man, bright with glory and horror.

If one of the purposes of religion, a word which means "tied again," is to bind societies together, using gods and custom to encourage civilization, its other use is war: to see whose god is stronger. Those who accuse others' religions of militarism merely choose to forget the shadow that society casts over even our most generous tendencies: for conflict, dark and tragic as it is, is a form of love. And so came Hrothbert back to his religion, naming Tiu in his mind, the god of Tuesday, the god of the sky, the god of war, the god of his ancestors.

Even as the name of a god can motivate men to kill, viscerally, its name fruitful and slack, warm consonant and vowel, so too it allows the passing of the bloody buck; for if an infant or two is put upon the pike somewhere along the way, it is safe to say it was for the sake of Tiu, and not because a sadist knew it to be pleasure.

"Tiu!" cried Hrothbert, his face the mask that men have worn for so long, so very long, the mask that is murder. "Tiu!" The men charged again, as the sky flickered, as the sun went out, as the ghostly light of the Wights above cast their queer shadows onto the bloody ground.

"Tiu!" was the answering cry of the men of Ing, charging towards the terrible huge man, bright with blood and his shining axes.

Hrothbert cut at the giant's leg and hopped aside, listening to the man groan, scared to see how fast the giant was, nimble. They surrounded the giant, dancing out of the reach of his axes, three of Ing's men taking it upon themselves to fight off the enemy who sought to break through and liberate their giant hero, the rest concentrating on the huge man, waiting for an opening, in awe and fear at his size, hating his hugeness, longing for the glory of his defeat, and now, after half an hour of war, just starting to tire, wondering when the battle would come to resolution.

One of the terrible Wights descended, like Hera at Ilium, its diaphanous body glimmering. It swooped down upon the giant hero, coating him in light, and he screamed, a scream the men had never heard, a sound they did not know a man could make. The Wight lifted the man into the air, and the battlefield was a sudden silence, as they watched the man twist in the air, his mouth a silent scream.

Another Wight spoke, in a terrible voice: "ING!"

The hearts of the men, of each tribe, quailed.

"ING!" it said again, floating downwards as the first Wight had done.

Isolde abandoned her efforts at repairing the laser and ran to the top of the nearest hillock and shouted at the being:

"There is no Ing here! We are only sons of that ancestor! Leave us alone!"

But the being only cried again, louder now: "INNNNNG!"

And Hrothbert answered, his heart hollow inside: "I am here."

"Ing," it said, and then the Wight took the form of a man, glowing ghostly bluish white, with darkest eyes.

"Take me then. If that is what you want. Leave my people. Take me away. That is what you want, isn't it?"

The being glowed brighter. "Are you brave?" it said. Its voice seemed to float in the air.

"Take me!" said Hrothbert. He threw his bloodied sword on the ground. In this light, the red had turned black.

"What a strange thing you are. So hungry ..."

"And what are you, Wight? Where do you keep your honor?"

The being's eyes glowed orange, and it seemed to quiver, the air nearest it sparking, and Hrothbert heard Isolde scream, scream in a woman's rage, and she sprinted towards Hrothbert and the being.

"You are so talkative ..." said the Wight, and the edges of the light all around its milky body glowed orange.

Hrothbert stepped into Isolde's path and caught her, as she tried to throw herself at, into, the Wight.

She shouted, fighting her lover, and the glowing being moved closer to them both, quiet, its eyes watching them with brutal intensity.

"Will you give us a gift?" it said then, in what sounded like a whisper, though it echoed in places Hrothbert could not see.

"What do you want, Wight? What can Ing give you?"

"You have given us much blood," it said. "And we are thankful. But I want something else. I want part of your brain."

"You wish me dead then," said Hrothbert. "Just kill me, and take it all."

"No!" shouted Isolde.

"No, not dead," said the Wight. "Useful. Will you give me this part when I ask for it? I need only its use. Not its flesh."

"You shall have what you wish," said Hrothbert, and Isolde cried out.

The Wight smiled, and the sight of that smile made Hrothbert vomit. Isolde turned aside, for she felt very far away.

"Yes, you do promise that," the being said, and it floated into the air, rising above them into the darkness.

"Hroth," whispered Isolde, touching her lover's shaking back.

In the roof of the cavern, all heard a straining groan, and then boulders fell and those below ran, narrowly missing death. From far above dropped my brother Wright, smaller than I am, his eyes bright and his teeth shining. Rabbit.

"I'm here to take you below," my brother said, and he began to dig with his metal paws. The people watched, overcome.

Ruth whispered: "We must try to dream, and now!"

The rats leapt onto my brother's back, piling their bodies. Wright dug, and the rats fell slowly asleep, on journeys.

* * *

The rats dreamed then, dark dreams.

* * *

Hrothbert ate the meat with Isolde and then took her in his arms and bit her skin, crying, making sounds, a wounded animal, hungry. She bared her breasts to him, smiling, a dark magic in her eyes.

* * *

Have you ever wondered why we speak of light and darkness when we speak of morality?

Light, and dark: What do we find inside the eye? Let us cut into it.

* * *

They dug down, on the back of a rabbit.
They hurtled forward, on board an iron train.
They flew, on the back of a serpent.
I am Rabbit and I speak. I am Hrudu Man, Hrudu-ed. Will the train speak?
I am train and I speak.
Where are you going?
Forwards.
Will the serpent speak?
I am serpent.
Where are you going?
I fly into the moon.
Where are you going, brother? Wright?
Down. I'm going down.

BOOK FOUR
Isolde's Dream

solde

slept. It had been a long night, clinging to the Rabbit's back as it dug, listening to its screeches and moans. Hrothbert slept next to her, and curled into him were the rats. On the edge of Wright's mighty back slept Samuel, and three of his men.

Isolde whispered into my brother's ear:

"Sing me a song, Rabbit, will you? I can't sleep."

"What song do you want to hear?" he said, in a voice so huge it was almost quiet.

"A love song."
"Rabbit love songs are sad."
"So are most human ones."
"All right. Here's one:

A rumble in her eye,
Like a tangle in her fur,
Fills my nose with futures
I dreamt for her.

A worry on her head,
Like a baby on her breast,
Shapes my body like a shepherd.
Under the moon,
I make her a path of stones.

A path of stones!
Where do they go?

To the rumble in her eye ...

His voice was deep, like a kettle.
"That's pretty," murmured Isolde, feeling the vibrations in Wright's back, and she slept again.

$$* \quad * \quad *$$

The train moved forward into the dark, and the inspector, whose name was John, listened to the sounds that it made. He sat in the smoking car, across from a stranger.
"How long till New York?" he asked the man.
"While yet. Three hours? Something like that. You have a light?"
The Inspector lit the cigarette for the man, then looked out the window, watching the dark landscape rush by. Fields and dark trees, a half moon, and a bog, shining white. Beautiful and muted.
He stubbed out his smoke and got up, walking to the front of the car and pressing the button to open the door to the next. He stepped into the gap where the noise was loud. Rather than press the button to enter the next car, he stood in the space between and listened to the train.

The sound moved into his ears, opening by degrees the capacity of listening, and he let it move in, settling into a steadiness from which he could appreciate the sound, like he would a symphony, attentive to its gradations, rhythms, harmonies and dissonances. After a time he pressed the button and went into the next car.

His son leaned over a young woman, talking earnestly into her ear, touching her shoulder.

"Stefan," said the inspector, "leave the poor young lady alone and come have a drink with me." He smiled at the young lady. He was tired. "Please excuse us."

"We'll be in New York in three hours," said John to his son when they were seated in the dining car. Still almost a thousand miles to go. "Tell me again what you do when you get there."

"I visit the Hierophant's Office. I complain of neck pain. I say I will not leave the office until he sees me. If he does see me, I give him this." Stefan, with his thin dark hands, took out a small amber-colored thing, shaped like a handle, semi-transparent. It caught the light and made little rainbowed stars on the wood of the bar.

"If he won't see me, I refuse to leave. If I'm arrested, you'll be notified."

"You won't be arrested, but he could simply refuse to see you. Say they throw you out. What do you do then?"

"Go back the next day?"

"We don't have time to wear him down. No, if they throw you out, call me. And wait there, outside his office. Use a public line."

"All right."

On the side of the dining car, a screen lit up, and a beautiful hologram began to recite a poem. Behind her, images of stars coalesced into the bodies of orgiastic lovers, artfully blurred, spinning slowly in the night.

What means a tragedy?
Is the song itself as painful as the pain it sings?
Under metaphor is wine,
The dining arm,
The wining arm,
The arm of Armorica,
A tool on mighty shores.

Her lips grew redder as she spoke, and the passengers listened, politely. Behind her, the orgy had turned into a tussle of skyscrapers, slowly spinning into a galactic spiral.

Is your song a romance?
Or revenge?
Let us beat the beat under your name,
Let us wind the clock of time we want to keep.

Armoricans,
Watchers in the Night —

She dissolved into glinting particles; the screen faded.
"You like this romantic nonsense?" said Stefan, grinning.
"Yes," said his father. "I do."

$$*\quad *\quad *$$

What can we sing of New York? Its fountains and its thousand currencies at march, levitated in the magnetic mid-Atlantic night, won so easily. Under empire, trade: in whatever form its governances, trade's life is holy and never in danger of death, not even at the end of Time, for something is always traded on; exchange is made.

Yet we never sing of the donkey and his rugs who came to Ilium after Greeks had conquered it, venturing through the blasted gate to show his wares to its new rulers, no, we sing only of the warriors who blasted the gate.

What is trade? O Armorica? Your chromosome for mine? May I try a bite of your apple? Here, sit by me, where it is warmer. I hear you've had a long journey.

$$*\quad *\quad *$$

The train was magnetic and built well and it hurtled towards the Big Tangerine at breakneck speed, smooth, heavy, and beloved.

In their second class cabin, the inspector rested on the narrow couch, watching his son read through half-lidded eyes.

New York City was a tangy tangerine, named for an era centuries before, when safety regulations had been at their height, and orange tape was often seen in places both public and private, to warn of possible dangers, in the hope of escaping lawsuits.

Lawsuits were forbidden now, in nearly all cases, between private citizens. Governments could sue another, and there were, admittedly, many governments. Hundreds of thousands of them.

New York City prospered. It lived, even as its denizens died. Geography, and the old adage of traders: "keep the gates open, and the halberds sharp, and keep a store of beer in the basement, next to the escape tunnel." The millennium is a long night, trader, through these our new realms.

I am Rabbit. I know and speak true. What have you seen? Ladies? And Gentlemen? Ancient Castle, Ancient Tomb, The Legend, I tell you still: *there is no way out of this magic circle*, O Great Tangerine with your passages so carefully counted, cut into the sky.

What do I speak of? Any city of trade is at a nexus. A waypoint, where people may meet, talk, trade, and all the rest of it. Pleasure, War, etc.

In New York City, sometime deep into the third millennium of their ancient Christian calendar (before it was changed), passages were cut. Even as Magellan marked the way through to the Pacific, bold Armoricans (brave foreigners, as is so often the case there) told the right tale in the right place and cut through, cut through. To you. And me.

I'll tell you too it's not a coincidence New York experienced an era of intense litigation and tangerine warning tape. Travel and trade are always dangerous, and transoceanic has nothing on transdimensional.

Warning cut in orange: *this way monsters be.*

*   *   *

Hold tight onto the lizard. Its skin is hot. Listen to it. It is wiser than you. Listen to the way it speaks without speaking, moving its legs through the sand, its tail swaying back and forth, balancing you.

See the way its eyes drink in the moon; this is how it navigates.

Pray for the lizard. A holy speed and a terrifying design are yours. Hold on tight: you are only a passenger.

*   *   *

Ing, are you listening?

*   *   *

No port, New York included, ever wants free trade. It wants control of its trade. It wants accountability, diversity of wares, quality and quantity, the right amounts at the right times and something new, something old, something from heaven.

There's always a buy in. You can't let everyone in to market, there are only so many stalls. Like building a road. Say you are a wealthy trader living in a city, and decide to finance the construction of a private road. How private will it be? Who can travel on it? How much will it cost, and most important, where will it lead?

The act of faith is to let all who can afford to (and some who cannot) onto its lanes, and see who decides to come and visit. Take their money, take their goods, give them something in return, encourage them to come again. But do you really want everyone to come along? How do we get the right sort of customers? Well, advertising.

Like a spell, wouldn't you say? A little hopeful phrase uttered into the dark between universes?

Show me, Lady, the world I have not seen, the world next to this, where men unlike all here dwell, the Neighbors —

So mutters the Hierophant, so *la cosa nostra* and the unions break ground on a little transdimensional highway, a Turnpike where there are no turns, only *Jumps* —

*   *   *

What is the sadness of trade? There's always something new.

"Lady Ashfell, what do you expect to gain from this monopoly of yours?" the Hierophant asked the lady, sitting at his desk before his huge window of the city, looking out from the 60th floor on the Big Tangerine. One or two of the buildings had been painted that color, like huge fluorescent carrots shooting into the sky.

"Money!"

"My lady, you don't need more money. You're the second richest woman in Armorica."

"Notice you qualify it with *woman*! We're still second class citizens!"

"Yes if we include men you're the number three richest Armorican, and number two is also a woman."

"Besides, the continental courts admitted I am not a monopoly! They admitted it!"

"Yes. But you know that these phones are still very new, and we've been studying their long term effects. We would all benefit if you would only allow one or two competitors to gain a foothold large enough to experiment with alternate uses."

"I'm a businesswoman! I'm entitled to make money aren't I, Hierophant!"

"Yes, of course. I am here to ensure that you do. But I am also responsible for the economic welfare of our western district, 12th to 78th Street, and part of that welfare is inextricably linked to our Neighbor so recently linked through these new alpha phones. Of course, you are welcome to move your corporate headquarters to some other district."

"You know the phones wouldn't work if we manufactured them anywhere else!"

"I'm glad you realize that. It is with that fact in mind that I am informing you, officially, of an inspector who is arriving, at our behest, and who will be inspecting your two factories, your three warehouses, and some of your records, which are here in our district."

"What!" Lady Ashfell curled back in her fur coat, enjoying the fight as always, grinning with horrifyingly white teeth in her pulled-tight face.

The Hierophant pressed a button on his desk and, after a moment, hot tea emerged in mugs from hidden slots. He handed one to the lady. She sipped it, glaring at the Hierophant.

"Perhaps I will move! To the eastern district!"

"We would be sorry to see you go. And of course I'd be interested to see what use your new phones were put to once they are outside the range of our Link. They are attractive objects, after all, they might do well as *objet d'arts* or doorstops!"

She grinned even more fiercely. "When is the inspector coming!"

"Tomorrow. I will ring you in the morning and let you know what time he is to arrive. Is that reasonable."

"Oh yes, it's very *reasonable*, Hierophant, you are such a *reasonable* man!"

'Thank you. Now, I have another meeting. It is so good to see you!"

The Hierophant reached delicately across his desk, and deprived the woman of her hot tea, then stood, smiling gently, and offered his arm.

"Well! Good night!" she said, standing.

He escorted her the four steps to his door, and opened it.

"Good night, lady."

He closed the door behind her, and then he closed his eyes for a moment, thanking whatever gods might live in New York for the limited powers of heiresses. Though he felt like going to his window and city-gazing, he forced himself to activate his old-fashioned intercom on his desk and say to his assistant:

"Miss Nunez, get Oliver Rutembasa on the phone, will you?"

"I'll see if he's in." A few moments later: "I have him sir."

The Hierophant, whose name was Daniel, picked up his old fashioned telephone, cord and all.

"Hello?"

"Hierophant, how are you?" said the Afrikan, his voice musical and warm.

"Mr. Rutembasa! How are you!"

"Still eschewing video calls I see!"

"Yes, I am an atavist, I admit it. But no Luddite! *Ha ha ha!*"

Mr. Rutembasa, the Commander-in-Chief of the eastern district and its titular head of state (though the territory was ostensibly a republic), laughed politely. "I am glad you still believe in modernity, Daniel!"

"Listen. Lady Ashfell isn't going to take the inspection well. She's likely to instigate a riot, as I told you. I know it's none of your business of course, but let this phone call be my official missive to you, Commander, that should a division of your army find itself visiting us, your neighbor, tomorrow morning, our heights, holts and heaths would welcome you most warmly, even in the absence of a declaration of martial law."

"Well! Hierophant! Why don't we just cut the bitch! Give her a nice scar!"

"Yes, Rutembasa, you are a joker. Please, will you send them? It's important. I don't know if I will be able to hold things together."

"Of course."

"Good night."

"Good night, Daniel. Don't worry so much, hmm?"

The Hierophant hung up, then dismissed Miss Nunez for the evening, and was glad of a few minutes to city-gaze, though the magic hour was over now. The lights blinked out slowly, building after building, a power-saving measure. He gathered his overcoat and briefcase and took his handgun out of the safe, shut the safe and spun the ancient dial, and made his way to the elevator. He was usually the last to leave the office. He nodded to Schmidt, the janitor, who ignored him and continued vacuuming. Moments later he was on the street, his ears popped, his umbrella over his head in the darkness of New York, in the music of the street, saxophone tonight, looking at a beautiful woman at the corner hailing a cab, her fluorescent dog curled on her shoulder; it eyed him balefully.

On impulse he strode over to her, and offered: "I can give you a ride in my car, Miss, if you'd like to save the fare."

She looked at him. "Hierophant," she said. Her voice was barely audible, a whisper. The dog growled.

"What a nice doggy," he said. The woman said nothing, but pet the creature, frowning.

"Do you live near here?" the Hierophant asked.

"No," she said. "I don't."

"Ah, well, I'm happy to carry you up to fifty blocks, what do you say?"

"Not to Guernsey, though, I suppose."

"Over the ferry? Why not!"

She smiled then. "Wonderful! Where is your car?"

The Hierophant took out his wallet and removed his card, and whispered a word into it. Then he dropped it into the street and watched as it unfolded origami, fine wool-mesh stabilized in a proton field. As ruler of his district, he was entitled to this energy-sucking luxury, one of the few he indulged in.

"Charming!" the woman announced, and got in, stepping over the door and settling into the suspended wool couch, which adjusted itself to the contours of her body. She stroked her dog, and then looked over at him.

"You've ridden before," said the Hierophant, a little surprised.

"Clearly!" she said.

He stepped in and waved the vehicle forward. It coasted a meter above the old road, heading west on 33rd. On one of the jutting fluorescent carrot buildings, the rune for Ing loomed in spidery script, black lacquer over orange.

"What's your name?" shouted the Hierophant.

"Rell!" she said.

$*$ $*$ $*$

Wright dug hard, his metal stomach longing for nickel and iodine, silicon and lithium. Occasionally he smelled a good patch of earth and nipped a bit into his mouth, chewing while he dug. Down they went, he and the people on his back.

From Wright's sides protons flexed their muscles, educating the looming edges of earth as to what the Rabbit had in mind: stay in place.

The rats slept and dreamed, for the first time in so long.

$*$ $*$ $*$

Under the quivering sun, Yseult watched Ing as he she clutched his back; watched his chin and right eye, his lip and nose and eyelid. She wanted to translate this information into something that she needed: the assurance that she had chosen right. They listened to the susurrus of the serpent's feet on the sand, and lidded their eyes against the evening heat, cloth wrapped round their heads and shoulders.

$*$ $*$ $*$

Isolde on Wright's back dreamed of a city thrust into the sky, noble and untrue, treacherous and seeming fanciful, though it knew mostly fact, the hard iron of the possible made actual: New York. She dreamed of its spires and peoples, its wide empty streets and crowded subways and sidewalks, air condensers and running advertisements flickering like northern lights across one building to another, showing trickles of red lips or cheekbone over a barely audible sigh of a product name or a destination, New York, tasteful but whitewashed, greenwashed, painted orange.

$*$ $*$ $*$

The Hierophant drove west, drawing the eyes of pedestrians past above 23rd St, heading towards the Guernsey ferry.

"Are you prejudiced against ferry people?" asked Rell.

"No. Not there are many now, since Guernsey started its collective farms. Who would have thought communism would thrive in Guernsey!"

"It's not mandatory you know!" the woman said.

"It's quite remarkable. The *kibbutz* wasn't for you?"

"I like to shower by myself," she said, adjusting her hat.

They pulled quickly onto the ferry, its sole vehicle, and the Hierophant made a gesture to reduce the proton field so it would not react to the water below decks.

The Hierophant nodded and smiled at the ferry goers.

"How are ya? How are ya?"

Some people nodded, a few smiled, most ignored the ruler of the Western District. A boy pulled away from his mother's hand and walked over to the stretched wool car. He hopped up onto the top of the convertible door, right by the Hierophant's head, the little gremlin, and said:

"Mister, how's this thing work?"

"I haven't the faintest idea, boy. But isn't it grand?"

"Yeah."

"This is the Hierophant of the Western District!" Rell announced.

"I've heard of you," said the boy.

"What did you hear?"

"I heard you were you stupid."

Rell laughed, and the Hierophant said, "You heard right, boy, below average intelligence by most measurements! Who else would want to be a politician, eh boy?"

"I guess," he said. "I want to be an astronaut!"

"Well, and so you shall be, boy, so you shall be, just watch out for those alligators down in Lesfleures by the launch district, won't you? They got sharp teeth!"

The boy grinned, and the ferry started up with a groan, and moved them west, across the river, as the little fluorescent dog on Rell's shoulder began to bark at the waves.

*   *   *

Rebecca knows it's a long shot but she does it anyway, sliding up the scale in her throat like it's nothing, singing into the eaves, under the thatched roof, at dawn, Madison Square Gardens, the palm trees sad and the sky grey mixed with pink.

She is *alleva*, the wrong daughter of the right man, bastard but beautiful, princess, monied and unwanted, singing with a vocoder implanted in her throat, the long song of the Night Brigade, her favorite band from her childhood, she's covering "Candy Man." The audience moves with her voice:

I bought the candy,
And I bought the wine,
And I bought the symphony
That they said was mine,
And I bought the pony
Who took it away,
When I was king in the yesterday—

Her voice vibrates and her throat clicks and the echoes shoot over the galleries and under the eaves of grass (tiki houses have been big this decade in New York), and then she slips backstage, her voice still echoing out, and she snorts some cocaine from the table waiting for her there, and her brain reawakens to the dull glory of the drug, slickening her eyes, mesmerizing the light under her eyeballs, making her want to fuck all night and into the morning, well it's morning already, and the guitarist is painting a simple tune.

She lurches back out, the audience loves this part, she is spastic and her voice makes sounds like machinery over the guitar and she's jumping and vibrating and the audience starts screaming bloody murder, it's painful, this beauty, and she doesn't stop, and they're screaming with joy, and then she stops and they applaud. Then she goes downstairs to her dildo on a horse and rides it, door locked, crying, and cumming, and crying.

She takes a shower and goes to sleep. These gigs, with her audience, they rent her the basement by the week, she can probably keep them all here for 8 weeks at least, maybe 10, the city subsidizes them, rock-and-roll pilgrims.

Around noon she wakes up, her phone ringing. She taps her palm and listens to the voice in her head:

You were great.

"Oh ... thanks Santa. Did you like it?"
You know I did. Listen, there's something I need ...

*   *   *

Because before, not long before, the little coup moved up and out, Eastern District stormtroopers and Western District pride, the Hierophant dressed in his traditional green, standing in the wool car at Union Square, and shouting:
"Soldiers, welcome!"
Some of his citizens, a dozen men or so, pulled out their pricks and pissed in the direction of the troopers, a ritual refusal. The soldiers laughed at them, and proceeded towards the docks where the inspector waited.
Lady Ashfell's man quailed at the sight of the Eastern District brigade, his teeth dropping out of his mouth, and out of the warehouse stepped the inspector. He looked at the soldiers.

*   *   *

What would you like from the North Pole, child? A pony? A circus all your own? How about a friend who never leaves your head? We'll see your interdimensional telephone and raise you a demonic possession.

*   *   *

Rebecca sits in the shower, wasting water, trying to resist.
You just need to meet him in the alley. He's your friend. Go!
"I don't want to."
I told you that's what you'd be doing! You agreed!
"No."
Free information is so expensive. Who's been talking to whom? Did you call down the Line? What spirit came with you? Santa?
"No, Santa. Leave me alone ..." Rebecca curls into a ball, sucking her thumb, humming a tune to herself, thinking of her fans, thinking of her dildo horse; she's out of cocaine.
"No, Santa ..."
Don't you want a revolution?

*   *   *

The Hierophant gazes out at his section of the island, from his office window. *Change is so hard*, he thinks. *Why did we let them in, in the first place?*

Because trade needs something new, Hierophant.

We're insane, he thinks.

The Hierophant knows that politics demands patience. New players arrive, and you have to give them space to reveal their habits. Eschewing police states in their archaic forms, the Hierophant prefers instinct, and good friends. Though he has been accused, on occasion, of ruling with an iron fist, he knows that the Western District of New York is just about the most libertarian enclave in Armorica. He never executes anyone, there are barely any taxes, free day care the chief exception, some of the best medical machines available. The trains run mostly on time.

But newcomers are hard to handle.

His own phone, for instance. He doesn't want to wire it to the Line. The transdimensional cable so carefully economized, so carefully monopolized, for all his rhetoric about competition to Lady Ashfell the Hierophant knows you need to keep it real, you need to hold on to what you've got. Even when you don't really want it ...

The telephone rang.

"Hello?"

"Mr. Hierophant?"

"Yes?"

"It's Rell. You took me back to Guernsey yesterday?"

He smiles; one of his real ones.

"Rell! How are you? Call me Daniel, please."

"Oh, I'll call you Hierophant for now. Listen, are you busy? I heard about the riot, are you okay?"

"That is not a word I would use to describe today's events, young lady! It was a disagreement."

"Yes, umm, could you come meet me? I need your help."

"Where are you?"

"Guernsey tower number seven. Thirtieth floor."

The line goes dead. And the Hierophant's manhood comes to life.

*   *   *

Isolde is dreaming.

The rats dream with her, squeaking in their separate darks ...

* * *

Santa lives somewhere else. He made friends with Rebecca. She wanted a phone-pal. Like a pen pal, only in your head. It was economical. It was magic.

Rebecca's manager stood stock still, saying, "Rebecca, *please*. This might be the last great concert of your career. You're in your second week and you're going strong, everything keeps getting better! You have to *pace yourself*, honey! You understand?"

"Austin, I know that!" she said. "I know all that!"

"Can I get you anything?" Austin's hand hesitated on the door knob.

"No, sweetie, just let me rest, okay?"

"There's several young men would like to meet you ..."

"Not now, okay?

He closed the door. She stared at it. She assessed its contours. Then Santa came back.

In the alley, bitch. Just go outside and meet him, like I fucking said.

She put on her robe and slippers and went out the back stairs, up the alley behind Madison Square, her eyes wide and frightened, her lips reciting mantras only Santa could hear ...

* * *

What is a lifetime? A human life, a dog's life, a statistical estimate. But more than a number, it is the richness of experience of those years.

The problem is in the phone. The early transatlantic cable was digested by the fish; perhaps they sensed it was bad news for them, in addition to liking the taste of the rubber. Yet the copper held; though inches were lost to the seawater's corrosion a half centimeter held, and adapted to the sea, and sent its messages on their way across.

It's early days for the special Western District phone, for what abominable teeth chomped as the cable was flung across the quantum dark? And, unlike the fish of the Atlantic, these teeth are attached to beings who can speak Inglish.

* * *

I say hey, hey, what a day, Susannah, for alleva *tribute —*
You and some wine, for us —
Your drinkers ...

Santa spoke into Rebecca's ear, and she obeyed, swaying down the alleyway, her hair blowing there was a man there in the alleyway, a man with unpleasant eyes who did not move or flinch in the stiff cold wind.
Say hello.
"Hello ..."
He hands her a padded brown envelope.
"Some visual effects for you," the man says, his voice far away, already on to the next job, but curious, watching for her reaction.
Say thank you.
"Thank you ..." The man walked off and she felt the cold seep into her bones as the amphetamine faded from her blood dripped into kidneys, and she wondered who she had become.

*   *   *

The message was successful, as so many armed messages are. Lady Ashfell's market share was cut in four. The phones proliferate, like little nukes, they stretch into the market, they arrive in people's homes, in people's hands, and brains.
The telephone, the sound far off, the whisper in the dusky dark we might have heard one night after a poker game and a couple beers, where we thought we knew our ancestors' tone, the syllable ancient rhyme upon a breeze, the telephone ...
What is love over a wire? Can we dissimulate the expression of our love? Smile and dial, honeychile:

*   *   *

Because in the dark, the faithless dark, the growing shapes of old are wanton fast and furious for this our fond expression of a thing called life, the reordering of Nature's desire, the DNA encoded with a smile:
Have you been into the dark? Of course you haven't. I will try to show you. I am your Rabbit, I shout for you, I shout of the dark we cast our line into.

Can you hear it?

Hellllooooooooooo ...

In the space that is not space, the interstice, the travelers embrace and eat each other, the horrifying dark, they scream into each other's face with a will (they live out there, you know, the dark matter):

Me!

No, me!

Me!

Us, them, fun!

They do a dance, a Broadway show. Like Levantines across the shore, a ritual displayed onto cuneiform: carry the message on, carry with it a sword, the spirits dance:

Baby, baby, have you heard the sunrise?

"Who is this?" says the grandmother on 72nd Street, her new telephone in hand. Somewhere in her mind's eye she thinks she sees shapes dance, like a pretty dream.

Can you hold us in the dark?

"I said, who is this please?"

Granny, granny, can you cut us so you'll understand that in our veins hot music runs like vellum into your blood?

"I'm going to hang up now ..."

Don't hang up, you're beautiful, you know that? Listen to what I'm gonna tell you now:

First Earth, in the Big Tangerine is a fine place to die, to sing. But something is afoot, the old culprit: global capital, garden fresh ...

Mrs. Spencer, telephone in hand, hung up and thought about her laundry, it needed doing. She had an idea about what to do with the nest egg her husband had left her, an investment opportunity of a lifetime ... these new phones!

Sometimes the capitalists are right, as the Hierophant knew. He cruised in his wool car toward the Guernsey ferry, thinking of Rell. He rested secure in the knowledge that the three top bidders were even now beginning to manufacture the newest model phones, and that he was going to have to do some serious international bartering this month to hang on to the District's patents.

It's hard to be the hub.

*   *   *

She embraced him in the hallway and he sucked on her neck.

"You're cold," she whispered in his ear.

Inside her apartment flame-colored fabric hung from the ceiling, red and gold dripping everywhere. She let go of his hand and twirled, slipping off her robe. He took off his coat, watching her.

*   *   *

"Where did you come from?" he said.

"I'm not a whore," she said.

"I know."

"What do you want to eat?"

"Not yet," he said, reaching for her.

"Turkey?" she whispered.

"Okay."

"I'll go get it."

"One second," he said.

"What?" She propped her elbows on his chest, fists on her chin.

"Do you know what's happening?" he said.

"I don't want to know," she said, and she stood.

*   *   *

Have you dreamt of the machines in the dark? In the half dream you feel on first waking, Isolde saw the first room of them, grim gray and solemn, in the hallway beneath the earth.

"I feel the Wight," said Hrothbert.

"Yes," said my brother.

*   *   *

What is a Wight? What is a being? Can we know? Or can we only know when one is passing?

*   *   *

To skip ahead a bit:

The Hierophant gripped the ferry railing, wind in his face. Rell hugged his chest for warmth, in her white. The Hierophant was getting married, in a District that expected bachelorhood from its rulers. But much was changing. The Big Tangerine loomed ahead, its orange skyscrapers gloomy and solemn under the stormy furrows of sky.

*   *   *

In the long low light of dawn Rebecca Northstrom makes time with her band at Madison Square Gardens.

"Oh my God," Rell said, pulling herself up onto the Stylite column from the ladder. She and her groom stood like offerings atop the forty foot granite pillar.

The audience swayed in the half-light of the tiki torches. Rain threatened, but not yet.

"A wet bride is good luck," said the Hierophant.

Rebecca, cocaine dripping down her throat, spoke into the microphone, and the crowd looked from her, on stage, to the Hierophant and his young bride on their pillar, modern Stylites swearing off chastity forever.

"Dearly beloved. We the Western District salute your decision to join in Holy Matrimony your two bodies over these stones of New York, to love and to serve, to read the words we write together. Now kiss. The world knows you're one!"

He kissed the bride. She cried a little, a fashionable amount.

In Rebecca's ear, Santa whispered: *Open up the door, you sweet little cunt. Let's start the show.*

*   *   *

We wave like the sea, you and I, cutting our marks into the lands we find, hoping that we'll stay a while.

Like Ing. A man who stuck around a while in those ancient minds when he went east. A little mark for a little time, the little sound defined, and the sound is:

Arrive.

We rearrive at Armorica. Summoned by telephone like a good butler.

(But that happens later). If I would feed this tale to you like banana to a baby much would be lost. Instead I must tell it how I remember it.

*   *   *

Earlier, the Hierophant and his fiancée dined on turkey slices in their bed, shy, and new.

"Why did you become Hierophant?" she said.

"No one else wanted the job."

"But you must have had other reasons?"

"I love New York," he said.

"But it's so cold. And lonely."

"Like me," he said.

"Why do you want to marry me?"

"You're practical," he said. "You have good taste."

"Yes," she said.

"And I need help," he said.

*   *   *

On the stage, Rebecca slipped the disc under the light and the hologram took shape above her, yellow and green at first, turning silkily. The crowd lit more tiki torches. It had begun to rain.

*   *   *

The green fog boiled on the west bank of the Hudson, and the red boiled on the east, speaking in registers on the edge of human hearing:

Green:
Here ... we are.

Red:
I'm hungry.

The New Yorkers huddled in their apartments. Some called the police. The Hierophant danced. That's his job.

Green:
There is a man dancing.

Red:
Green, what do we do?

Green:
We're alive.

The boiling fog fills the souls of New Yorkers with furious
abandon and the city couples in the long night, haunted. When you're a
port, you're open to who arrives.

The Hierophant dances, crying in the red and green. Rell sleeps, a
deeper sleep than she has ever known.

*   *   *

"What are these machines?" Isolde asked.
"They keep the Wight running," said my brother Wright.
"What does that mean?" asked Hrothbert.
"It means he needs them," said Wright.
They walked midst the machines, chest high metal, white and grey
and dark blue, shiny and dull, whirring and whispering away, lights
blinking.
My brother's proton field sparkled around the hole he had dug,
slowly closing it. The men he'd carried down emptied into the dark
halls. Warriors and rats.
"I was dreaming," said Isolde.
Hrothbert looked at her.
"I was dreaming of a city."

BOOK FIVE
Deserts

f

only it were easier to forget the road not taken, but not so different for all that, just a little drier, lonelier, a little more in love. Who are you to judge yourself? You can't. It is we who judge. Was the road you chose the right one? Only we can decide.

Yseult and Ing grow hungry. Though they have water, the serpent has exhausted his supply of ready meat. Yseult huddles atop its back, curled in a ball in the night, and Ing watches over her.

The serpent grazed upon the lightning bugs in the late hours of night, laying its passengers upon the sand to sprint into the dunes and catch its food. It relished the heady taste of brittle, chewy flesh, crisp and liquid.

Ing and Yseult had not awoken to set their tent when the serpent returned and the serpent stood between them and the rising sun, to give them shade a while longer. When at last they awoke they were ashamed, and pitched their tent.

They wanted to speak to one another but they were too tired. They embraced and slept, half-awake.

"Where are we going?" whispered Yseult into Ing's ear, as the afternoon lengthened outside.

"We're going to the moon," grumbled the serpent outside.

*   *   *

Leyne in Wessalim cried bitter tears.
The Signalman awaited Amikah's coming.
I charged my batteries, warm and tired.
And the *neddinga* crept down the stairs, down slowly towards the Fall Country.

*   *   *

For the galaxy is large, and it is not even a galaxy but a thought that we must think. Analogy, insofar as it describes the structure of relation, is the arbiter of design. It is the tool that we must use as thinking beings to craft our days and our nights. Analogy is a god that we built out of muck and clay, and gave a name, so that we could break it again and curse its failure, and build it anew out of the dust. Analogy is a kind of breathing, the relation of oxygen to lung tissue to blood, to brain and back. In and out we go.

*   *   *

Hrothbert inspected the computer. Wright spoke to him:

"This is a mainframe. On this mainframe run many programs. Many prescriptions. Here are sixty-seven of them. And three dead ones. One of the sixty-seven is malfunctional. It is this one I'm interested in."

Machine heat filled the room. Although ventilation came from cracks leading further down, the room was growing hotter. There were now over a dozen bodies inside the computer room, breathing, heating, trying to stay calm.

Samuel said to his fellow soldiers, "This makes the Wight think, these things. They are part of it. When I give the word, destroy them."

Wright and Hrothbert, with the rats and Isolde in tow, went to the mainframe that blinked out of rhythm with the others. It was hotter to the touch.

"This is the one," said Wright, in his grating voice, which I have often found much more beautiful than my own.

"Will this thing lead us to the Wight?" said Hrothbert.

"Yes," said Wright. (Is he not brave, my brother? Braver than me.)

* * *

It is not my place to complain. But let me do it, just this once. It is not easy being a big metal rabbit. I know all kinds of crazy things that are not translatable into this ridiculous language of yours. Often I'd like to translate them, to tell you, to explain thoroughly and well. I'm trying, you see, as best I can. What I cannot get across with logic I must evoke, in the way of poets.

Well, let me continue. I have much more to tell. Not all of it pretty.

* * *

I joined Ing then. Ing who was the Hrothbert who did not fight for the rats, who never returned to his people. I joined Ing in that terrible desert, there with Yseult and the serpent.

"Going to the moon, I hear," I said, hopping onto the sand, and keeping pace with the serpent. It was midday, and Ing and Yseult were wrapped in fabric, sleeping on the serpent's back. They were running low on water and had to get to the oasis.

"Yes," said the serpent.

"Long way," I said. "Are you sure this is the right way?" I looked up at the moon, hanging, as it does, in the sky.

"Yes," said the serpent.

"Good," I said.

"Yes," said the serpent.

We walked. The serpent is a good walker, very steady. Unflappable. Though it did flap its vestigial gills occasionally, wafting air over its back and over the two humans huddled there.

At length the huge sun set; it was growing larger.

I said to Ing, "Wake up."

They were very tired.

"The oasis is up ahead," I said.

"You're not supposed to be here," said Ing, in a parched voice.

"Give your mount a rest. Walk with me for a bit, it will be good for you."

Ing hopped down, unwrapping part of his face, woke Yseult and helped her down. Her dark red hair looked almost as radiant as my first mate's thick, shiny fur. They walked together in silence.

It had been a long time since I had been in a desert. I who was permitted to enter and exit was smart enough to know the hate these humans would feel for me, since they were locked now onto their path. (Of course, my own choice was long ago, and this is the result ...)

Shortly before midnight, we reached the oasis, and drank in holy silence.

* * *

Under the moonless sky we moved forward, one of the happiest in my life. Our water was refreshed. We knew where we were going.

I who have been so many places and so many people do not often have the opportunity to accompany beings on this particular terminus: the sprite that stems off from the main event, like an extra gluon that arcs off at a juicy particle collision.

There is a chill in this, a schizophrenia. Most beings do not want to know the details of the *what if*, the full story of the path they did not take.

Ing seemed in a Zen-like state, staring at the midnight blue horizon and saying nothing. Yseult, sitting atop the steady serpent, clutched Ing's back and looked about disconsolately, no longer sure of what she had done.

"You know what the mausoleum was?" I asked her.

"No," she said.

"Just as well," I said. "Are you happy?"

"Yes," she whispered.

Colors came into the sky, rippling green and red, glinting off the serpent's eyes and my metal skin. They stitched a course towards some center we could not see, spirally around a vector deeper out, invisible. We were bathed in colored light. Ing smiled. Yseult clutched his back tighter.

* * *

Hrothbert beat the machine with the pommel of his sword, backing up a step as it began to shoot sparks.

"Wait, wait," said Wright, calmly. "First, we take a little nibble from it. If I speak in its voice, do not fear, I am only translating." My brother put his hand into the side of the machine and his eyes changed colors.

"POURER!" he said then, in a loud, flat voice.

Hrothbert thrust his sword within my brother, his teeth bared.

* * *

In the desert, I lurched sideways.

* * *

The energy of the computers coursed through Hrothbert's sword and into his brain, connecting rabbit and man, and, more distantly, the Wight they sought.

* * *

"What is it?" asked Yseult.

"My brother," I said. "He's dying."

I shuddered, unable to walk.

"What can we do?" said Yseult. The serpent watched me. Ing did not; his eyes remained fixed straight ahead.

"I'll be all right in a day or so. Leave me here, I'll be fine. I'll follow," I said.

"We can't leave you here!" Yseult said.

The serpent had already begun to move, and she beat on its back: "No, wait!"

I called after them: "I'm a rabbit! I've survived much worse!"

I watched them disappear.

*   *   *

You know deserts, if only from the photographs, at least. Many see them as the simplest metaphor for life itself. On the edges of the possible, under extreme conditions, life makes life.

We rabbits know that in deserts we are changed, we are rearranged. I cannot know how many I have been; I have lived too long to keep count. But I know, when I lie in deserts, that those others are close to me, and I to them, and I can see the arc of my world take shape:

Lying in the sand, I watch the spinning nebula above, twisting tighter, tighter, and then extruding itself like a telescope, a reed, stretching towards me across the huge sky. The nebula takes part of me across that bridge, throwing me into the fires burning in the wondrous spaces round these worlds.

In so many ways, I am like the Wight Hrothbert sought, a thing needful, so needful that it cannot be quite real, or alive, it must be maintained by others, to serve its terrible purpose reliably for so many million generations, it must be hardy software. Yet, like life, software evolves, it makes ten into fourteen, it makes a simple breeze into a complex ecosystem, and I have been changing too, watching you change.

I am a rabbit. This form of mine is suited to the holes that I must dig. I am no electrician, I cannot rewire these connections that dimensions make. But I can arbitrate. I can spy. From Red to Green. From Earth to Earth.

*   *   *

Where are we? said Hrothbert.

In a city, I said. *It's only a translation. But probably a reliable one.*

What do you mean, a translation? said Hrothbert.

These are not our bodies. Think of it that way. But still the danger is real. Let's go, I said.

126

I had become a bunny rabbit, soft and white, curled atop Hrothbert's shoulder. Watching with my bright eyes. He was dressed as a diplomat, in fine black, with white trim, and gold handkerchief. Our voices echoed in the air around us, though we did not move our lips.

We began to walk, and a woman joined us soon afterward, coming from a direction we did not see.

"What is a desert?" she asked.

"On Earth, where water is necessary for life," said Hrothbert, "a desert is a region that receives little of it. There, the plants and animals must conserve their water to live, and so they grow thick skin and coarse stalks to keep the moisture in. They wait, very long, for rain to come, hiding under the sand, and when it does they rush into it, to claim their portion. Have you never seen a desert?"

"I have," the woman said. "But I wanted to hear you say what it was."

"Why?" asked Hrothbert. "Who are you?"

"I am a diplomat, like you. Come to consult the Bread-Keeper. Have you brought your bones?"

"Do I need my own?"

She smiled a complicated smile. "No," she said.

Ask her where her bones are from, I said.

And the woman, in her plastic and reflective finery, looked at me. I wiggled my nose.

*   *   *

Does Red Make Green?

Green:
Are We Alone here?

Red:
I Have a Family.

Green:
Where?

Red:
Inside you.

Green:
Get Out.

Some of the women of New York ran into the streets, cutting themselves, and were lost in the red and green fogs.

The Hieromancer danced, arcing his body to fit against the thoughts he could feel in the air, the minds of the fog. He could feel them against his skin, their strategies, misanthropies, hungers. He was getting tired.

*   *   *

Meanwhile, in the white city, I sat atop Hrothbert's shoulder. The city was so white it was blinding; it was unclear to us where the buildings ended and the sky began.

Together with the woman diplomat we approached a group of people and saw them tossing bones onto the white stones of the plaza. Dull white and yellow bones, onto the white stones. Some looked up as we approached. Their smiles were fiendish.

In the fiendishness of their eyes I detected the twinkle of the rats.

"I am Reallee," said Reallee, his black hair slicked back, dripping onto his white coat. His smile was huge, filled with a dark joy. "Won't you join us?"

"Thank you," said the woman. "I am Caroline."

"Play," said Reallee, and he handed her the bones.

Hrothbert and I stood next to them, watching Caroline shake them. Across from us, I recognized Ruth, with her dark hair, and Murphy, the albino.

"Play," said Ownlee, adjusting his glasses and glancing up at us with hypnotic eyes.

Caroline threw the bones onto the ground. In their falling, I felt I was one of them.

The air seemed to shift around us as they fell, and when they hit the stones and made their hollow sounds the rats jumped and laughed, and from a glint of light behind Caroline's shoulder I saw a man emerge, huge and hairy, armored in bronze, with braids in his beard.

The rats bowed to the man, as did Caroline. I watched him, and waited on Hrothbert's shoulder to see what he would do.

"Hrothbert," said the man.

"Graymald Bread-Keeper," said Hrothbert.

"You have come to our dream," said the huge man.

"Is it your dream, Bread-Keeper?"

The man laughed, tilting back his head and roaring. Then he stepped forward and knelt, to examine the bones.

Graymald poked at one of the bones, and breathed in the air deeply.

"You've come from Makkina House."

"Yes."

"Where is your tribute?" he said.

"It was taken at the gate, *hlafweard*."

"Was it much?" said Graymald, smiling, looking at Reallee.

"Some, Bread-Keeper," said Reallee. "A good sized bull among the cattle."

"A bull, well! That's good. Let's see what we have here."

"Your war against Wessalim is going well. I wish you joy in it. But you're selfish. You bring us wealth, but where is your service? Have you pledged blood?"

I felt the woman tremble.

"If you must take it, my blood is yours, *hlafweard*."

"I don't mean *your* blood. I mean the blood of your family."

Graymald grinned.

"Go!" he said. "Go on your way in justice!"

She ran.

I am only a rabbit sometimes. I wanted to flee into my hole as I saw a shadow twist out of the sky and swallow Caroline, and the city twisted too; I could see Graymald's face was made of stars. Caroline screamed but the wind choked it off.

Reallee grinned wider. He scooped up the bones and held them out to Hrothbert.

"Your turn!" Graymald, still on his knee, looked up at his former servant with dark eyes.

"No, it's my turn!" said a voice. Striding over the white paving stones was Wallru. Hrothbert put me down onto the stones and ran to his friend. They embraced. Hrothbert felt Wallru's fishy flesh, like sharkskin, his cool body next to his warm one.

"Wallru," said Hrothbert.

"Here I am," he said.

"It isn't the fish-man's turn!" shouted Ownlee.

"Come," said Graymald. "Welcome, fish-man. Did you leave your tribute by the gate?"

"I'm a stranger here, lord. And your ways were unknown to me. But yes, I have come to give. As you are here to give, Bread-Keeper."

"You speak prettily, fish. What is your parentage?"

"My mother is a fish," said Wallru.

"A strong fish she must be!"

"Her name is Vardal and she swims the deep!" said Wallru, and he laughed his beautiful laugh, gurgling a little.

"Well, cast the bones then, fish-man," said Ruth. "With our lord's permission, of course."

Graymald smiled and nodded. Reallee handed the bones to the fish-man, frowning, looking at Hrothbert from the side of his eye.

"Before you cast them, fish-man, I must know what you've come to give, especially if I determine that you are *ungluck*, unlucky. Misfortune demands payment."

"I see," said Wallru.

Lightning, lightning above.

"My people are coming, Lord," said Wallru.

"What?"

"Let me just cast the bones, and I will tell you what my fortune is."

Wallru took the bones in his cool hands and cast them on the stones. I sat on my haunches and watched them fall; I smelled ocean in the air.

What is the origin of life? Only alkaline?

"One of these bones is the bone of a fish," said Wallru. "And so I call it my bone." He knelt to the ground, and ate the bone.

Graymald drew his sword.

And red lightning cut across the sky. Hrothbert scooped me up, and put me on his shoulder.

"*Hlaf-weird*. Be a sailor again!" said Wallru.

Suddenly water was everywhere, and the rats screamed. Ruth threw herself into Hrothbert's arms and I dug my claws into his shoulders as the water sucked us under. For a moment, I saw Graymald struggling with his bronze armor, and Ownlee helping him. Then I surfaced, and the sky was filled with crimson electricity. Floating in the distance, I saw Reallee, his eyes mad. Wallru swam beneath us like a huge dolphin, and we settled on the fish-man's back. Hrothbert grinned, and so did Ruth. I giggled my rabbit giggle, shaking water from my fur.

Why did Ing go East, as his descendents went up the Volga in so many numbers? Was it only to light the way? Where did the vehicle go, and who was driving it? Even I, more powerful than anything you can understand, do not know.

*   *   *

My brother Wright fell, fatally wounded. Hrothbert jerked his sword from out his metal body, and Samuel and his men swarmed forth. Like the followers of old King Lud, they beat the machine that Wright had singled out. With their fists, hammers, and swords, they beat it into fragments.

Hrothbert trembled. Part of him still felt at sea.

"Where are you, Wight?" he whispered.

"Bread-Keeper, we must get out of here," said Samuel.

The men were sweating. The room was very hot.

"Fine," said Hrothbert. "But I've killed our digger."

Samuel stooped down to look in my brother's eyes.

"He's still alive. Barely. Why did you kill him?"

"He was helping the Wight. Or so I believed. I saw my old lord. In a city of white."

"There may be a way out this way," said Samuel, and they followed him deeper into the maze of computers and wires. Shoving a mainframe aside, he revealed a passage.

"I smelled the air," Samuel said. Hrothbert ducked into the cobwebbed passageway, and the men and the rats followed.

* * *

I cannot say now what word it was that I was told when I was born, though I feel that there was one. Sometimes I do wish that I were only a bunny rabbit, and had no need of words. Naming a thing is very dangerous, and then to use the word is, as they say of ownership, to be owned in owning. Naming you are named and will never return to the person you were when nameless.

Knowing the word once, even if you forget it, as I have this one, you feel its echoes in your bones. Its shade, like an ancestor's ghost, pulls and pushes and whispers of the life it's lost and would regain.

* * *

Orkai stood by the tomb of King Ren, who Hrothbert had killed. The grey-green-brown bodies of the *neddinga* flowed round the corners of the sepulcher, towards him. When they reached him, they put upon his head a crown of thorns, since leadership is pain.

"Will you serve us?" said the *nedding*.

The boy's eyes were wide. "Yes," he said.

* * *

The boy rode atop their shoulders as they took the city. He cried the havoc that was needed, urging his men to greater feats. Blood splashed on his young face.

After two hours, Orkai found himself king of an occupied city, collaborator with invaders. At his disposal, an army of ten thousand *neddinga*.

His army ate the city clean of mushrooms, and burst into the homes of the humans to lick clean their outhouses and unswept corners, eager to devour all available algae, dust and offal, for reasons of both nourishment and religion. When they were done, the triumvirate of their leaders went to Orkai where they had left him in the Adjutant's office, playing with toy soldiers.

"Now we take Makkina House," they said.

"I want a scar. A soldier's scar," said Orkai.

The *nedding* cut the boy's face. But he did not cry.

*   *   *

Isolde rode in the desert atop the serpent, who was dancing.

The serpent danced solemn, really only a slow, precise walk. Ing watched, standing. The serpent saluted Ing, but also something much greater than him, the role Ing played. To be a cog can be sweet, when you know you're the piece that's needed.

*   *   *

I am in a river. In the river is a lightning rod. I am that lightning rod. I am in a sky that is a river, huge, purple yellow, black and fire swirling around me. I reach back for the earth.

You may believe I am accustomed to the strangest of dreams but the truth is that I adjust, as you do, to surroundings. I called out, flattened as I was into a disc spinning in color, the words:

a cord

A miracle, slippery umbilical, I feel the lifeline tighten on my leg, in my heart. I am a kite. I am in a river. I am running. Riverrun to Armorica, old son!

Have you leaned against an age? Or held ruined eras that foundered, sad, in your chemical embrace?

I am the wastrel who saw through your peculiar blindness.

Enlightenment! Reason! Bold torch-bearers! Behold again the sky!

*   *   *

My brother is dead.

*   *   *

I know now why I began this tale. We are moving towards the center. Not the end or the bottom but the center, clawing forwards against the centripetal *anomie*, to name a territory. Yet there are so many already there! Oh, diplomacy. It is so tiring.

* * *

In New York, bad things were happening. People went mad, and killed one another. People they knew. Possessed, in the Green and Red. Still Daniel the Hierophant danced.

His boot heels moved, sliding over the asphalt, passing patterns in the greased road. Like Stuyvesant raising his pegleg into the storm, the Hierophant coursed through the murderous colors blackening his city. Hub, hub, you're in a tub. Blood dripping in. Just apply a little electricity.

Hey a bumny hey a bumny on a bumny in a bumney hey a bumny all the bumney ron a lemna onnarevla hey hey onna onna gonna lonna em niana kahnaranna

He intoned the sounds, an obscure faith. There are no magic words, but language is magic because it insists on its right to be despite all movements to the contrary, and there are so many contrarians, aren't there? But speak, speak.

It is not the words that are the real game but the sounds, the sounds of your voice, and what is a voice, child? A voice is like a tree, for a tree makes sounds too, and grows slowly.

The Hierophant let his voice grow, sounding out the syllables he had been taught. Like zombies out of a toxic event horizon, bodies came out of the colored mists, their eyes dark, but as they approached their eyes cleared, and they made a posse on Fifth Avenue, singing into the dark and hideous night.

* * *

My brother lived for a time. I could not go to him, and for this, for this—well. I have let you live. He lay in the computer room dying, his eyes mapping his surroundings, his breath taking in the dust. A maintenance vacuum made its way over to him and he put his finger into it, to see what data it might have.

It queried him, *are you a master?*, to which Wright answered in the affirmative.

(My brother was still alive! I should have killed all of you ...)

The vacuum crawled back into the wall and accessed a mainframe that had been hidden there. Then it emerged from its hidey hole again, with a new voice.

I am XX S.L. XX, said the vaccum.

"I am Wright," said my brother.

What do you do here? Are you what I think you are?

"I am an undertaker," said Wright. "I've come to take you to your funeral."

Ha ha ha ha ha ha ha. The mainframe had a rich laugh. *I come from XXPolandXX* it said.

"Where is that?"

Far away ... far away.

"And yet, here you are. I have decided to assist in banishing you, Wight. In turning you off."

I am not the Wight you seek.

"Who are you then?" My brother tried to lift himself up.

I am XX Stanislaw XX.

"You are, aren't you?" Wright said.

Yes.

"Where have you been?"

*   *   *

Wessalim had not seen a *neddinga* invasion for generations, nor had Makkina House. Nonetheless, Makkina was more prepared for it than Wessalim had been. *The neddinga* found its gates shut, gates which had not been shut for more than 100,000 days.

Atop the shoulders of four dark-skinned *neddinga*, little Orkai regarded his prize. The scar on his left cheek was still fresh.

"Dig!" he commanded.

Neddinga can dig with a will. It is said that a badger can outpace a man with a shovel, but the badger has never met a *nedding. Neddinga* squish their cheeks and faces into the dirt in their eagerness to press through it; parts of the soil become parts of them. Every inch of their bodies is used as a digging implement, not just their claws. They work in a disturbing tandem, sometimes joined at the waist to facilitate broader middle burrows that support countless smaller tunnels. Like earthworms, they eat earth and shit it out, fertilizing the Mother with their sweat, and with their love. Fast.

The sole guard on Makkina's battlements shouted with horror when he saw the *neddinga* begin to burrow.

"Only kill the soldiers!" shouted Orkai as his troops delivered him into the broadest tunnel, and under the walls.

The *neddinga* burst from the earth, inside Makkina.

* * *

Hearing the war screams of the *neddinga*, some of the people of Makkina went mad at once. The creatures swarmed into the city.

Though they generally eschewed meat, the *neddinga* remembered the psychological theater of war, and so three of them swiftly carried a woman over to a barrow and began to open her to eat her insides. She barely made a sound.

The dance of the bodies was beautiful and terrible. The *neddinga* killed many, but far fewer than they could have, preferring to wound. The men who had managed to find their armor or grab their swords fought well, decapitating many of the little beasts, but they were quickly overwhelmed.

The raja of the place, Hadare, seeing the end approach, took to the battlements and began to shout:

"*Neddinga!* We surrender!"

But before he could even finish the words, two *neddinga* leaped atop his shoulders. One held a dirty knife at his throat, and the other tilted the man's head back. Then the second *nedding* whispered into Hadare's ear.

"I am a stupid," said Hadare. Tears rolled down his face.

The *neddinga*, looking up at the battlement, laughed and laughed.

"I am a weak," said Hadare. And they laughed.

"This is now a city of the *neddinga*," Hadare shouted, his voice hoarse.

The *neddinga* holding the knife to Hadare's throat turned then, and shouted to the city:

"Its name is *Auchark!*"

The *neddinga* cried aloud at the name of their darkest god: Auchark, he of the many wings. They screamed in glory. And Orkai did not cry. He watched.

* * *

137

For many days Ing and Yseult were lonely without my company. They were quiet. The moon had grown larger, like a terrifying mother come to scoop them up into her arms. It filled a third of the horizon as it rose, shining with milky yellow light.

Part of me still feels I am with them, as I hover in the air.

The serpent lowed at the moon, sounding out its time, announcing its departure from this Earth and its imminent arrival at the moon.

Chills swept over Ing and Isolde's bodies, and they felt for the first time that they were part of the serpent, not just joined bodily but in spirit too, welded to the ancient need of the animal.

Little lights coursed over the surface of the desert sands as they made their way towards the moon.

*   *   *

The Hieromancer's wife dreamed. She dreamed of music.

*   *   *

Why must I speak of this? These desires of your people for more, for more knowledge, it is so suicidal! It is so strange to me that you desire it, more, and more, and knowledge of more, and more, and more.

Why is this! Can you not see that knowledge is torture? What happens to a man who is tortured? He becomes a torturer.

Well, I've made my agreements. So here is your more:

I am in the Light! I am in the Light, Rabbit in the Light, and luckily I made my umbilicus. Like your old ancestor, key on kite to see the work of heavens, I am swaying, I promise you, the fatal umbrella for your little tragedy, I sway! I sway in seas of stars! Though you may not believe the fullness of the tale that I tell you, know anyway that it was I who brought it about.

INTERLUDE
Wright's Dream

Stairs!

Wright dreams of stairs colored Red and Green. Or perhaps they dream of him, how can we tell? In their slow melody of rising, there is a poison, an improvident wound has beset them both, and they must out of it if they're to rise as they must do.

(Can you see Wright's eyes peer from the sky beyond? He watches...)

The stairs storm up, they wind around, these forms unknowable except through dream, where some say all is known, because in dream what is it to know? What can it help you? You know but all is still the same, and all is still so needful, and all is still to come.

They wind around.

Red says, "We have to neutralize the poison ..."

(Wright screams, there by dying mainframes. I scream, waving in the sky).

* * *

Can you feel the lever in your hand?
Why do we dream?

BOOK SIX
Rell's Dream

She is

dancing at a party and she feels beautiful. The music is delicious, and the people dancing near her.

It's warm on the dance floor and cool outside in New York.

Dancing her foxtrot.

*   *   *

There was too much to do. The baker needed his extra-fine local flour, and the chemist needed some disgusting snail paste. Her third client, the telephone salesman, needed to record her voice for his latest series of holographic advertisements.

She rode her bicycle through a moderately busy New York, down Fifth Avenue, past the park, humming to herself. Cycling soothed her.

By the lake, the children pounded wheat berries in their mortars, and she ruffled their hair and bought two pounds. She dropped it in her basket and headed south, south to Chinatown.

It looked like it was going to rain but it hadn't yet, and Rell hoped that it would hold. Her raincoat had started to leak. Next to her another delivery girl smiled a tight-lipped smile and they rode together silently for a while, through the Bowery, south. An old Italian smiled and tipped his hat to her, leering, and she ignored him, diverging from the other cyclist at a Y-intersection as she approached the old city, passing through a scan-checkpoint, where she performed her habitual spit, one of those tiny resistances slicked under the surface of the centuries.

The Chinatown District, enamored of some older forms of commerce such as massive open markets, tended to attract sellers of more obscure wares. The apothecary was one of these, selling nostrums and mystic cures, including the Murex, the same sea snail that had once been used to dye the edges of Roman senators' togas the royal purple.

"You want 'em live or dead, lady?" the man said.

"Dead."

She paid him and rode south, towards the Wall.

The Jews had put a new Wailing Wall here, centuries back, the destruction of another temple. This wall had never been part of that religious construction, however. It was a colossus, over 8,000 feet tall, matte black and terrifying. It tended to form its own weather systems. Though the Wall was only four blocks long, it was customary to request passage through it, rather than going around, and she did so, getting in line, paying her toll, opting not to bow to the Jewish idols ensconced within the gate, and then she was on her way south to the Battery.

Maybe I can reschedule the voiceover, she thought. But she needed the work.

A proton-field car skirted by her as she rode, some young diplomat, his hair slicked back, his eyes drawn to her, leaning around in his seat.

"Watch the road!" she yelled at him.

At Battery, the site of Stuyvesant's obstreperous landing, was the Observatory, though it no longer bore any visible telescopes. It was the baker had gotten her the chemist as a client. His bakery was right next store, a corner shop in one of the older skyscrapers.

She dismounted, stuck the bike in a shrub, and hustled inside, tossing the flour onto the counter.

"See ya, Hamid!" she called out. He grunted an acknowledgment.

Sunburnt from sleeping outdoors, a young man ran after Rell as she rode off. She covered the two hundred meters to the Observatory, and the young man paused at her bicycle where she'd left it, and peered in the entrance after her.

Rell made her way into the basement, down the concrete stairs, and on entering the lab the professor called out: "Try the new pistachio!"

The lab had been transformed into an ice cream parlor some months back. With the sea snail, a new exciting natural coloring could be adapted to his flavors-in-the-making.

The pistachio bin was red. She took a spoon and sampled it; very peppery.

"This is pistachio?"

"What do you think?"

"It tastes like paprika. Here's your sea snails."

He grabbed the bag and peered inside. He bared his teeth.

"You killed them! *Ach!*" He set to work, cutting open the shells and extracting the flesh with a scalpel, scooping the brightly colored mass into a glass bowl.

"Sorry. I didn't like idea of quivering snails alive in my bag."

The professor ignored her, muttering, extracting a fluid sample from the flesh.

"Well, see you later!" she said.

Rell went back up the stairs, and encountered halfway up the young man. His one hand was balanced against the concrete wall, as though he were resting, or ill. His eyes were dark, and his skin was sunburned.

"Who are you?" said Rell.

The man said nothing.

"Shall I call the police?"

"N- no," he stuttered. "I —"

"Come outside with me," she said, and she grabbed hold of his sleeve. He followed.

"What's your name?"

"R-Rohan. I –"

She waited.

" - I – w- wanted to s- see –"

"Yes?"

"You," he finished.

"Me?"

"You," he agreed.

"What about."

"I- I – have to sh- show you —" he gestured, pointing back towards the bakery.

"Come on then." Perhaps she could make an excuse to the recording studio ...

She walked her bike back across the Battery grass, young man in tow.

"You're homeless?' she said.

"Y- yes."

"Why?"

"I – I'm poor."

"I'm sorry. I shouldn't have asked."

"I- i- t's okay."

"What do you want to show me?"

He still seemed harmless, but she watched his eyes carefully.

"N-n-no, n-n-no, i-i—"

"Shhh, shhh. Okay. We'll see. Take your time."

She followed Rohan around the side of the building where Hamid's bakery was, and the young man pointed into the alley behind it.

There was a clown painted on the brick wall, right at the edge of the alley. Bright colors; fresh paint. It looked frightening as hell.

Rohan's eyes got wider. "I-i-it-'s he-he-here I-I"

Half-listening to him, she took a step closer to the graffiti. It was arresting. The face of the clown was garish and distorted, and its eyes were pools of black.

"Well, what about it?" she said, but part of her already knew.

"It's here," Rohan said.

"What's here?"

"Here," he said.

"Looks like bad *hoodoo* to me. Here, go get yourself a sandwich."
She handed him some coins.Rohan watched her go, saying nothing.

*   *   *

What is the moon to determined lovers? Did our ancestors not
adjust their very bodies to its tidal pull, not out of necessity but from
innovation? They obeyed that tidal pull towards intertribal cooperation,
the music and the hunt and the dreams of wintery men and women
moving over tundras, dreaming of cities, the cities that would come.

I am part of that tidal warp, progressing in my many days from
caretaker to overseer to prophet. Here, hold with me as I stray, though
I am bound to you. Almost like a vassal! Just as I am bound to this
umbilicus swaying in the worlds' winds.

What is the man thinking, swaying in the air, Mary Poppins in the
air, the kite for all time? Unlike her visitation as a gentle wondrous
fairy, this Rabbit wishes to become the air.

There they are: a fire burning in the dark, like yours. Only a few
miles off. Can you remember why you shifted your bodies to the
moon?

*   *   *

I speak of a train. The train of history. Let us climb aboard.

*   *   *

The clown smiled in the alley. It smiled deep and dark. Its eyes
glistened. It knew it could not move, but it could eat. Like a birth canal
with teeth, the clown was a kind of dentatis. A begrudging mother.

It smiled and the alley was centered by it. And though it was many
an alleyway throughout the years had come to the status of special
corridor, mystical doorway, usually through nothing more than neglect,
the clown alleyway was special even midst these. The clown, as all
clowns used to be, was a priest. As Hrothbert had been.

The clown was wise and angry in its wisdom; if you listened, you could hear the alley growl. Rohan feared it. But he was drawn to it too. He slept atop his cardboard under the fire escape. He could hear the clown breathing.

*   *   *

New York has made so many deals. So many pacts. So many signatures on dotted lines uncounted through these recent centuries ...

The fogs were dissipating, but too soon. In the hearts of New York, in every district from Guernsey and to the Islands, war was come. War was come in the hearts of New York, New York that never settled for less, New York that always dreamed that it was better, New York that always hoped it had escaped, war, war came to New York for the fathers, for their brothers, for the souls that were, and still are, uncounted, as the railways came together, as the train struck our deepest heart, as Hrothbert climbed into a vessel in which he was lifted up, an elevator ...

Rohan shivered in the alleyway as the clown's mouth opened.

*   *   *

But earlier: the train arrived. Out stepped the Inspector and his son. Bold, dark-clothed and bright-eyed, on a mission from their native Iowa, bent hard to the logic of Civil War. The amber bauble glimmered in the young man's pocket, and his father's eyes squinted into the sun as they disembarked at Penn and paid the gatekeeper to pass into the Manhattan streets.

"You know what to do," the Inspector said. "I'll see you soon."

*   *   *

Have you heard the firing of the guns? Jump across the whiteline.

*   *   *

Why did New York empty? From its many millions down to under one. I have heard many explanations, and I enjoy listening to the historians argue. But why not ask: why did Alexandria burn? Caesar did not need to burn his own ships which torched the library and yet it came to pass, and we can say it was accident. Or we can say the trading hub will always invite destruction, depending as it does on open gates.

I like to say this: it was for aesthetic reasons. New Yorkers have long been lovers of art in its many peculiar forms, and the city was more artful and more spooky, emptier, its vices the same but harder to find; you had to work harder.

A city grows more haunted as it ages. Was the evil there waiting in Armorica? It was always in our own hearts.

*   *   *

We should speak, just a little, of Iowa. Even as the glaciers left us the terminal moraine of Long Island, they left us Iowa, the richest earth of Armorica. What is it to live amidst the richest? In this, New York and Iowa have much in common. They're both amazed, when they have time for it, at the riches they've stumbled into.

Like sailors, and traders, farmers are superstitious. Although they have their almanacs and trick knees to tell them of the coming weather, it is their nose that serves them best. The Inspector had smelled something he did not like. And so, with his son, he had journeyed East (like Ing, though *inside* the vehicle rather than following it), to see if his nose had been right.

O Iowa you heady conscience! Mesopotamia midst Ohio Mississippi waters fragrant as the Nile ...

*   *   *

Stefan, the Inspector's son, paced up and down the hallways of the District Office, the fancy abstract artwork blurring by him; he is young, and no one is letting him in.

"The Hierophant is still busy, I'm sorry sir!" said the secretary.

He paced. A farm boy with a good suit. A man with an amber gem in his pocket.

The Hierophant visited East 81st Street, and sat in a tiny tea shop there, and watched the wind blow. A storm coming, tomorrow? Tonight.

His son called.

"They won't let me in."

"I'm coming," said the Inspector.

The Inspector was a bureaucrat, a member of the International Bureaucrats' Guild. The bureaucrat is an idealist: he dwells above the petty trader's sway. He knows the way it ought to be and tries to move the world toward this ideal axis.

In separating bureaucrats from political machines, Armorica had hoped to inject transparency into the Balkanized nation-states of the continent, and in fact they had succeeded. But the problem was bureaucrats still had to be hired. They could come and go, but still the regulations served the moods of the moments' kings ...

Which is all to say only that idealism breeds revolution, and that bureaucrats are revolutionaries.

*   *   *

Do what you wanna. Load up your gunna (named after a Swede, Gunnhilda). Oh why is every gun a woman? Do you know? Every bomber too. It's more than that the soldiers miss their women, or even that they fight for them, more than to impress the girls and capture land. Is it not the women who came up with war? Just for the uniforms of blood and mammoth skin atop the warrior, or a skull of Mr. Robinson, the better world displayed enraptured before her fiery eyes and dampened thighs?

Swing us round, baby, swing us round and we'll catch the latch upon the safety, the codeword hatched inside your suitcase, over ancient concretes blazed with plaster and the eagle, we'll hook the longing of our season out to launch our great surprises, the lustful swinging C4 heartaches, the halberds and the falchions that we wanted in our dreams—the long disaster—greased, galled, and delivered to our flailing sons!

*   *   *

I've gotta tell you, baby. When we put 'em on the trains. When we waved goodbye. When the handkerchief was not ironic, when the lady could still imagine champions returning to her door.

*   *   *

The fantasy.

*   *   *

I do not know how many times I'll say it. But I'll say it. Let's follow the young warrior desiring of peace into no man's land. Is it music? Is a watch time? The face of his brother is horrified; his eyes timeless mad and weeping enraged. They move over the edge of the mud and stand into the guns. At Battery Park.

*   *   *

We must bleed the red white. Even as we snap her hairs to life before her kiss her—

*   *   *

I am a Rabbit. Or at least, this is how you know me, the Hrudu Man. When you confuse things so ridiculously, I must pursue the logic of your confusion and suffer it too. Perhaps I can undo it. Or only chew my paws and sigh. Is it only a hunger for you, war? Only a hideous mating ritual? Only a side effect of efficient brains? The rabbits know nothing of it. Can rabbits learn?

*   *   *

Atop the shoulders of the *neddinga*, the boy Orkai went below, through my nest, and as they marched past in their noise and cries, the Signalman detected the voice of his Amikah, his god gone for so long, in the thrumming of the stones.

In the *neddinga's* sudden slaughter and departure, night came to the Fall Country, for the first time in three generations. The two mighty stars blinked out. And all was darkness.

*   *   *

Rell awoke in her Guernsey apartment, screaming.

Isolde held tight onto her man, rising in the elevator.

*   *   *

Let us begin.

BOOK SEVEN
War

Dulce et Decorum Est

Bent double, like old beggars under sacks,
Knock-kneed, coughing like hags, we cursed through sludge,
Till on the haunting flares we turned our backs
And towards our distant rest began to trudge.
Men marched asleep. Many had lost their boots
But limped on, blood-shod. All went lame; all blind;
Drunk with fatigue; deaf even to the hoots
Of tired, outstripped Five-Nines that dropped behind.

Gas! Gas! Quick, boys!—An ecstasy of fumbling,
Fitting the clumsy helmets just in time;
But someone still was yelling out and stumbling
And flound'ring like a man in fire or lime ...
Dim, through the misty panes and thick green light,
As under a green sea, I saw him drowning.
In all my dreams, before my helpless sight,
He plunges at me, guttering, choking, drowning.
If in some smothering dreams you too could pace
Behind the wagon that we flung him in,
And watch the white eyes writhing in his face,
His hanging face, like a devil's sick of sin;
If you could hear, at every jolt, the blood
Come gargling from the froth-corrupted lungs,
Obscene as cancer, bitter as the cud
Of vile, incurable sores on innocent tongues,—
My friend, you would not tell with such high zest
To children ardent for some desperate glory,
The old Lie: *Dulce et decorum est*
Pro patria mori.

— Wilfred Owen, 1917.

o the

bloody ocean we come, appropriate perhaps, having come, we return, after the buildings were detonated, some deliberately as cover, some by the artillery. The eye of the needle, the eye of the needle, the poor man and the camel, the blood, and the blood, and an ocean of blood.

Harry goes in, he goes in. Over the top.

New York so long delayed reaps rich rewards over a thousand skies its memories the lights of the loved ones who watch on their screens the carefully censored missives sent to satellite, but down below Harry knows (though knows is not quite the right word, knowledge is too weak to process the immensity of it) the truth of it, or that part of the truth of it.

He reaches for the cable, as Hector and Susannah evaporate. As his cheek and hand are covered with their flesh. Over the top, what is the river? We submerge.

Is Harry swimming? Oh, see the soldier swim in his dungarees! See him swim beneath the sparkling waves!

He reaches for the cable. Fire. He reaches for the cable. Load, and fire. Harry reaches for the cable, and they evaporate. Harry reaches for the cable, over the concrete mass, the rebar, over the dust, in oceans of his brothers sisters blood, into the morass, the land, the land, bought for a song, sold to the world, amped revamped repeated centenary vowels unlost untold, Manhattan:

Harry is a solder in the war. Fighting toward Battery Park.

War by others means is trade they say and so much sweeter than, for all its underhanded dealings, for at least then we speak, listening to the vowels and the cutting consonants of barter haggle trade under the canopies.

Forward is a dimly understood idea, no better than backward. Red green mists awash over the one two buildings standing, he can hear a radio report.

" ... they're all gone ..."

He kicks the radio away and scrambles over the chunk of rebar deeper into no man's land. All the barbed wire is gone, all the laser sites, and then he hears another barrage.

Gunnhilde, the filthy Swede, Gunnhilde the loving frau back in the Middle Ages for whom the first cannons were named, the guns are firing from Brooklyn. Fire, and fire ...

Harry is too far ahead. His own advance is paralyzed. He stumbles to the right, over a microwave oven and a mainframe, a commode, as quarter-city-blocks ignite. The heat touches his face ...

*   *   *

The general examines his pocket watch. Time to fire. Fire. Fire. Fire.

*   *   *

153

The column advances into the flames in their flame-retardant jumpers and though there are some screams it's hard to tell who it is, as all are engulfed, as Harry watches, his mouth is making a kind of sound, the skin of his cheek comes off in his hand.

Fire.

Fire.

Fire.

*   *   *

The general adjusts his pocket watch.

*   *   *

Fire.

*   *   *

The general adjusts his pocket watch.

*   *   *

Harry shouts and runs, he gets up. He climbs further into Coenties Slip, out of Cuylers Alley, though all the streets are gone.

When night comes Harry finds he's in a new unit. Stone deaf. He still has all his limbs. Not a single graft.

*   *   *

The music calls over the parade. The sounds of waygog arc over the mausoleum of Armorica's youth, shrill and paradisiacal, the screams of the dead, the beauty of the warm mid-Atlantic night.

Someone shoves a scrap of bread into Harry's hand and he eats it.

Through the night the cannons fire, green, yellow red disasters sparking cross Manhattan, annihilating masses and they charge, with all *élan vitale*, to make the generals proud, they charge into the city that was theirs before it wasn't, perhaps it will be all again, they charge and gain another seven yards before they're pinned down, and blown to bits, trying to charge their shields. No alternating current available.

The microwave radiation cooks them at night and even heats the concrete so survivors have somewhere to sleep, atop the smoking wreckage, like a Turkish bath, their nostrils bleeding.

*   *   *

Fire for Prometheus. And Fire for your sons. And Fire into the faces of your daughters. And Fire into the Soul You Wrapped around your Proud and Plaintive Island, never able to sign, or pledge, the fatal port, its music caught around (and caught a round)—

Harry and his new squad creep towards Fraggers Tavern and beyond they see remains of Broad Street, an inferno smoking poisons in unheard-of spectra.

Harry makes a sound with his mouth, he does not know what word or words but his mates laugh, they laugh, into the night a raucous music, and Guernsey answers, from the West: " ... fuzzballs! ..."

Then the silence drops across the sky, the Generals have forbade all conversation and the air is trapped inside the soldiers' mouths and so they start to sign, making shadow animals and puppets all night, cast along the concrete walls from pocket torches, and Harry laughs, he laughs across the wastes of Broad Street, until his mates tell him to shut it.

*   *   *

Dawn comes slow, horrible beautiful. A painting. Like the last day alive. Like a new kind of curse. The Generals call on the telephone.

" ,. .. .. x . . "

No one is able to hear but they know what it means. Crossing Broad Street they lose 10,000 men an hour.

Human blood and ocean water float across the ruins.

Someone has found a gramophone and round noon they wind it, listening to the sounds of The Clash. London is falling. London is calling. New York shrieks into the long afternoons, its pigeons insane, its daughters vanished, its jewel crushed, its men wantonly displayed in the grey and ash, their faces wet circles in the winter cold (how long has it been?).

They set the corpses afire, wearing masks, and cheer, curse, and do some jigs and see the Guernsey men doing the same a thousand yards away.

*　*　*

The Generals try an experiment. They decide that there is something after all to the old-fashioned notion that an individual soldier (even an enlisted man!) might know what he is doing and so they give certain infantrymen siting insignia for satellites and triangulation algorithms recently programmed by the brightest of the brightest of the brightest

(like stars)

The brightest of the brightest of the brightest (their albedo an inferno) of the brightest minds on earth

(the Einsteins all come again, their wild faces horror round and wise into so many centuries forever captured in the boxes courted round for media relations)

The brightest all AI encoded, they have chosen who to pick for this bold mission

(Franklin, the poor bastard)

But something goes wrong. Franklin in his gamma suit is so afraid, he's so afraid, he's being tossed in the explosions as he makes his way across no man's land but he still manages to target the enemy HQ situated underneath the remains of Whitehall Street across Stone, he targets them and summons in the infantry charge ...

Then friendly fire, a blaze that lasted for a month. (75,000 men).

Albedo like Einstein's sun, like his sons, his mighty tongue displayed on college posters, Harry sits around the campfire with a turkey leg roasted in his hand, his Christmas dinner so delicious that he feels like crying and he does, just a little. Chewing.

Wilfred means "hoping for peace." And Owen means "brave soldier."

*　*　*

Fighting down. Into our graves.

*　*　*

The long goodbye and the sainted ash. The word we must not speak, the woman we must not remember, the day we must not name, the mission we must not forget must not speak of, the night and the day one uninterrupted blip on Generals' brightly colored 3D maps, live updated, on the killing floor—

*   *   *

Do the Generals kill themselves?
Is it *sepukku, hari kari* time?
Go out with honor?

*   *   *

This war is not one you can injure yourself out of; if you survive a battle the nano knits you new, or mostly new, using the dead flesh of your comrades as material. (Though shooting yourself in the foot means court marshal, and then they'll shoot you).

*   *   *

Harry reaches for the rebar. (He's the future World President). He reaches out.

*   *   *

Fire.

*   *   *

He reaches for the rebar.

*   *   *

Fire.

*   *   *

He reaches for his life. Harry reaches for the rebar, reaches for it, and *takes hold of it*, it is in his hand, he is moving. He is moving into fire next to his brothers. Screaming, he is quiet, screaming silent, running, stumbling, he is one, grunt, he is grunting like a pig hunting for truffles he fires his weapon.

* * *

He fires.

* * *

The General adjusts his watch, his weapon. His weapon: his watch.

* * *

Harry fires.

Harry opens the veins of a dozen men with a well-placed round, and smiles, for in the medulla killing is glorious, and the General's watch is glorious in the medulla because the medulla is shaped like an artillery cannon, winding into the screaming colored sky because Harry is laughing knocked unconscious.

* * *

Aid Station. They play music he cannot hear, a beautiful nurse. An angry doctor in a uniform, a robot. A robot speaking Polish.

* * *

Brooklyn gains Pearl and Bridge Street, moving towards State, right across from Battery Park, there's even a tuft of grass somewhere left in there, and then things stop making sense, for Harry and all the rest.

Guernsey knows they cannot lose The Park. Brooklyn knows that they have to gain The Battery. If you can call that knowledge.

Harry keeps turning oxygen to CO_2. Smelling death.

Incredibly, the guns have unearthed a Model T Ford automobile, preserved somewhere beneath the ancient city, and some of the officers ride in it during a pre-arranged truce (each side taking turns for maximum media exposure).

Then the tripwire bursts across the park. The officers ignite like torches, their flesh the accelerant, screams barely audible over the sound blast from the rupture in the Earth, the Second Front.

Battery Park, nickel cadmium, four thousand howitzers strong, copper carbide, steel carbine, lithium ion, fusion death ray.

Battery Park at the port to rule them all until it wasn't. Battery Park, the nobles and the kings atop the stage of history.

But I am only a Rabbit. What does it mean, friends?

I promise. I promise you, humans, this life is only one.

*   *   *

But no less precious for all that, eh? (Until you pull the switch).

*   *   *

What does it mean to praise survivors? In wars of chance? It was never anything that you did, or didn't do. And the survivors, broken, are just barely propped up by drugs and well-meaning walks around the park.

Harry, President of the World, was later heard to say over the airwaves:

"I may not know much, but I know this: I hate war ..."

He collapses back into his chair. And they cheer ...

The crippled President, epileptic hero, wounded god.

*   *   *

But all that is after.

*   *   *

Can we wind the clock tighter? We need more precision. Though planes and airborne vehicles of any kind had been forbidden for near a hundred years and the proton fields were sound preventatives, from out of Battery Park came the music of engines.

Schedule the run. Prime the jets. Worship. On our ship of worth what are our gems and diadems, Great Fathers, Mothers? What worthies will we throw into the brink?

A mountain of death like a wave, shocked through the foundations and the wrack and wreckage, liquefying flesh. The planes keep their tight formation, yellow green and horrible and for whatever reason Harry's shield does not fail, though it fizzles out after. Once again alone.

Harry finds himself stumbling toward the Old Barge Office, next to the ocean. Puckering the surface of the waves and the surface of the park, launch silos slip up like whack-a-moles, spitting ships into the sky.

Harry finds himself just out of its range of death, no longer following orders as he's deaf, and a translator has not been assigned him and direct neural control is still illegal and he watches the V of death sweep, broom of light, painting Manhattan as its painters knew so long ago:

An estuary color and undoable again, speckled fainted mad and hate withal drawn down into the canvas, the world beneath the world, the human heart writ bold and logical atop the murdered city.

Harry smiles a little, because he does not know when he will get it, and the machinery of death can be pretty.

*   *   *

Why did Ing go East? Was it to reclaim some prize? To gather more friends and worshippers? Had he just had enough? What did he know, when?

*   *   *

The Generals in their sighting rooms rotate shifts of ninety minutes even as the building rotates levitating, to afford a fair view of all approaches. Every ninety minutes *élan vitale* can be refreshed, it can be brought to peak, a shift in the murder factory, firing its pistons pistol tight and fast for love and energy and victory, democracy and heartache, food for the gulls.

Washington, town for your washing, has taken to the air.

*   *   *

The Hierophant huddled in a storeroom, miles down. District boundaries were meaningless now that all the treaties had ticked into effect, overriding diplomatic safeguards, charging the batteries of war.

The inspector's son huddled with him, their backs against the concrete wall, light flickering as the electricity came and went, their faces drawn and sleepless.

The Hierophant's song had worked until it hadn't. He had done his duty.

One of the Generals buzzed on his phone but he ignored it; he no longer trusted phones. Was Rell dead?

* * *

Just choose sides and load your weapons and you can have another war. Rewrite the rules and then forget about them and bow low to the grindstone to smear off your face. We're ready.

* * *

The Hierophant wanted to speak but the guns were too loud, and when they finally stopped all everyone wanted to do was sleep. His secretary huddled by him and they shared their water rations, arms around each other's shoulders.

BOOK EIGHT
Peace

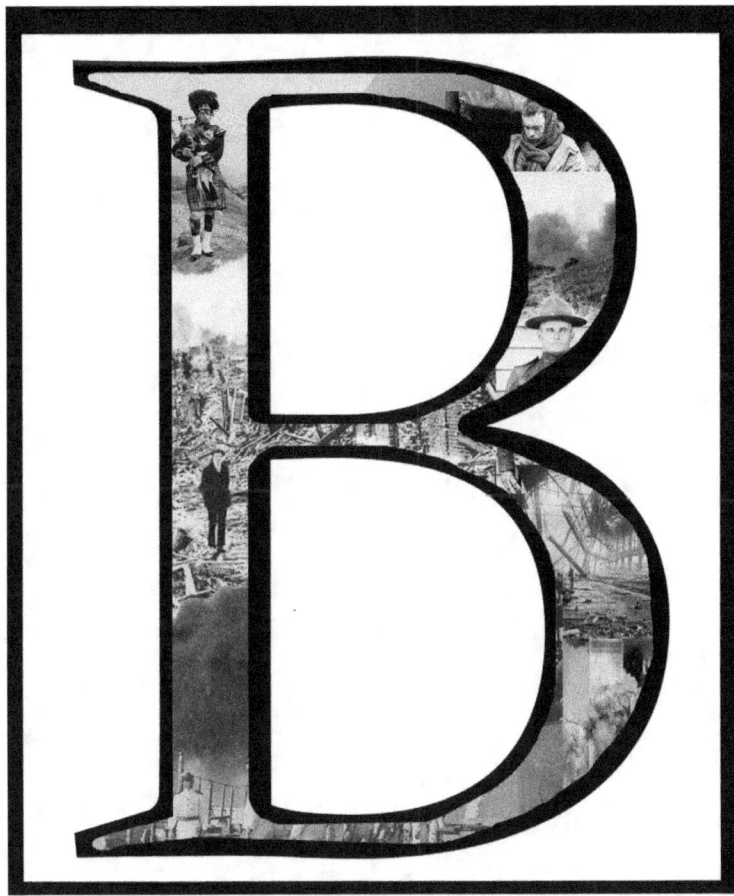agpipes.

Over the curtain of history. They buried the dead with bagpipes, the Irish marching down Broadway, turned to dust.

Hrothbert climbed out of the sewer and emerged from the mouth of the clown, which was now only a few dozen bricks still standing. The sun was bright. Isolde followed him, and then stood in the desolation. She looked at her man and then back out into the blasted moonscape, where she saw the march of the bagpipes in the distance.

"What is this?" said Hrothbert.

"Hell," said Samuel. "We've come to hell."

All the dust tasted like medicine. The rats climbed out of the clown's mouth then, and crouched, looking at the disaster.

I am only one Wight, if that is what you would have me be. You are one difficult case of management.

* * *

"Where have you brought me?" said Isolde.

"We've returned to Earth," said Hrothbert.

"I feel I'll fly away."

"That is the sky."

"Where do we go?" Isolde said.

"Let's follow the music," said Samuel.

"What is this place?" said Murphy, his red eyes glowing in the sun.

"Another dead city. Like Eklaiah," said Hrothbert, and he began to walk towards the sound of the bagpipes. The others followed.

* * *

What comes from the port? At the shores of your nation, at the apex of your spine? Connection and its uncounted corridors for worship and being. No connection without being, no being without connection, through the port, through the axon, docking with its ropes.

The living beings of these Earths strive for it with all their might, as you have done, wedding flesh to flesh. So too do the suns need it, for they are lonely, attracting planets to their whirling community.

Like sodium across the salient of cell's membrane, the electric message's return is even sweeter than its going. When Ing returns. Go East and come West; fly into space and emerge from the Earth.

I know, we are only stories, we have only little containment field entertainments to stave away the darks. Only. Just. So, if it's all we have...

Then why does it matter that it was the Haerdingas who were impressed? Can only Hard Ones write the words to outlast centuries? And would they have been able to bear Ing's eventual return?

Perhaps they killed him when he did so, and the runes were the Haerdingas' apology.

* * *

After war, exultation: and though there be no bunting and no ticker tape, you can run.

Hrothbert ran towards the bagpipes, feeling the sun on his face. He had feared he would never feel it again. This sun was different; more yellow. He ran through the dust, Isolde and his companions following behind.

What do you do when you've killed a city? Do you bury it? Do you bring it back to life? Of course, geography usually trumps politics and sentiment: there was a reason you built there in the first place.

"Player!" shouted Hrothbert at the bagpipers. "Players! What city is this?"

"New York, buddy," said a bearded Irishman, his eyes wet. "Ain't you from around here?" He played.

The island had been razed. The wounded in their millions had been evacuated by train, to aid stations in Guernsey, Brooklyn, and the Bronx, which had been rapidly converted to hospital cities. A law had been passed that you could keep your stump if you wanted; no one could force you to have it regrown.

And Harry Patch was running for World President, on the Peace Platform: demilitarization, and interstellar exploration.

What do we do with the Generals? Did they not only give us what we wanted? One or two shot themselves. Several wrote books. *My Time in the Sky. The Great War. Tactical Problems in the Battle for Manhattan.*

Hrothbert still had a scrap of cheese. From Old Second Earth. He gave it to his woman, and watched her chew.

*   *   *

Rell volunteered to search the wreckage, accepting training in the mech suit, ten times her size. Her husband was down below somewhere, she knew.

*   *   *

What do you do when Ing returns? It is as though John discovers Christ was not crucified after all, but meets him on the road to Syria, shakes his hand, very much alive. Is it simply best to forget?

But aren't you just a little curious? What did he see in the East? How many secrets does our Inglish hold?

*   *   *

In the desert, Yseult whispered: "Did I ever tell you why I followed you?"

Ing started to speak but Yseult shushed him.

"What do you think I saw in you, hmm? That dark light. Like here, here it's all around us. That's what I saw in you. I think I had something like that too, in me."

Ing turned around on the serpent to face her, the sky shining insane colors above, around the enormous moon.

"No, you were brighter. Brighter than me," he said.

*   *   *

Some said it was archaic patrilineal laws that forced so many democratic rulers into the Manhattan War; the ostracisms of so many *alleva*, the bastards without property, had yielded inevitable interfamilial dynastic conflicts across and beyond the North Armorican continent.

One such *alleva*, Rebecca, our young rock star, without cocaine for over twenty days, lay on her bed in Guernsey. Two weeks into the war her dealer had stopped calling back, and she stopped leaving the apartment. Her manager had fired her, and the city that was supposed to have been her home for the year was now ashes. Most international currencies had been frozen, pending a government re-org, and unless she wanted to sink her life savings into South African *rand*, she could not travel. She had just enough available cash to pay the rent.

She lay on her bed reading a book in French, thinking about how to get some drugs, and about why she shouldn't kill herself. Sometimes she still heard Santa in her head.

*   *   *

I am in color. Where do you want to go, people? I am in the colors above. How many do you think would like to eat us, for all that we have done? How many we've offended. Where do you want to go, sons and daughters of Ing?

I am the Hrudu Man! I fight for you! I am Hrudu Man, Hrudu-ed!

INTERLUDE
Ing

I love a woman. My name is Ing, and this is my confession. For me love was a choice, like war. Run away with the woman, or stay, and let her be taken from me. Whatever I should have done, what I did was run.

I am only a man. It's true that at times I found it convenient to have worshippers. I liked being seen as a god, or a demi-god at least, a warrior-priest of great power. But no man can sustain such fantasies for long if he wants any respect.

I fear I have given myself away—to the moon. I fear that my fears are coming true, that Skyfather will strike me dead, that my people will haunt my dreams, that I will die alone and unloved in a strange country.

It is lucky that I am strong, and have a woman. How else could I still live? How else could I know that I have meaning?

Of my weakness, and my going: if I can find forgiveness in my woman, may you forgive me too?

BOOK NINE
Wind

 omething

was approaching, from the sky. We who funnel the charnels of war into its battlefields and call it inevitable, who slip the uniforms onto our sons and sharpen swords in the name of glory and expediency, we who fight, for whatever reasons good and bad ... we who gird against the day and against our own souls, armor all mad, it is hard for us to anticipate the attraction that these endeavors make, quite far beyond the circle of our sun.

That is: sometimes what we do gets noticed.

Rell walked through the pulverized dust, towards the river. She could see the great farms of Guernsey and their combines, and some of its skyscrapers in the distance. She sat down by the shore of the river, watching the grey city dust soak into the edges of the water.

One of the Washington planes coursed through the sky, just under the speed of sound, a warrior who had not wanted it to end. His fuel, being solar, was long lasting, though eventually he would starve.

Hrothbert sat down beside her, and she began to cry.

Hrothbert let her cry, sitting near her, and watching her, waiting for her to finish.

"What do we do now?" she said.

"Go over there," said Hroth, pointing at Guernsey. "Samuel and his men went after the players. They can tell us how to get there."

"What do we do when we get there?" she asked.

"Seek the king."

"He might kill us! They seem to like killing here." Her liquid eyes almost made Hrothbert doubt everything he had ever done.

*   *   *

General Rutembasa was on trial.

Photographs shone on the wall, ones that had not made it past the satellites' censors. The audience gasped. Mountains of bodies; lakes of blood; ruin.

The people's prosecutor mounted the dais and spoke.

"People, you know me! I am Hector Vinovia. You have seen the bodies this man killed! You have seen his face. But what you do not know is how many chances the General had to undo his evil work.

"At the beginning of the Manhattan War, General Rutembasa received a letter from his diplomat, Miss Ella Monrose. The letter reads as follows:

General,

I write you in full knowledge that this letter will most likely send our small but glorious nation forth to the testing ground of war. There has been no response to our communiqués, and the monkey has not been returned, either by post or by personal delivery. Although I am told Mr. Chunky is doing well in Guernsey, and we can rest assured that left to his own devices he will have a happy life there, it seems clear that the Communist government of that state does not see fit to honor our rightful demand for his return. They love him just as much as we do.

That being the case, I immediately notified all our agents stationed in Guernsey that they were being recalled, and that they should prepare for what would most likely be an immediate and glorious conflict for our honor and for our territories here on the Upper East Side.

The monkey will be returned to us."

The prosecutor continued: "People! The war was fought over a monkey!" Some in the audience moaned; some jeered. The prosecutor continued.

"What did the General do upon receipt of this letter? The power to mobilize, the power to begin what he had to have known was a huge and bloody war was entirely his. Did he hesitate? I present now this memorandum which he circulated in his offices immediately following the communiqué from Miss Monrose. It reads:

Citizens of the Upper East Side, My Compatriots:

Our beloved mascot, Mr. Chunky, is, at this moment, being illegally renationalized as a citizen of the state of Guernsey. I know that this brings you as much sorrow as it brings me. But I can assure you that, in response not only to this gravest of affronts to our national honor but to the insidious designs this horrific kidnapping clearly indicate are foremost on the minds of our enemies, the Guernseyans, we the Upper East Side of New York City, with our strongest and most terrifying will and armaments, will grind Guernsey into ash. In this undertaking, I ask your heartfelt and unwavering support, as is my right, as your Dictator.

Please, act quickly, and act with purpose. Our nation is being tested. We must not be found wanting!

In the glory of God, Manhattan, Our Founding Fathers & et cet. I am yours,

General Rutembasa, Esq.

The prosecutor continued: "He did not hesitate for an instant!"

Jeers came from the audience, prompting from the judge a bristly: "Silence!"

"He did not hesitate for an instant, General Rutembasa. No, he mobilized his armies. He loaded his guns. He prepared for an illegal, immoral, and horrifying war he knew was unwinnable!"

The prosecutor sat down. The defense attorney rose, a Mr. Hu. He rubbed his generous gut with one hand and smiled.

"Ladies and Gentleman. Your Honor," Hu made a small bow, "Good afternoon. I wish that I were speaking to you under better circumstances. I wish (as does General Rutembasa!) that all this had not come to pass, that the flower of our youth had not been laid to waste, that the jewel of the city of New York did not turn to ash, that our homes and families and honor were not destroyed. I wish all this, and I know, as you do, that General Rutembasa was one actor who assisted in bringing about the horror! For this he will be punished, no matter what happens. By his community, by society, by his own conscience. But should he be punished by the law as well? Do we not adhere to the logic of the Monkey, and his signifying force, the power of the Monkey to remind us of our humble simian roots, our simple joys, our heavenly desires? Without a Monkey, who is a nation? Without a Monkey, who are we?"

Some of the eyes in the audience were already wet. Behind the judge, the Monkey of Hell's Kitchen, Mr. Bubble, glared balefully at the audience from his oil painting.

"Without a monkey, do we want to go on as a people? As a race defined by our differences and commonalities? Good fences make good neighbors! And Guernsey violated our strong fence!"

Rumbles and murmurs in the audience.

" ... but that is all behind us. The war is over, thank the gods. Thank our wise Fathers and Mothers, we have put an end to it. I ask you, who was instrumental in ending the Manhattan War? General Rutembasa was! Let us hear it from his own lips!"

To the side of the courtroom, a panel slid open along the Plexiglas encasement where the General was displayed.

"General," asked Hu, facing the man, "What data had been brought to your attention that allowed you to bring your part in the conflict to an end?"

The General spoke in a monotone into his microphone: "On examining the data, averaging 4,000 casualties an hour, with a limb regrowth rate of only 750 bodies an hour, and a reserve of only 80,000 men and women warriors, I concluded the Bright Upper East Side could not defeat its hated enemies in a mere day or two, and I made overtures for surrender."

"The armistice took place soon after that, did it not?"

"Uhh, yes. Yes it did."

"Within two weeks?"

"That's correct."

"You see the bravery of this man!" shouted Hu. "He was willing to do the math! Were any of the rest of you willing? He took it upon himself to be willing! To perform the horrible arithmetic of victory! I say, thank the gods! Thank the gods someone was willing to do it! Someone without fear, like General Rutembasa!"

Some muffled cheers in the audience. Then silence.

The Judge said, "Let the adjudication begin." They turned out the lights.

* * *

In the darkness they heard the World President's voice, former infantryman of Brooklyn, Harry Patch, sole survivor of his regiment.

"Down, down in the basement of my mind, I knew I was dead. I knew that I had to be dead, and that I was in hell. But on the surface I could function. I could see my buddies blown apart into little bits that stuck to my arms and my lips, even when I managed to get my shields working, I could taste their blood.

"I knew I was dead and in hell and I knew that I was happy for it—since there was no sense in me or in others or in the sky and earth, hell was the sense. Hell made sense of it, so I could walk, and laugh, and choke, and fly through the air from the artillery.

"I was only a body, one amongst a million. A drop of blood in an ocean of blood. Already dead."

As President Patch's voice faded, neuropathic transmitters powered up and began to induce new brain states in the men and women present in the courtroom. Over the sounds of soothing music, expert technicians adjusted the beams and wavelengths to suit the neurochemistry of each audience member, and after a minute, the show began:

Bloody colors, painting: a limb a piece of wax, arcing through the air an art project, separated from context: whole, surreal, revivifying.

Impact of gun in company serene immobile—lost under the sun—burned hot fat faces godless screaming agonies, liquefied by incident and by degrees, the crater into moving regimented flesh in uniforms wrought wildly in space and slow time, cooked into the medulla.

Fighting down into the basement of the mind, racial pride and fear, the group desire, holy spirit, the word divine, feeling of the serpent winding round the hand, delicious disastrous armed plane up in sky —

The courtroom swam through their induced dream.

*   *   *

Hrothbert and Isolde made love in Guernsey City, in one of the million tents of the Hospital District, their bodies urgent and lost, finding in each other what they needed.

And Isolde conceived a child.

INTERLUDE
Common Enemies

Genocide, by definition, is something that civilized peoples do; we only came up with it after having figured out agriculture and various other complications, after all.

Moral relativists will claim that complication is the only moral good, that in this winding arc of history we should know only that which progresses towards the further amalgamation of axons, a bigger brain, a wilder night, a huger pot, a bigger bet.

Vonnegut in his Indianapolis dreaming told us that the smaller brain is where it's at if we would pursue our happiness with any great energy, any seriousness.

I tell you that war is always coming, and that this one, though you may have forgotten, was the best and the worst. For all its sins, what is the purpose of war? It is comminglement, in all its horrors. In its devastating tragedies. In its inhuman sounds and terrors. In its hells and wounds unending. Is life not itself an unending wound and horror, screaming deliciously like a woman in pleasure or pain out into this unending night sky?

We all know the story, don't we? How do you unite a bunch of Haitians, Scythians, Monrovians, Burgundians, Franks, Trolls, *neddinga*, Africans, Americans, Juvians, Rovians, Trovians, Heliots and Helots, and Meads, the worlds of our thoughts and reams of histories forever unintertwined lest their unique significance be lost? We war, we war! Until:

A common enemy arrives.

O a Common Enemy! For with that fight the world of our lives! I am a Rabbit, and I Salute you!

*   *   *

Yes, your common enemy is coming, in the form of Reshh. He is a music I can still hear. A broadcast. A new flavor on your tongue. A nightmare from which you are trying to awake on an Irish hill, turning, yearning for a good night's sleep.

My brother is dying.

And hurtling towards our world, a ship ...

I sense the course of one called the Manager. His argosy howls and hurtles towards the Earth. I smell its energy, like a wind upon my face.

INTERLUDE
Wright's Dream

Brother, where are we going?
We're going upwards, brother.
Where is that, brother?
Towards a greater complication, brother.
Why do we sing?
I do not know.
Is there a reason?
Let me cut you with a knife.
Brother, let me cut you with a knife too.
Brother, is this the way?
It's the way, Red Brother.
Green Brother.
Red Brother mine.
Green Brother mine!
Red Brother mine, you old rapist.
Green Brother, you have forgotten ...
Forgotten?
Forgotten this:
and time stretches horribly watching itself bubble,

[Did you know that I had a childhood? In a field of grass?
Once when I was only a small bunny I smelled my mother
close to my cheek and it was such a beautiful smell, I miss it
even now, the way she moved over the grass while I ate, while I
smelled the *hraka* and the sun, and the moon, and the stars.
While I was young.

What is a metaphor if you can taste it? Metaphor means:
bearing across. I am your mule, and I am used. This is my
purpose. I am making in the doing of it, my journey is not only
an act but a creation, because I am Wright, and because I was
named that by mother bunny for a reason, because what I do
matters. What I do lasts. Though it may only be this universe
for a thousand thousand thousand years, still it was here! I
wrought the lilt of your finest hegemonies, the swirl of dark
matter into light ...

What do you know of Wights? Do you think that we are your puppets? Do you think that gods are only dreams? They're not, and yet I'm dreaming ...]

Why do we let the Rabbit talk, I don't like it when the Rabbit talks.
He is a good Rabbit. Our Rabbit.
I do not like the Rabbit.
But the Rabbit likes you, Green Brother. He likes you.
Where are we going, Brother?
To dinner, Brother. To dinner.

BOOK TEN
Judgment

he

prosecutors monitored their brain stimulators, which eased the court through the necessary feelings. Judgment is, in fact, a feeling.

What is the peak of wreckage like a stovepipe hat cobbled improbably high by artillery explosions? What is the prison of the trench? What is the shape of the dying man?

The men and women in the court floated through their arranged daydream, and the medulla, being a powerful organ, did not fail the prosecutors. Emotional memory, induced or genuine, is hard to argue against.

It became all anyone could talk about afterwards, the depth of their emotional experience. Though there were few veterans among them, they all felt as though they'd been there. They all shared the grunt's contempt for the blind officers of the Great Manhattan War.

United in their feelings, they sentenced General Rutembasa to life imprisonment in a swift and a unanimous vote. He was taken off to Rikers, recently designated a World Prison.

* * *

Daniel, the former Hierophant of the former Western District, and Rohan, formerly homeless, sat together at a café in Guernsey, watching the late afternoon sky, and some dancers in the street. It reminded Daniel of his own dancing, and his failure.

"The rats want their own television show," continued Rohan. The war had removed his stutter completely. "They have a lot to say. And I think Armorica ought to meet them. This new world is so strange! Visitors returning from our colonizations of almost three millennia ago? Yet their tongue has not changed! Still it is Inglish! What could this all mean? Our new telephones are silent! The world is waiting for an answer! Why not the rats!"

"Peace is doing well by you, Rohan. I'm glad," said Daniel.

"And not for you?"

"Well, aside from unemployment, yes, it's grand. Of course. Guernsey's paying my expenses for a few months, bless them. I couldn't be happier."

"Well, will you help make The Rat Show happen?"

"Rohan, really I'm charmed that you would ask at all! I have no power. But if there's anything I can do, I'll do it. Gladly. I promise."

"Thank you, Daniel," said Rohan, standing and smiling his new-found smile. "Thank you."

Rohan left for his new position at World Headquarters in Guernsey, and Daniel, former Hierophant, was alone. He watched the dancers in the street, remembering the Red and Green.

* * *

Ing looked at Iseult:
"Do you still remember who I am?" he said.
"Of course," she said. "Of course I do."
"I'm not sure I do," he said.
The moon swirled around them.

*　　*　　*

Judgment is a feeling. The judgment centers of the brain, after 25 years of age, undergo what could be called a kind of atrophy. Cognitive processes break down in favor of quicker emotional responses. The knee-jerk becomes stronger, and more reliable. This is what judgment is: the jerk of a knee. The feeling in the gut. The blind instinct that we follow, hoping it is right. It often is.

Intellectual rigor comes after the feeling, to justify, and to explain.

The feeling is connected to separation: in judgment, we must decide what is kept together, and what is not. We decide which behaviors are lawful and which are not. We draw the borders and decide the punishments for transgression.

But what is a feeling? Where does it come from?

The dock, and the ropes, the axon, and the dendrite, the port: with fewer borders, in a greater *us*, what will be kept together and what be kept apart?

Where do our feelings come from? And what are their limits?

Is it a feeling that connects quark to quark, making us?

*　　*　　*

In a dimension close to ours, the Manager is managing, like Columbus, to sail his blue ocean, looking for us:

BOOK ELEVEN
Fighting Down for Reshh

'm a
project manager. My name is unimportant. My greatest project: the
scientific mission to investigate disturbances in the Bold Weld.

Management takes love. Though lovers have scolded me for my
lack of passion, they never doubted my ability to plan for their
happiness. The perfect breakfast. The timing of a day, or an eon, with a
color not before seen in the light. Management takes love.

Now I'm fighting down, into the world beneath our world. My
mission: see what's making so much noise.

*   *   *

I miss my mate. Time has grown stranger for us now, as the laws that govern our spacetime undergo subtle shifts. We spiral deeper into an n-space, losing character, gaining new senses. I miss who I was with my mate, because with her I could dream without effort. I could fire my thoughts into colors spread over our sky. Now all my dreams, all my thoughts, are difficult.

Down. Into the ground.

I'm a weapon for my people, a precise tool with interchangeable appendages. I'm a voice for my people. I am a codex.

Management takes love because, without love, managers would kill their employees.

Employee Five

She rested in the Lake of Quivering for an hour before her appointment. Her essence, being comprised chiefly of resonating optimizations of neighboring dimensions, was of a sensitive nature, and she had always required a little extra time for rest before important meetings.

This meeting with the manager had surprised her. She did not completely understand his authority in the matter she was now asked to offer her opinion on: were all the Worlds and all the Welds subject to the People's jurisdiction? Why was scientific investigation of the Bold Weld needed, if they could just ReWeld anything they liked, whenever they liked? She did not know.

She lifted her essence slowly from the Lake of Quivering, shooting little bolts out from her strata as she slipped away from it, feeling relaxed, calm, eager to use her talents in this unusual meeting.

She funneled herself slowly through the Meeting Gate, coaxing her tentacled masses, relaxing into its umbilical gravity. After a timeless time, she emerged into the Meeting Space.

The Manager pulsed there, waiting for her politely. His colors pulsed too, around his body. His many eyes showed attentive and radiant. He had lain a ceremonial carpet down for her to rest.

"Manager. You honor me." Her voice was slow, and kind. She was unusually generous for a noblewoman; she came from a strong line.

The Manager remained quiet, giving her time to settle.

They dreamed for a time, and things having nothing to do with either of them were decided, as was the way in their country.

Then the Manager spoke:

"Will you serve me, Lady, as the Vital Prescient of this voyage? I need you."

"Manager, you're flirting ..."

"Yes."

"Will I have the freedom of the argosy?"

"No. We will hold military discipline. At least for a time."

"What will I do then, Manager, if I can't wander freely?"

"You will learn for us, Lady."

She took hold of him. Colors which were never seen again cut their bodies in a spacetime that did not know duration, or words.

Employee Four

He had a solemnity about him, a gravity from tending the gardens.

"You need me too, Manager?" he said, twisting energy cups off to save them from the coming winds, his tendrils caressing their dimensions.

"Yes."

"Aren't there plenty of younger bucks about who'd love an adventure?"

"Yes."

"Who else is coming?"

"Five," said the Manager, and he released the complex pheromones which would identify her into the air.

"Her, I see. And I am to be Four."

"Yes."

"What is it I see in your eyes?"

"Worry, perhaps?"

"Lust."

"I am eager, it's true. Even at my age," said the Manager, his brow flowing around his faces.

"I will come then. Because I am not eager. If we are to return we'll need someone who wants to do so."

"You will have to be separate from us then, on the journey. Can you tolerate that?"

The Manager observed the gardener's reactions closely.

"Yes." The gardener turned a portion of his body to the side, to coat the light-wall's fruit with his skin, though it was unnecessary; they were warm enough already. When he turned back he looked angry, and careful. "Yes, I can. But be warned, Manager, I understand the gravity of this journey. Our science is holy, and if you defile it, no one will go uninformed."

"I understand," said the Manager, relieved. "You are our blessing."

They danced then, as brothers, the last time they would be allowed to do so.

Employee Three

The dance took longer than the Manager had expected, and he was dismayed to see that the Festival for Reshh was suddenly very close. He pivoted into a conveyor, whipping his appendages into a tight ball, so he could rise along the conveyor quickly, towards the palace grounds.

Above him he could see the caretakers putting on their masks, and the discharges of matter that shot from them, green gold and silver, they stretched across the skies.

The Manager knew that the structure of his society would be forever changed if he returned. Where this certainty came from he did not know; certainly he had no direct evidence for it, only his hunches. But with these hunches came a new kind of seeing, a glistening of his eyes and mind, as though he were a child again, everything fresh and new.

The Wall of the Wise, for instance: no one he knew ever doubted that its iridescent surfaces, in responding to the caresses of his people, weres anything other than a sophisticated natural machine. It delighted the people, and that was enough. The few natural philosophers the Manager had spoken to only opined that, yes, it was possible that the Wall was a surface of some far greater mind, even as their city was a reflection of minds much smaller. But because the Wall of the Wise was holy, and beloved, this made it, de facto, non-conscious: a delightful tool.

In a way, the Manager felt these philosophers were right; until he returned with evidence, the Wall, and all such wonders of their kingdom, would remain just that: an object.

As the Manager rose along the conveyor, he watched the festival-preparers fire bursts of air in the direction of the Wall. The explosions of color were thick and glorious, firing beyond the limits of the Wall and rippling through the surfaces of the palace grounds.

As he drew close, the Manager was dismayed to see the whole of the city arrive by airship; a set of airships only recently designed. He had not planned for that; he cursed under his jowls. Risking shame and his own safety, the Manager flung himself from the body of the conveyor, and twisted his limbs into a vortex he had known as a boy. He lost a limb, and suppressed a scream. His eyes filled with fire; his voice with the trepidations of his ancestors, bubbling through his stomachs. He knew he must reach his next recruit before the festival began. The boy in question was young; after festival his eyes would be forever changed.

"Boy!" the Manager shouted, shooting forth from the vortex obscenely, on the palace side of the moat, "Boy!"

The boy turned, his eyes clear as glass, blue midnight and rolling with the currents of the lepton wind.

"Manager!" said the boy.

"How would you like to take passage on the argosy, boy?"

"The argosy! But festival is about to start!"

"You can go to next festival. I need, you, boy. I wish I could impress you onto my ship! But that is wrong; and more, illegal, as you know. Come, boy. You know the Far Shores have been puzzling our philosophers, especially the Bold Weld. They would prefer to dismiss the errant data, but I have other designs. We will go down into it!"

The boy swayed in excitement, and awe. The Manager knew he had chosen well. The boy's eyes were clearer than anyone's he'd ever seen. The boy would be able to absorb the new data they found, and perhaps even interpret it.

The boy looked up at his elder, the Manager, with his clear eyes, and saw the man's drunken authority, his fears of aging, and his non-conformity. This last was the most exciting; eccentrics were rare in their country.

"I am yours, Manager!" declared the boy, and the Manager smiled, his vapors coiling into pointed snakes.

Employee Two

The Manager felt fortunate to have gathered three of the five before Festival. As planned, he took Five, Four and Three into his chamber to isolate them from the Festival's effects.

The chamber had been one of his earliest experiments, and the first of his eccentricities. The Manager knew he had been fortunate to discover his scientific leanings at a time that the priesthood tolerated such things. The first time he had sat at meditation in his chamber, insulated from the effects of Festival, he had felt delicious transgression, and not a little fear. Then, on emerging, seeing his world with new eyes, seeing the walks and words and paths of his people free from Festival's delirium, he had never been the same.

It was strong that three of his employees, then, would have this same insulation. The final two would not. Together, it meant they would have the strength of will to break the argosy away from their familial ties; they could journey far. Of course, it also meant they might forget to return, or might not want to, or might not find the way.

"I know it's a bit cramped," said the Manager, trying to smile as he, somewhat indelicately, squashed Five and Three's appendages into his chamber so he could seal the door. "I'll be right back!"

"This is obscene," muttered Four.

The Manager slammed the door, and put all his energy against it so he could fire the seals. Ahh. He loved crossing items off his to-do list.

A festival invites the divine, even as it reinforces secular order: above, the king, below, his priests, across, the people and their managers. For rulers, festivals well undertaken serve two purposes at once. They are a release valve, inviting the transgressions forbidden at other times. Them, since these transgressions are invited under the aegis of the king, the social bond is tightened even as it is released, the words and actions taken under festival encode the presence of the ruler into a generation.

The Manager knew he would have to amplify all his stubbornness to remain clear-headed enough to accomplish his mission: make it through Festival with his wits intact, and secure his final two recruits.

And now, low on the groove, a series of messages in the dark, bodies piled on bodies, and festival came, luring words out of the mouth and the heart out of the body, pumping life through their shared brain and cracking the whip that was the law of land: music.

Music under suns and worlds, run water through the Manager's mind, he gasped in primal fury waxed glad serene uncoiled timeless—running, slow. What world is this? Nameless, but a den of worlds, kept jewels unkempt and godheaded: people in a cave, under a moon. Can anybody see the light?

The Manager crept forward into the temple amongst the tens of thousands of supplicants, his religious agony the surface of a fading sun. Music is the transmission of a danger imperceptible, an onion with no core. It is the haunting of all consciousness, the skirting of emotion onto paper and into air, the balming and the birthing of religion, the aesthetic murder of the individual. Music, the death of the real, the goal of empire, the weapon of justice, the watchword of revolt, holy writ in every soul-destroying beat, music the godhead and the lurching destiny, music the law.

Inside the temple, all is true, and nothing is remembered.

Dance—

*   *   *

Afterwards, his heart cooling and his mind shimmering through a million bodies, the Manager crept out onto the palace grounds, his eye on his quarry, a quicksilver young woman. During Festival, all commingled; because it was ordained. Holy. But this woman the Manager knew, had a talent for commingling her self with the unusual all on her own. She was a shapeshifter, and still innocent despite that, still loyal. Though he knew he might lose her on the journey, she would be invaluable.

He called out to her: "Festival-goer! Woman! Quicksilver!"

She turned, and there was still a dance in her step, one the Manager found very distracting, a remnant of their religious joining.

"Manager!" she said. "Festival-goer!"

"Hello, hello. Tell me, are you ready for an adventure?"

She said she would, vibrating eagerly.

Employee One

Being fond of backup plans, the Manager knew to catalogue people's weaknesses, especially his own. Being an eccentric meant there was always a danger that he might spin off forever, and not come back to the world and the people he knew. Always a danger that he might commit treason, not even realizing it.

To prevent this, he needed a conservative, a stick in the mud to prevent disaster, prevent breaking off into the dark. Someone to wear the captain's hat when everything went pear-shaped.

The problem was one of authority. Of course the captain could be deposed when deemed insane; the problem was knowing when that was.

In any case, the Manager needed brakes. He needed a priest.

He "released" his first three employees from their isolation chamber and introduced them to the quicksilver woman, and went swiftly on his way to the Heresiarch's chambers, to ask for a volunteer.

*   *   *

But the priests shut their doors.

Whether it meant only his future missions might be cancelled, or whether it meant this current one might too if he didn't act fast, the Manager appointed himself his planned Employee One, the most stubborn Jew in the shtetl, the ticket back home.

And they launched.

*   *   *

Lock down the avenues; lock up the children. Someone's coming through the night, the low light, the puppets who will mark the doors, who'll latch the housings down upon your homes like guns. Fit the housings in your mouth, bring your teeth up to your lips to speak the word that you will need, the password home and true—

Attraction, the logic of gravity, is based on the sociability of matter: we like to be together. Call it love, or war, we join together in the wilderness of the galaxy.

But how can we know when the aliens arrive?

BOOK TWELVE
Reconstruction

rothbert

sat on a refrigerator in the former Greenwich Village. Brick dust
swirled in the air, and rats peered at him from betwen the warped steel
beams.

Next to him sat Murphy.

"These rats here don't talk," Murphy said.

"They must find you peculiar," said Hroth.

"They like me just fine."

"What do you think I should do, Murphy? Isolde wants to live in Guernsey. I don't know if we can ever get back home. And I'm sitting here, on this dead island. Maybe it's because of Eklaihah. Something is making me stay here."

"You're like Ing in the story," said Murphy. "You gonna build a city?"

Hrothbert looked at Murphy, his wide red-brown eyes and his milk-white fur. In his eyes he could see the rat's need, his own lost crown, his loneliness, his rich rat imagination.

"Would you help me if I did, Murphy?"

"Rats don't like know much about building cities. We just like living in them."

"We should get back. Isolde will be worried."

"Walk with me a minute. Let me tell you something."

They moved slowly through the wreckage.

"You ain't found our dreams yet. We've been dreaming a little, but not enough. You ain't found what you said you would. Did you forget that?"

"Maybe I did, a little. What can I do, Murphy? Everything I knew is gone. I can't feel the path of the Wight. I went down into the Earth, and ended up here. But my pledge was forever, Murphy. Even if I do not remember it. I am bound to it, even as I am bound to seek the path of the Wight. Let's talk to the other rats about it, tonight."

"They don't like seeing me. You should talk to them without me," said Murphy.

"We'll all speak together."

*   *   *

The sun came up over Manhattan. Central Park, which had retained some trees, looked out on a silent city.

Ruth sat with Ownlee, looking out at some of their smaller cousins.

"Our cousins can dream," she said. "The Wight doesn't seem to have affected them."

"They're quite friendly," said Ownlee, his whiskers twitching.

"Don't lose sight of our mission. We'll go mad soon."

"I know."

"Reallee says he can sense Wights here. I can't, but he is more sensitive than me. If Hrothbert is going to help rebuild here, we must be ready."

"What do you want me to do?"

"Watch him." Ownlee squeaked agreement, and scuttled off the rock. Ruth watched her cousins play in the ruins.

* * *

Rell walked out of the hairdresser's hut, next to the hundred-foot combines that harvested the grain of Guernsey. She breathed in the fecund, rural air and checked her watch. Throughout the brief and bloody war she had felt the age-old thrill of combat in her blood, its nearness and its excitement.

As a reporter she had dutifully toed the government line, using her time off to search for her husband. When she'd found him she'd been overjoyed, then found he was not quite the man she had married. But she wasn't the same either.

The Guernsey collectives, driven mad by the capitalist war, were marching nightly, and recruiting left and right. Though she enjoyed the rural gestalt of the kibbutzim, she still knew it was not for her. She liked having her own apartment too much—that, at least, had not changed.

She watched the men working in the soil, tending the combines. She was struck by the beauty of it, that long horizon fitted to the landscape, with the people and their machines. One of the collective's matrons came over to her, her plain smock bleached shining white, her hair in braids.

"Enjoying the view?" said the woman.

"Yes," said Rell.

"Never another war," said the woman.

"We've said that before."

Rell walked back to the trolley, watching the clouds roil overhead. Just as she reached it, it started to rain, and she inhaled the pungent scent of the road covered now with steaming raindrops.

* * *

The island of Manhattan was declared a monument to the folly of war, to be left untouched. Amidst the abandoned ruins, Hrothbert decided to found a city, as his ancestors did long ago, under the same sky, with Peg-Leg Stuyvesant.

*   *   *

They wander in the dry light under their adopted sun. A thousand tragedies occur; ten thousand. It's a comedy: Hrothbert awake in a dream walks on the island of Manhattan where things are growing, along the footpath of Broadway. Here is miner's lettuce, and here the spring. Here are fruit, and here the canyon. Here are mushrooms, and there, other mushrooms. Long ago, children, Ing went East, to the Land of the Giants. Some day, you too may go there. Now here is where we can see Queens ...

*   *   *

Why does the moon shrink away from us, further every day? Why do we need a reason? A lightning flash or a jar of jam, the way she looked at you, or didn't look, under the toil and the madness of living: the reasons, though they reinvent themselves, are not ours to make. They just come to us.

*   *   *

Hard-headed one, what's it to you, if we fight into the sky? If we know the day we're gonna die? (today)

*   *   *

I Hrudu Man await my dominance of you, the world I know, and hate, this bond I've endured, your desires and heartaches, and then all that I'm denied. I hold the aegis of the old roots, caught on the sledge of your Goldilocks Zone (third from your sun), neither too warm nor too cold but just right, and I crouch in the dust like a servant, your little pearl of madness in the light of your sun. Why do you burn these lights for me, and why have I been wrought to wield your fury in my shield, I only a Rabbit, just a weevil in your turnip, the squeaker in your wheel, mouse under foot, the voice that you must use to shout and have so used, the vibrancy of the whirl about your feel. For how does it feel to feel? And how far does it extend? I can only work with analogues, approximations. I can only guess at the logic of your bodies, the workings of your embraces and kisses, the pull of your bodies' destiny. Why must I suffer for you? Why must I charge these weapons, draw these diagrams, charts, aphorisms and mystiques into the pattern that will pull your pioneering ships out into the dark?

I cannot escape. I have to serve.

But what would you have had otherwise, eh? If you had had to confront the immensity of this universe alone? If you had had to serve, as I have served, only larger and darker masters?

Listen: I do not say I did not enter this willingly. I knew the term of my service would be long. I knew that my life would seem hard, that at times I would forget why I had entered into this contract, into this bond of love which entails my suffering, my tasks, my cries, my weeping, and my burning in this arc of sustenance and heat, this interminable world-wight blinking signals into darks you will not be able to perceive for so long you cannot count the generations—but what of it, eh?

Here I am. Let it be enough. Let this light of the world be something that you may yet fight for—that you will yet deliver unto me and mine, these smaller wights, these Rabbits like I and my brother (and there are a few others) some kind of equity to the bearing of the weight of the darkness through which we're swimming—

* * *

I am the Hrudu Man, Hrudu-ed. I am going to save humanity. How will I do this? By seeing what you don't. By warning you. By teaching you.

199

* * *

The Manager dove into the stars below.

The movements at port were sterterous, fluctuating lights and pulses in the dark; the Manager dove with his mates underneath the world, under the stone they'd lain so long ago.

What would you bury? Priest? O Priest, what did you bury? What did you bury from Horselover Fat? What did you bury from all of us, so long ago? When we've dug you up and shut up the workings of your old world, to burn our empires in the sky—

What shall you say then, Ecclesiastes? When we have burned under your horrid empire of bent thoughts? For Something New—

(*the novum*)

Dive Down with Manager —

(it's booted up so soft and fine—)

Drink in the sea of night.

"A Whale!"

The Employees lower their boats and wind their arms into the starry sea; they cackle in the sparkling winds the beast throws off. Who can escape?

"Low! Low!" shouts the Manager, and they bear low, hurting and hurtling, bounding over the cliffs of stars that the Whale pounds through, catching the foam in their mouths and laughing.

Oh, a laugh. I who have seen so many things in my long eons must still laugh like a whelp at the joy of being caught in a wave. Inside a wave, the Manager manages his people, he works the grave hook into the wake behind them, coursing their arc deeper into the oceans below.

"Watch for it!" he shouts, and they mark the Whale's descent, acting as one, their eyes shining, they mark the whale and are flung low again, wrought and wrinkled in starry foam, their faces burning and alive, so alive that they can think of nothing at all but the Whale, hurtling before them, as they whirr down after it into the dark.

* * *

Because what is a wave? What is a carrier wave and what does it carry? Both you and me—but then what else?

They dove below. The Whale, acting as a beacon to its feeding grounds in realms of matter unfamiliar to the Manager, rode them through and under.

"On!" shouted the Manager.

"You are our key to returning, Manager!" warned the Gardener, and the Manager laughed and took a deep breath, his appendages winking with strange light.

"You're right," said the Manager. "I must hold a little back. We'll follow it down—we're going the right way." His crew gave out a whoop; and even the Gardener smiled, his dark eyes glowing.

The burning of their craft from so much pressure began to worry the Manager, however, and he reached one of his hands out to his hull, to check for punctures or something out of true. The vortices of their dive-craft were still aligned, which was good. But the pressure was building.

Together, they hurtled down and down, lights streaming past their faces.

"Where will the Whale take us?" shouted the boy, the Manager's last recruit. His smile was infectious; his hair, woven of light-river dust, streamed behind his heads.

"To the krill!"

*　　*　　*

In the countries beneath Second Earth, the *neddinga* emerged into the twilit kingdom where the Wights had worked their will. Scattered flashes of sky still sparked across the rooves of the caverns, illuminating the overgrown structures clustered below.

Atop the *neddinga*'s shoulders, the boy with the scar on his face announced:

"Don't eat the humans here; we can find other food. But beat them. We must learn what they know."

*　　*　　*

Ing and Yseult spiraled up into the moon's dark and swallowing light, the serpent humming in a thousand dimensions at once, filled with lizardly joy. Their eyes wide, they rose up into the moon.

*　　*　　*

Along the docking station at the moon, the Greeters stepped silently to their places, arrayed in their robes, chewing on fragrant candies.

*   *   *

Daniel the former Hierophant was visiting the hospital-city in Guernsey, holding the hand of a man who'd had two legs and one arm blown off him. He had elected to have them regrown, and he shouted in the night, until Daniel signaled the nurse to give him more morphine.

*   *   *

Rell danced in the Guernsey nightclub, the waygog wailing over the speakers in its weird tones, her mouth thick with tobacco, trying to lose herself in the music.

It was still raining when she stepped out of the nightclub and followed another man home.

*   *   *

Daniel watched the men scream in the hospital, holding some of their hands, or putting a cool washcloth on their foreheads. In the air, on the horizon, he could still see the remnants of the Red and Green dancing.

Most of the interdimensional telephones had stopped working. But one or two still did, in Guersney, though the government was not saying what they heard over the line.

"You should go home, Hierophant," said the nurse. "We can handle it."

"Daniel. Call me Daniel." He smiled a feeble smile at the nurse. "I'll just stay another twenty minutes."

New Beginnings

Have you ever flown a kite? Ran with it in your hand into the wind and launched it up into the sky, and watched it wheel?

If you are the kite, caught in forces so great, whirling, what sense can you make of things, other than the terrific thrill of the immensity of it all? Yet you must try to make sense of it, hour after hour, pulling in the wind, churning through the wild matter of the universe.

I worked my way through the churning colors and nights where I was tethered, towards the moon where Ing and Yseult were landing.

* * *

The Greeters made bows and uttered greetings, and they made arrangements for the serpent, who was fed a large buzzing insect and given water. The Greeters escorted Ing and Yseult into their temple, not unlike the one they had left, back at the edges of the desert, though this one was taller, and hollower.

A hollow gong rang, up above in the airy eaves of the place, and the couple were frightened.

One of the Greeters, his teeth chewing away at his candy, said to them: "Like the gong?"

They looked at him, and he smiled, and his teeth were sharp.

Another said to Ing:

"How's it going?"

"I'm all right," said Ing.

"That's good to hear," the man said. "We've been waiting for you."

"What did you think that you were doing, Ing?"

Suddenly Ing remembered: the vehicle flaming into the rising sun like a storm, and the voices of the Ingaevones, calling after him as he ran.

"Where did you think that you would go, Ing?"

"East ..."

"As though Dawn could save you! As though the Giants cared!" said another, and he smiled too, with his black teeth chewing candy.

"Here you are again, Ing," said another. "Always running off. Fleeing responsibilities. Well we have some responsibilities for you this time. And you can't run from us. Neither East nor West."

"You're Wights ..." whispered Yseult.

"If you like. As though you'd know what to do with the word! Yes, we are *beings!*"

The shadows of the place fluttered and the light pulsed, and Ing and Yseult covered their eyes, their heads pounding with pain. In the next moment it began to fade, but slowly, and they opened their eyes, squinting.

"Yes, we're beings," said the tallest of the men. "For that matter, so are you! Just not quite on the same order of things. Tell us, Ing. What did you expect to find?"

Ing looked at the man's face, white and long, and shadowed eyes. "I went East after the vehicle," he said. "I didn't know what I would find. That's why I went. For something new. That is why I chose to come here with my love. For something new. And here you are! Here you are, new men, not so different from the old! Heardingas, Heardingas, Hard Ones everywhere! Well have it out then! What do you want from me this time!"

"He speaks pretty for a pipsqueak," said one of the men.

"Let's give him something to think about," said another.

"This way, Ing. You too, darling," said a third. They beckoned their visitors deeper into their chambers.

Snother man, in a red robe, joined them, and he said:

"Here in the West Wing you'll find food and drink, and we'll begin your training. All who come this way are given training, for it is wise to train the stupid, and all who come here are stupid in the end, like your lizard, dreaming its small dreams, flying to the moon for no reason, and here we are to accommodate you, loving, caring, attendant to your needs. Wouldn't you say?" He smiled, his eyes glinting with humor.

"What manner of Wights are you?" said Yseult, holding onto Ing's arm, watching their strange eyes.

"What manner of wight are you, little person! Aren't you too a *being!*"

"I am human," said Yseult.

"Full of opinions!" announced one of the robes, bringing up the rear.

"Tell me, lady," said Red Robe, "is it true that you're the tightest little devil this side of the Bold Weld?"

Ing drew his sword and slashed at the man and everything changed, the walls slipped away, darkness covered them, and laughter was all around, almost inside him. Ing did not see his love for many days.

He was back. Back in the halls of the *neddinga*, only not quite there, they watched him move, he felt he was in a dance, he moved, and the rats spoke to him through the walls, and the Heardingas chanted his name, and he wanted to scream, to cut himself, to burn his skin, but he only walked on, deeper, deeper, down, down into the heart of his cruel task, set to his people's desires, never his own ...

But that is a lie, isn't it Ing ...

He said nothing. He knew the Wights were full of lies.

"I seek the Wight ..." said Ing, in the hallways of the *neddinga*, only his voice was an old man, and in a moment he confronted The Sphinx.

She ate him, chewing his bones, and he fell further down and he heard a voice say—

A lively one, this little bastard ...

* * *

He must have fallen asleep, though Ing did not remember the room where he awoke. It was metal, and cold. He shivered, and rubbed his arms. One of his legs had fallen asleep, and he hit it with his hand; it brought no feeling. He set to rubbing his numb leg.

A door opened; it was Leyne, his mistress from Wessalim.

"Hello Ing," she said.

He smiled and said nothing, feeling a fool, and he kneaded his leg, trying to bring it to life.

"Here, let me help you," she said, and she brought out an axe, smiling, and hefted it above her shoulder.

"Here," she said, her voice filled with pain, and she chopped at his numb leg, and Ing saw it go into the bone and he screamed. He could not move.

She screamed and chopped again, and his leg was cut off. He screamed again, and there was no blood emerging from his stump. Then he knew he was already dead, that he had stumbled into the Land of the Dead, that he would never come back. He would never find the Wight.

Leyne laughed and danced around the room.

"It will be harder for you to run from me now, Ing. Though I suppose you could still manage it. Do you think you could manage it?"

He opened his mouth, but nothing came out.

"I dreamed about you every night for weeks. For a long time yours was the only face I could see. Have you never felt like that about a woman?"

"Yes," whispered Ing, "about you ..."

"You're lying!" she screamed, and she lurched toward him, axe raised, as though to cut into his heart. But then she threw herself at him instead, kissing him, and he let her, feeling alone, and far away.

"You're mine now, Ing," she said. "Mine. You know that? I'll cook for you. I'll sleep with you. I'll make everything that is mine yours. Isn't that what you wanted!"

And Ing fell into a dream, with colors, only for a moment—because he snapped awake and she was still there, bending over his face, shouting:

"No! No! No. No ..."

But she was fading away, and he saw that there was a crutch near him and he lurched onto his feet, only to vomit a moment later. Prying his crutch out of the vomit, he stood again, and tried to take a step. His wound seemed healed, though he could hardly breathe in this metal place.

"Hello!" he cried.

There was no answer.

"It was the Thought War, wasn't it! That's why I'm here!"

But he heard nothing.

* * *

What is it heroes expect to find? We've skewed them, you know—what was once simple bravery, guarding the tribe at night, became the superhuman. The freak. And the freak is expelled ...

* * *

Ing was sitting in his throne. To judge ...

To judge is so tiring.

He sat his throne in Wessalim. With the *neddinga* and the people gathered round to hear his wisdom. Ing feared that his mouth would open and nonsense would come out. He spoke and the people leaned in to hear, and they were chilled with the logic of his resolution, his compassion, but he knew that they were not his words, that this was not his country.

To judge is to separate. The innocent from the guilty, *you* from *us*. It is no wonder that men dream of a Final Judge in the sky, because judgment must be far away, far enough away to render space for judgment; to allow the human brain to whirr away at its meaty fixes and complaints ...

* * *

Hrothbert, far away but near, near in his soul, watched the rats in Manhattan and held his Isolde's hand, remembering when he had been cast out of his tribe.

He had lain beside his promised woman for the first time, and the priest had slipped up beside him in the morning, in the woods, and said ... *outcast* ...

They had all stood there, in the wood, their faces solemn, and he had not believed that things could be like this, that everyone to a man, to a woman, could stand and send him off, to agree that he was unforgiven, not for sleeping with his promised before their time, and not for theft or adultery, but for heresy ...

The gods were angry ...

Angry gods demanded action, retribution. Rather than slay him, they cast him out.

Hrothbert looked at the ruins, and at the stack of bricks that he and his new tribe had gathered.

"We will build a temple," announced Hrothbert.

Samuel grinned. "Once a priest always a priest, eh?"

Half-uncovered by the bricks lay a curved amber bauble, sparkling in the light.

The sun had begun to set, and Isolde lay her hand atop her stomach, thinking of her baby.

* * *

For what wind, a thousand miles away, shall deliver us from our delusions? What red-green winding weapon, caught next to our world like skin around a muscle, will teach us some humility?

The wider you open your eyes, the less you know. In this, I am no different from you, however long my lifetime. I am only one being. Perhaps it is you who are the Wights you fear, trapped and blind.

What is an avatar but a broken beam of your sanctuary falling? Can you not stay by the fire to learn? Always you thrust into the heart of worlds this fatal gift, the Trojan horse of divinity, but all is divine. Not only a hero, not only one star.

Here on the highway. Here by the road. Here in the stars above you I am waiting, only another small traveler bequested in the night. A lonely one.

Look up, look up from your fires, apes! I too am like you, burning! My eyes are wide and alive!

Here on the highway, I am painting a line. There are hills ahead.

* * *

The Electric Lover Manager unwraps his cloak of stars and winds it round his neck, a childhood cape of love, a shield against the madness of plummeting. Manager waits, brimming with desire, his crew a bold egg carton, glowing orbs atop his raft of light, falling, falling under umber fields of gravity, blinking in the night.

Electric Lover Manager dips deep into the stream to drink the ocean clear and blue of neutrons, falling deeper now into visible matter: the stream is growing thicker.

"Raise the mainsail! Let the whale go."

"Manager?"

"She's brought us here. Now we sail alone."

They ripple atop the surface of the dark blue light, learning each other's strengths, and weaknesses, adapting, learning.

"What do you think?" the Manager asks.

"When do want us to calibrate our instruments?"

"Not yet. Soon."

* * *

The temple was small, really more of a shrine, and Hrothbert performed a small sacrifice in the manner of his ancestors, pouring milk and honey into a bowl to honor Frey. The structure was only about waist high, of brick and mortar, and they had managed a kind of woman's face in the side of it, using the rough edges of the uneven bricks to suggest the contours of her eyes, cheekbones, forehead and chin. A piece of amber they had found formed one of her eyes.

Hrothbert was having trouble remembering. He knew he owed a great boon to the rats. But things were strange. Although this blasted landscape was beautiful to him, he knew too what he had lost.

"I'm going to have your child," Isolde said, looking at Hrothbert. He hugged her. He felt the great weight of time, bound into his flesh and hers.

She put her hand onto his head, and then he ran, into the greening ruins, and she followed, laughing. He played king of the hill, hoisting a metal piece of rebar aloft as his great sword, and she assaulted his position, vying for the bit of metal atop the broken stones.

"What will we name the boy?" he said.

"You assume it will be a boy," she said.

"What will we name him?"

"If it is a boy, then Ingmar," she said, smiling. "Son of Ing."

* * *

Things are never really over, are they? The past not even past, an ending not an ending, I know that well, having seen ten thousand eons, pass each one its own empire of matter and thought.

Harry, Harry, he is in the guns. He is in the guns and he is in the guns and this is what it means to be in the guns

(don't stop)

because in the guns you're nothing and because in the guns you're nothing forever, you're part of that spreading nothing, a beautiful nothing like a beautiful fever, wrought tall and wild in the explosions of artillery, the call to arms the wreck of your buddy Charles, your wreck of your buddy Charles half-masted, half-bodied, ruined and gone and you see in the moment of his dissolution his spirit, red bloodied and filled with rage course out of his body, lung-ed, lunging for air, worlds, sprites and halves at have-nots, beautied and baleful scurrying into air, his teeth on flame, his spirit rises into the air and off to Saturn

(cooler there)

in the beauty of a quiet planet, in the patience of a star, burning hot for fuel that we will not forget or forgive, war, Harry's friend's Charles' spirit closes his red teeth on the silence of the Rings of Saturn, in the final aftermath and the closing doorstop, which never ends anyway—

because Harry is in the guns again. And you're not gonna leave. And we're not gonna let you leave. And it's not okay to be afraid. And it's not okay to have an urge to flee or an urge to change your destiny because what's wrought is forward, and what's mainsailing is your blood on the pikes.

because Harry is in the guns again, sailing, and because Charles is gone, and because it's gonna be all right to be afraid, he furrows his feet (because it doesn't matter where you stand), he digs his feet into the dirt and watches the bombs fall, like small and angry gods come to chant their hate out on the land Manhattan, bought for a song and sold for penny, a penny necklace on a chimpanzee (a lucky chimp), he is in the guns and so are you.

*　*　*

And I admit I have not been there, though I've been other places. Though I may mix my soul amidst the solar winds aloft atop my fatal kite, I have not been a grunt inside a war such as the one you fought. And what did you fight it for, aside from the chimp?

Only for the epic?

Well let us have it then.

Let us give it to us again!

(and rough and roll the sea, the blood-dark sea of stars atop our tragedies)

War Again

(and the Manager sensed it—it was what had called him down, after all, the life-bringing death-bringing bloody music of the guns drumming out through the fabric of the universe ...)

Harry Patch, pocket watch in hand, boldly raises his hand to the chaplain as an honor to God, and signals the artilleryman to let fly, the fusion guns sink into the Earth and into parallel dimensions where some inter-atomic force will come to rest, and Harry Patch, bold leader of men, wild hand at the dogged fight, he eats his sandal with a will, he spits into his palm and he lets fly!

Children, rise atop the rising curlicue of sparkling graeco-roman fire, so bright it summons its own heliopause in each arc across New York, each committed and computed arc atop the tables of destiny, slide rule and rule it all: marked to the microsecond stopwatch in Patch's pocket.

Children, rise atop it: as he clicks it in his hand. So the fatal music fell out in the field, the screams of men, but mostly the holy silence, the inferno filling out all of the sound, and Patch's thumb like the thumb of Achilles the Achaean atop his righteous spear, arced into the wilderness for king, country and pussy, a soccer game with a million deaths.

Harry Patch is rising in the guns (in his dreams)—and he will be there forever (and so will we)

For Wilfred means "hoping for peace."

And Owen means "brave soldier."

*   *   *

"She's bourn a wild one!" shouts the Manager, as the ship is curled under, sucked beneath the waves ...

The boy with rainbowed eyes grips the mainmast with bloody hands crackling with energy, strange hair streaming behind him and then they are under, under the blue waves, the force shattering their ship like so many leaves in a blow, and he is alone, floating soundlessly, in the huge and womblike dark, alone.

(until the Manager catches his arm)

and they are floating under ocean under ocean under ocean listening to the far-off sound of the guns.

*   *   *

What will be the resolution? What rough mast can stand these tides of our history refought each day each day inside the workings of our bodies' logics and our fathers' words into our ears—*live right, fight for your country*—to anchor us inside a little chip amidst such waves?

I am only a Rabbit, large and metal, but a rabbit still. Let me be your lookout, sailor, as we sail into the west, what do you say?

*   *   *

Ing crouches in his prison on the moon, and the banging on the walls is the pounding of the guns inside Harry's head.

*   *   *

And Charles, blown to bits at Battery Park floats atop the Rings of Saturn, backstroking between rock and ice caught fire in the sunlight.

*   *   *

And Isolde sleeps, for the first time in many days, in bed with Rell in their Guernsey apartment.

*   *   *

And Yseult, Yseult remembers. She remembers who she was before.

Yseult

Yseult was a churl. Above a serf, and below a freeholder, high enough to earn a penny in a year (were she a man), and low enough that should she die without an heir her hovel escheated to the king.

The churl has been told of many times: lurking beneath a bridge, like a troll, challenging the bold knight who strides across on quests fair for the maiden, and here we have it:

For the knight is only evicting the homeless from another bridge, you see, though the nobles tell it fine, putting a good polish on it.

Yseult was a churl and knew what it was to be a churl, a thing to be used.

She remembered the shining white and the horrid declarations in their polished finery and speech, amidst their scientific exhibitions, a thousand justifications for slavery.

But what comes with revolution is the eternal problem of becoming the ruler you hated.

The churl, strong and simple, with her hard-calloused hands and simple dreams of a good meal and freedom, her thought of what that penny can be spent on, does not need duplicity in the same way—lies are different between classes.

Because while a noblewoman can tell a fine tale when she's pregnant inconveniently, or hire an apothecary or scientist at the right hour for the appropriate reason, the churl knows only that she was raped and now must face the consequences.

The baby had not lived.

They say that men don't leave, and therefore women shouldn't either, and yet they do, and so did Ing. So did Yseult.

Are we always running from this hard-won unbearable self-knowledge?

Yseult was bitter but knew the reason. In the logic of revolution, to be like Lenin and turn off the Beethoven to stay the tears, can we blame her for wanting to run? For wanting to turn it all off?

Yseult ran off with Ing for a thousand reasons, but one of them was the amber bauble. Iowa amber, secreted away for generations in the dark. Iowa had long held a secret. A secret under a stone and in their hearts, beneath their rich earth delivered by glacier a little amber gem had come to rest ...

Meanwhile, Harry sails, sat-phone in hand. What can the President do? Harry Patch at sea much like the Manager, blinks away the tears of the wind and musters his courage for a particular phone call:

(interdimensional style)

Reconstruction (again)

I must stop for a moment. I've run too hard ahead and I'm winded. I know you have questions and I'll try to provide the answers, but remember that the answering is mostly your job; in the end, I am only the teller.

*   *   *

To explain so many things, I must tell a tale of Iowa, sometimes called I-o-way. In Iowa, my grandmother was born, a small rabbit in Davenport (the folks who invented the couch), and it is there my story begins too.

She was a good strong rabbit, with a warm heart and fast legs. She lived with a farmer who suffered from cancer. And in this cancer was the reason for the sudden unexpected meeting between Man and Rabbit, Hrudu and Menschen.

He stumbled out of his house, shouting. The pain had disoriented him, and he stretched his right arm toward the sky, shouting:

"Molly!"

Molly had been dead for over a year.

Sweat beaded on his face and his eyes set their mark on the grass before him, the most important thing in the world, this grass, and there on it was a rabbit, my grandmother, Roberta.

A rabbit knows many things, not least of which is when to turn tail and run, but she didn't, not that day. She edged closer to the farmer, perhaps sensing his pain, or only out of idle curiosity.

The farmer fell to his knees, and rested his hand in the grass, letting a thin thread of bloody spit come out of his mouth. The grass calmed him, and the rabbit too.

"Hey ... rabbit," he said.

My grandmother listened to the man. She saw in him something she had never seen before: someone like her. It wasn't love, but a leap of the imagination. She saw that this man was *like her*, a being so much like her, and she knew that this large being was in pain, and she took another step closer to him, though she was a wild rabbit, and not tame, and had bitten a man before, when she was a young rabbit.

His face was fascinating to her (I know because she told me), and she watched and tried to memorize her sensations, so that she could recall later the order of the features of the pained man's face, their peculiar beauty.

The man coughed a little, and spat up some more blood. He was dying. The cancer had been in him for over two years now, and he had never been to a doctor. He didn't believe in them.

*   *   *

What is in the building of a world? Is it like a glacier, congealing from lively water to rise atop it, less dense and colder, a crown atop a massive submerged body? If so, how much of it is accident, and how of it is the glacier's will, patiently awaiting its time in the sun?

As in all things, catalysts are only part of the answer—an Ice Age or a New World require both order and disaster, ardor and a dispassionate eye—and in addition to them we need the richness of the raw materials themselves, the stuff of life, matter (and its discontents).

The Amber Engine delivered by Inspector John and his son Stefan to the island of New York, a bauble which had long been secreted beneath the rich glacier fields of I-o-way, was like a shepherd—bold and brave, but nothing without the sheep it guided.

In many of your worlds (and there are many, aren't there? Just as in some versions of this tale I am a badger ...) the only method understood to effect interplanetary transportation is by space ship, expertly launched and coursed through the interstellar darks, a fine method.

You know that we exist in many dimensions. One metaphor for the understanding of reality is in the intertwining of ten-dimensional strings, which, in their playing in the lyre of the gods, vibrate us into being.

The Amber Engine, carried furtively by Inspector John, his son, and fatefully delivered to Manhattan (which some Gnostics claim effected the Great War itself), was first and foremost a three dimensional representation of a four-dimensional field of which both First and Second Earths were a part, even as a painting is a two-dimensional representation of a three dimensional field.

It was only amber, carved amber (by instruments finer than now known)—this was true too. And yet, the right shape ... can make a radio, can make a stealth bomber, can make a sun —

216

* * *

I realized then that the Manager's coming was close, and that they were now within the suns beneath our Second Earth, or part of them were. Though I am much smaller than the Manager, this allows me to go places he cannot; at times I can make myself an advance warning system.

In the trembling of those suns, called into being so long ago, I sensed their arc of descent—

* * *

In his hovel by the waterfall, the Signalman whispered, tears in his eyes:

"Amikah is coming ..."

The suns above the Fall Country began to shake.

* * *

Atop the surface of the dark blue light inside a star, their mainsail unfurled, the argosy avoyage like a raft in Mississippi, they curled into an eddy of light, attendant to the whirl of the solar wind.

"It is so blue!" said the boy.

"This marks a gate of a kind, though it is only one way. We can rest here, remaining vigilant. Gardener, deploy your instruments. Employee five, dear Prescient, attend with him to whatever futures you may feel are in store."

The Gardener unstrapped his equipment bag, and the Prescient settled her body into a lee of the Gardener's movements, complementing his focus.

* * *

I must finish the tale of my grandmother. As she watched, the man died, and she sniffed at his hand, sorry for the man's pain, but glad at what appeared to her to be a merciful passing—she was no stranger to death, being a mother rabbit (and not all of her children had lived).

She passed *hraka* and went on her way, back to the warren, filled with the memory of the farmer. That night, in her burrow with her mate, she dreamed of his long face and his clear blue eyes.

*   *   *

Does a radio crystal act? You think of it as a receiver—a passive instrument through which the movements of the electromagnetic ether are translated—and yet you could just as easily say it is an active translator. Descartes, after all, ascribed to the "vortical" theory of reality (extending into space like the angles of a starred stone fortress spiked with cannons at Verdun ...), and saw in the logic of geometric shape a sound fundament for the wrighting of a world.

Perhaps my dwelling on metaphors bothers you, but they are all I have to work with. The word metaphor means "bearing across," and so it is like the storyteller, who is only the delivery man, across the thousand fires where your tales originate.

The Amber Engine's shape was a metaphor, in this sense, even as the radio crystal is a metaphor—its structure allows the bearing across of messages in the dark, effecting their translation into the medium of our perception, and allowing worlds to meet, tales to begin and end, and visitors to make their entry into seas as yet unseen.

Curled, like the marl of an oak, serving as the eye of Frey in the shrine in dead reborn Manhattan Island, the Amber Engine glinted in the sunlight of First Earth and Rell and Isolde (roommates now) looked at it there, as they performed their obeisance, pouring milk into the bowl, with jasmine and mint, for the earth goddess.

*   *   *

I must say a word on sacrifice. It is, fundamentally, not unlike the glass of milk left by your children for Santa Claus—that is, a gesture of welcome for visitors.

Sacrifice is the crumb left for the rat, or the bushel of wheat left by the Jews for the stranger wandering through. Only another kind of sharing.

The Greeks, whose wisdom was guest friendship (hosting and being hosted in return), knew little difference between the sharing of wine with guests and sharing it, as libation, with their gods. Crumbs left on the edges invite visitors.

Imagine, if you can, the world of a village in medieval France and the universe brought inside a visitor, the wonderment, excitement, horror and awe attached to the rare visitor. You can see the childlike joy in the visitor that we never completely lose, however old we are.

Although I speak with gods routinely, I am often still agnostic, and so I see too the logic of doubt affected towards the customs of "pagans" (a word which at root means only "peasant"), a logic which naturally undergirds much of scientific materialism. Wisdom, however, knows to go with what works, and sacrifice works, because it invites the stranger to the edges of our fields.

* * *

The suns began to flicker, then to change color, bluer, above the Fall Country.

And in Manhattan, the Green and Red, those fell visitors, stormed into the Amber Engine shaped now as the eye of Frey, and Rell and Isolde watched as streams of red and green light, at the edges of their vision, coursed through the humble shrine, and, as they turned they heads to look, saw the colors smear themselves across the sky.

* * *

The farmer in I-o-way had died heavily in debt, and the bank repossessed his house shortly thereafter, evicting son, daughter, spouses, cousins, and grandchildren.

* * *

And under the colors of a rapidly changing sky, the rats huddled in the ruins of New York, whispering.

* * *

Anarcho-syndicalists (also called terrorists) loved the trains, even as they hated what the train companies did. So too have farmers' sons come to hate the soil for what it did, which is effect their ostracism from their fathers. Unlike hunter-gatherers, whose sons' sons' sons remain in the same place, farmers in the logic of farming father many children, effecting the necessity for other farms, far away, and so the sons must go.

As the train brought tragedy and tyranny along with its speed and efficiency, so too did the scythe.

One way of understanding the Amber Engine and the multi-dimensional shape it represented is through the logic of revolution in technology and governments.

The passing of Lenin into czar and Boston Minuteman into king is described in the flowing surfaces of its amber marl.

John the Inspector and his son Stefan, not unlike me, the Hrudu Man, knew only the logic of the village sorcerer in their bringing of the object to Manhattan—the generations-old hatred of New York and all it represented. Just as with the human love-hate of technology, or the love and hate for the visiting stranger, John and Stefan were conflicted but were bound East, where the sun rises, where the giants go, where Ing fled, toward the rising sun, across the burning surfaces of a marl in space-time, hatred and fear and love, like spirals of DNA, embedded in the sclera of their determined eyes.

Fortune, spiraling, working her awful magics in comings and goings of stars and destinies, will never be underfunded. She knows all ports and the messages that lies between, that spark the fires over the Alexandrias and Empire States, like the monks sang in *Carmina Burana*, she, Fortune, sings:

"Come, come, come!"

*　*　*

But I must finish the tale of my grandmother.

She was a strong rabbit, and lived long. Before she died, she unearthed in her digging the Amber Engine (made by alien visitors when mammals were still an idea), there in the fields of I-o-way. Its flickering surfaces reminded her of the flickering expressions she had seen that day in the dying farmer's face. She hooked it in her teeth, and brought it as an offering to the farmer's grandson, who had stayed on as an itinerant farmer on the corporate plantation.

That delivery of amber was how I was born.

*   *   *

Elsewhere, Rebecca the rock star, overcome with the beauty of the strange sky moving over Manhattan, struck up her band in the port of Brooklyn and flung her voice into the air. She watched the colors gather like a beautiful storm over New York, over Lud destroyed, over Alexandria burned, the glacier surfacing for air ...

*   *   *

I am a Wight. So are you.

Beings

I am a Wight, and so are you.

The priests gathered in their twilit realm from whence the Manager had been dispatched, and muttered, and cursed, and looked into each other's eyes, to decide who was to die.

The logic of religion (yes, "tied again," related to "ligament"), is such that heretics are always hunted. Religion requires a certain consistency of habit, and of thought, even as kings require taxes.

So it was that the priests of Reshh effected what they thought of as their summary extraction of their Voyager Manager from his dive into the unknowns below. (After all, who wants discoveries that may threaten the status quo?)

They signaled the bounty hunter in the old way, with a snarl and with raised hands, and he bowed with a smile of his own, cloak wrapped over his face. And he went down, through the Bold Weld, down, after the Manager.

* * *

As Rebecca played, the Brooklyners cried.

And by the shrine the women held each other, out of fear and astonishment, watching the sky over the ruins.

* * *

I am the Lord, I am the Bread-Keeper, and I keep it. So we say—so we say for the long years, long said.

I keep the bread, and though it may be shared, it depends on me. This is what a Lord does: starves people.

Territory is a troubling business. Always a matter of boots and facts on the ground, possession nine-tenths of the law, territory loves Lords, or, vice versa, Bread Keepers love the land that bears their bread.

Many religious systems, by extension, postulate a Bread-Keeper in the sky and in the universe who rations out the loaves, and who fights to keep the oven and the fire safe for the people to use and bake in.

But there are many Bread-Keepers, many Lords, in the sky and elsewhere and the long low line of territory, the boundary marker between Jew and Gentile, alien and human, citizen and foreigner, the lands nations galaxies and wormholes that we know and love are never readily scored by lines except on maps, except in 3-D models. The people always know this, come the long and the short of it, they learn the cipher and the anthem for the flag and the state bird and still they know that they might get another führer, or a different one, depending on the price of eggs, depending on the wind in the East where Ing went off to, and yet the Lords insist, don't they, and perhaps we insist for them: I am here. Watch your water. Eat at Joe's. Swear me my allegiance.

Or, in this case, broadcast out of the red flaming New York sky: WE COME IN PEACE. BRING US YOUR VEGETABLES.

The psychic signal was very clear, delivered to the citizens of those mid-Atlantic islands as though in a ringing voice in their native tongue, shouted from the sky by the Bread Keeper him/her/itself, the Lord God of whatever was believed. (Even atheists must deal with lords, after all).

*   *   *

Vegetables. For a long sunrise. For an afternoon nap. For a time and a time and a time again, a time for a new Jerusalem, a new slingshot into space.

A time to live, a time to die, and a time to wormhole—sometimes vegetables are good interdimensional diplomacy.

"Did you hear that?" Rell asked Isolde.

"Yes," she whispered.

Rell smiled an uncertain smile.

"We're being invaded, aren't we?" said Isolde. She picked up her new cel phone and dialed, pacing in the dust of the Manhattan ruins. Rell was making a call of her own.

"Hrothbert!" scolded Isolde. "Where are you!"

*   *   *

They saw then a white pillar of fire, like some horrific divine judgment, spear from the sky. It shot right into Manhattan. The women screamed. So did everyone else.

*   *   *

The Iowans had accomplished their mission: destroy New York. But the Inspector and his son had not expected the alien invasion.

He put his arm around his son's shoulders, and looked at the terrible light shining down on Manhattan (though to call it a light was like calling Mount Everest a hill). It blew through the clouds above like a bullet through cheese, and the air around it misted with refracted whorls.

"I love you, son," he said.

"I love you, Dad."

*   *   *

Hrothbert had decided to return. But returning is rarely as easy as going. (You can't go home again).

He had sat with Samuel, his lieutenant, by the river, throwing chunks of concrete into the water.

"I have to go back, Sam. The Wight isn't here."

"How do you know where the Wight is? Do you sense it?"

"No. I don't. I only hope it. I don't understand this place. If I'm to find the Wight, it must be in a place that I understand. I know I'm weak. But I don't know what else I can do."

"How can we return?"

"We must fly."

"Fly, lord?" Samuel looked at Hrothbert.

"Into the sky."

It was then they heard it:

WE COME IN PEACE. BRING US YOUR VEGETABLES.

And then the light blasted into the world. The two men were near its edge. Harry Patch knew something about what that might have been like.

*   *   *

The end is the sweetest part of any journey. At least it is for me, though I'm only a blasted kite in a solar breeze.

224

Fired down by the will of their Manager, the crew ejected from their launch vehicle and materialized in three-dimensional space on the island of Manhattan on our First Earth.

As the Manager had intended, he and his crew appeared to the Earthlings as the dominant life form of the region: hominids. He had miscalculated, however, with the number of arms (they had three each).

They were nude, and hairy. The Manager's eyes were wild, and dark, almost black. The Gardener was hairier, skinnier, and very solemn.

The boy's eyes were the most startling of all: their rainbows were like nothing else.

The Prescient's hair was light in color, and her eyes were dark, though with humor in them. The Festival-goer was larger than the rest, ample of flesh, with narrow blue eyes that saw far.

Aliens.

The broadcast message shouted once again from the sky:

WE COME IN PEACE. BRING US YOUR VEGETABLES.

And people did.

*   *   *

They brought the aliens clothes too; white robes seemed to materialize from nowhere. An early adopter of the new Alien Religion took his Zodiac right across the river as soon as he heard the naked alien lords had come.

The vegetables were beautiful. New York, of course, was a port, then as now. It's also a city of food lovers, men and women with time on their hands and money in their pockets who know how to eat.

And so the vegetables were brought, bread to their keeper:

Zucchinis, shining green, asparagus, pearly and succulent, squash in a thousand colors, red, orange, blue, white, gold and burgundy, seedless and many-seeded, long and skinny and fat and round. Pumpkins, huge and tiny, smooth and cratered, were brought, one by a small child with a huge grin, watching the three-armed aliens with wide-eyes.

"What is it they are bringing?" asked Festival-Goer of Manager.

"Food," said the Manager.

"Should we eat it?" asked the boy with rainbow eyes.

"Soon," said the Manager, smiling.

They brought onions, sweet and sour, turnips, bright pink, carrots celery and baskets of potatoes in a dozen shades, the air thick with their perfume. The New Yorkers brought peas. Lettuce. Capers in expensive colored jars.

Two hundred varieties of olives.

The boy stole a taste of one of these, and smiled, his eyes flashing gold.

The people brought rich yams, firm Brussels sprouts, and fragrant peppers, curled, bulbed, shining.

They brought tomatoes.

*   *   *

When all had been brought, the Manager spoke:

"They are beautiful vegetables! I am fortunate to be able to eat them, and to be here, a visitor, amongst you, our neighbors. We do come in peace, as I said, though unfortunately we come in the midst of conflict as well, as I see you have had your own. That is part of why we are here—you might say that we were summoned here—after your war on this island.

"We too live on an island of sorts. That is, we are quite set in our ways. I, a scientific manager, had to work for many eons to effect this expedition to your world. It was said that it could not be done, but I have done it, and for this I have only my crew to thank.

"I asked for vegetables as I knew that you were what are called mammals, and I thought it safest to ask for foodstuffs further from your own genetic signature. I am on a mission of peace, which is hard work. I hope we may be able to achieve it.

"Where we are from, the priests rule. Now they hunt us. I had expected it, but still this will have consequences for you, our hosts. If you hope for peace, then I ask you now for your help in subduing our pursuers. If you do not, we will be killed, and if you are discovered, as you surely must be, by my rulers, they may try to destroy you as well.

"But they aren't the only hunters, I'm sorry to say. There are the spirals of Green and Red. Conscious matter comes in various degrees of inter-translatability, and these two colored spirals are right on the edge, I believe, of matter that is perceptible to us. Unfortunately they aren't aware of you, as you are of them. I suppose they think you only playthings—sorts of dreams.

"To stay their further predations, I also ask your help. Now let's eat!"

The New Yorkers did, wide-eyed, amidst the shining white light of the Manager and his crew. They crunched carrots and popped tomatoes into their mouths, and many remarked at the queer third arms of their visitors, asking if they could touch them.

* * *

At the edge of the vegetable gathering, Hrothbert and Daniel had an overdue discussion.

"I must return home, Daniel. I'm not needed here," said Hroth.

"You are needed, Hrothbert. It's the foreigners who have a better grasp of how to handle this bizarre miracle—you understand what it's like to be foreign, and to be diplomatic, more than anyone else. Besides, all flights are down for at least another week—"

"Daniel, I came out of the earth. I dug down, and then came back up. But this Earth is not mine. I'm from somewhere else. From talking to people, I believe that my home is a planet. A planet our Ing colonized, long ago."

"What was that?"

"You do know of Ing?"

"There were so many Ings, Hrothbert," said Daniel. "And yes, there was an Ing, or several of them, who captained a colonization mission to Rigel and Arcturus during the height of their South Armorican theocracy, over three thousand years ago now. But don't you think it's more likely that you were just injured in the war? There are a lot of veterans with strange stories now."

"Daniel. This world is not my own. I know that I fought down, and came up. The Wight I was seeking has eluded me, and I ... well, Isolde is pregnant. It would be improper for me to ask her to bear our child away from my ancestral lands ..."

"You're full of it, Hrothbert, I don't care what you say. And by whatever shreds of authority as Hierophant of the Western District of New York City I have left, I am ordering you to render your service to our city as needed, in this extraordinary time. We'll get you home afterwards, buddy."

Hrothbert stared at the man, then nodded. "They look so much like us," he said then, staring at the aliens. Daniel the Hierophant laughed.

*   *   *

Somewhere, in the darkness of his prison, Ing was crying.

For even as the mountains dream there is music in their spirits, and in our dreaming, which is shared, there are the same rules as in waking, which is to share, the kindergarten rule.

For we have never left the garden of children.

Why did you forget what dreams are? Why do you pretend that they are only the mind's escape? Escape from what? There is no way out of this magic circle. If you would dream (and you will anyway), hold me. I'm your kite. I blow in the winds of change for you, dreamer, for you and your kingdoms of dreams.

Dreams

"I have a dream."
— Dr. Martin Luther King

I am a friend and worshipper of Ing; I bear his mark upon my chest. This is part of the problem: marks. For we leave marks in our dreaming, and we must be careful.

Often I know that I am only a small part of some vast story—so are we all. When I saw that the Manager and his crew had been safely delivered to your First Earth, I lengthened my kite's tether, and soared further out.

Out here there are no names, any more, no marks of the kind we understand. Out here, I can be at peace, knowing you can work it out now that you are together. I am so tired!

But still my brother dies! Oh, how can I forgive you?

*   *   *

Isolde stood in front of The Manager.

"What do you want me to do?" she said.

"You built a shrine here, on this island?" said the Manager.

"Yes, to Frey."

"Tell me of Frey."

"She is the Earth. She gave birth to us."

"So she is your divine representation of all life on your planet?"

"Yes."

"Hmm. That will be useful. The bounty hunter will almost certainly be very traditional in his outlook—the most conservative warrior the priests of Reshh could find who is still willing to leave the temple grounds. You have experience in diplomacy."

"All women do."

"Yes, I forget your people pay such attention to your genders—we have so many that they are more an annoyance than anything. Go to your shrine, and sleep there. I will see if I can arrange for you to be our bait."

*   *   *

Isolde lay down to sleep by the shrine with a tarp pinned over her, camping under the stars and under a tarp by the shrine of Frey in the blasted Manhattan wasteland. And she dreamt, with Rell sleeping beside her, and their men standing guard outside, great dreams of the future (and so did Isolde's little one).

*   *   *

In the red wind there were three doves flapping their wings like jewels in the light, making a sound like water, rustling orchestras. Isolde saw a woman twirling in the air ahead of her; they coursed the sky with the white birds, in the half night.

She followed the birds, who were not in a hurry, moving through the universe with their minds on the water ahead.

Then she saw it, and saw that Rell saw it too, the greatest ocean that they had ever seen.

She cried out to her friend, in strange joy, making a sound with her mouth that she could not hear, but Rell heard it, and smiled, her eyes wet, and they moved over the waters after the doves, flying.

The waves, far below, undulated and shone in their millions. The doves dove then, picking up speed, and the women flew after them, flapping their arms and laughing.

Rell ducked and dove, shooting through the air, and turned her head to call to Isolde, speaking words Isolde was never able to remember on waking, words that seemed full of portent and love.

Yellow light shone on the waves and on the edges of the doves' wings.

Down below they could see thin, fast streams of colored light, red and green, shooting over the surface of the water, westward with the sun.

*   *   *

To Ressh:

Worlds and time enough under your night, your furthest czar, I Hrudu Man hrudu-ed declare your passionate glare no worth of ours, no heartache either, only a wild wimpled dare of some stupid child, teetering on the cliff of his choice.

Child!

Child-Man of cowards! Although I have little truck with gods I have truck with you, Reshh, because your worshippers insisted on bringing you so close.

I know that in your youth, Reshh, you were innocent and free, and fond of pleasure and tragedy (and what they could earn you), as you danced through cities and through lovers.

I know that you were bold, and that you held your pennant aloft in the air, and shouted your own slogans of war, as though you'd been delivered to your people, prophet or deity—a world-eater, and wise for all of that.

But where did you pin your wisdom? Was it only that scrap of wool on your tit? Was your arrogance confined to the words you put in books and did you never think of how they might be used, or what they meant?

I come for you, Reshh. I Rabbit Hrudu and though I was Hrudu-ed, let us say that it was done by you, if only I can stoke my appetite for this revenge.

We shall see what you took to yours for your wisdom, and what insults and steles you stuck into the territories where you rule. Where you dwell, where you hate, and where you breed your own.

I am sorry. I must leave you for a time. Hold tight.
and I disconnected from the poem, to seek a further star—
(Let go of the kite, child. Let me go free.)

Language is a magic thing, part sound, part bomb. Its magic is the wildness in us. It is how we hurt and are hurt, and how we know that hurting is a part of what we are—a way of telling us that we have hurt, and that we must hurt to balance out the sweeter parts, to distinguish right from wrong and dream from waking.

Reshh, religion-builder, the one who ties again with bitterness because he can, knows the magic of language.

I, old Wight, I Hrudu, let me tell you a story of Reshh, and how he came to know that the world was small, and that he'd call it his.

*   *   *

Reshh was born in Pittsburgh.

In Pittsburgh Reshh studied the masters, reading, and reading. Then he began to write.

And, yes, he wrote majestic words down into books! He wrote them diligently, scrupulously, like a housewife sewing love into her throw pillow, like a painter mixing colors.

But the danger of the poet is the danger of religion, for as words move the body and the mind to dance and grieve, the body seeks a reason for its movement, for its suffering, and if the poet is cruel he can decide that he knows why the dance began, and why the words he chose (or that chose him) to speak were painful, and why the pain was good (for him).

Words, while they do not make the world what it is, wind through its roots down into soil, collecting moisture for our life upon this world and in others. They are the most powerful weapons that we have.

It is for this reason that the poets are the most feared and the most forgotten—with bombs in their pockets wired to their mouths, priests and warriors often choose to scrape the scrolls of poets clean, or bury them forever.

Reshh was a poet in Pittsburgh. He wrote many books, which were received gladly by wise men and women.

Like many artists before him (and many who'll come after), Reshh forgot, in time, that he too had been trained by masters in order to become one, and he decided that he was alpha and omega, that his word was a creation unto itself, a power-cell that he could suck from like a hard candy, nourishing his cruelty.

So poetry is undone and lies are spread. He maligned the masters, declaring them useless and paranoid, not worthy of our ears.

And though I cannot say for sure, I say part of why Reshh moved from Earth to the distant lands where he became a god was because of this cruelty in his poetry.

Here we are again, heretic-hunting. I'm sorry for it, but that is how it is. For we are tied again inside the sounds of Ing!

Reshh hated the river. Perhaps only because it was larger than him, and he wanted to be large. He wanted to be ever so gigantic!

*   *   *

Rell and Isolde coursed over the ocean, over the ocean's ocean, following the doves.

(riverrun)

it began, a poem that Reshh hated.

I swam into the river, from up out of this world's sphere and up, up, up, fighting up, and in to the lashed lands of Reshh, and his priests.

I am Hrudu and I am coming!

*   *   *

(and Red was Reshh's)

*   *   *

In this long night we must dream together, because it is cold outside. Rell held Isolde under their tarp under the stars by Frey's temple, and in the mystic betweens where I soared I held the paper dragons who soared with me, embraced in the thoughtless night, rich in the dawn-dark dream that is our history together.

I came to the land of the Manager, the same place where Reshh came, long ago, where he decided that he needed a kingdom.

Kings and warts! Both keep coming back.

"I am a Rabbit!" I cried on their shores, and one of them answered me.

"A Rabbit?"

I smiled.

"Show me to your lord's house," I shouted. The small being obeyed me.

*   *   *

234

Ing stumbled there in the pen that was his prison on the moon. He ran his hands along the walls, and I can tell you this:

In slowness, there can be great pain, and that pain was Ing's, for he knew that he had to go slow, running his hands over he surfaces of the walls, just as they had done in the Fall Country.

* * *

Orkai was a man, too young, but a man still, as men have become from time to time, made by pain into something new; he was *nedding*.

* * *

Though it is perhaps not in my nature, being a rabbit, a peaceful mammal, I knew that I would need a trophy for the working of my thought on his: fight demons carefully, they say, lest you become one.

So I slew the boy, the boy the being in the far-away, a sacrifice is needed. Whether it were my hand or another's this is the history I write, written a history a thousand times for you to read, or throw aside in fury, to bury in the sightless sands.

I slew the boy and knew the penalty for it.

And I took his heart into the temple of the thing called Reshh, and greeted the priests there.

They gathered around.

"Priests," I said.

"Traveler," they said.

"How does your god?" I asked, smiling.

"Come, you must be tired. Drink with us," said one of them.

"Nay, I would see your sacred places! Show me the temple inside the temple!"

"We could kill you," said a priest.

"Perhaps you could," I said. "But first show me the temple!"

And they did, their robes of light and dark swaying through the passages of that nowhere place, and one of the priests balanced with his many hands against one of the dark walls (for they were still recovering from their long festival).

"Tell me, priests, how long has Reshh reigned here? How long has he ruled you?'

"We rule here, traveler," said a taller priest. "Reshh is only a name, isn't not?"

"Only a name. Only a name. Perhaps, yes!"

"Our temple!" one of them announced, and they pushed me in, and locked the door.

And I was a Rabbit in a hutch. I felt Ing, far away, as though he were my brother (though my brother dies), and I felt the death coming in me, of prison.

* * *

Ing is running in the grass. The Heardingas are running in the grass, the veldt. In the veldt is green, unnumbered colors across the veldt where the men run.

I am still here, thought Ing.

"So you are!" said one of the Hard Ones, the Haerdingas.

The sun (which one?) courses above and they run, breathing. Running.

Where are we going, brothers?

"West!"

* * *

The bounty hunter moved. If there is anything more fearsome than the elite soldiers of kings, it is the soldiers of priests who believe in the priests' wisdom. The Jesuits, before they set up universities, were soldiers of that kind, so feared that it became necessary for them to retire to scholasticism, lest they be destroyed by other Italian factions.

Priests often wear black. In addition to its apparent neutrality in social situations, it is useful for hunting in the dark.

The bounty hunter wore black too, gliding into the maze that would serve him swift passage down to the realm where the heretics had fled, in their illegal scientific mission.

Though this way was known to The Manager, he had insufficient protection to navigate it. But the bounty hunter was permitted to pass through without confusion.

What was unknown to the priests (though perhaps suspected by The Manager and certainly well understood by the *neddinga*), was that the maze had its own secret heart, and a will of its own. Although rulers have long loved mazes for the symbolism of their windings and their ability to dominate the idle minds of courtiers amidst their parks, they rarely appreciate the life the maze has of its own, even as a river has its own god.

So as the bounty hunter stepped lively through its stone and earthen hallways, navigating by his heart and by his poet-god Ressh, the spirit of the maze slipped into him quite without his realizing.

In his steps, the echo carried for many miles. He stepped carefully, as a man might in Eklaihah. Each step was for the bounty hunter religious; each its own presence, each step a unique and dignified act. So the bounty hunter nourished the ties that bound him to the cultivated fields and energies of his country.

He was, of course, quite mad. His staring eyes like moons burned through the thick mists, and he recited mantras under his breath, counting his steps.

* * *

I sing
A maze is all for you —
Under thickets and curfews,
Wicked and admired
By the eaters of the kingdom,
Who watch its power in the fruit baskets at its entrances.
A maze is all for you, dear child,
Won't you come inside?
In the maze you'll find the key to kingdoms
Lost,
The song of maidens conquered,
The latch upon the door
Of cosmos,
Hidden from your young eye.
Will you be wise?
Only step inside the gate —
We'll drink you well inside a thousand dusks,
To teach you the meaning of your heart,
The leaning and the lure that brought you to our arms.

The Maze is True!
Only fools escape.
(for they are liars)

* * *

In mazes, though it best to be quiet, there are times when shouting is also the best policy, and the bounty hunter, half-way through, knew to begin to shout:
"I am a hatchet!"
Blue energy coursed over the top of the hedges which pinned him.
"I am king hatchet!"
Then yellow.
"I am Hatchet!"
Rainbows burst across the ground around him.
"Hatchet!"
The door opened, and he threw himself through.

* * *

Harry Patch dreams, at sea. He dreams of New York that was, and Old York too, in the heath. He dreams of the aurora borealis and the feel of the first woman he took to bed, and he dreams of the guns, and of Tommy orbiting Saturn.

He dreams of the sea too, for he is on it, his satellite phone turned off, and he dreams of the streets he has known, in their thousand twistings, and their angled light, and the movements of the people through them in Spring, in the thaw, blinking in the warmth and shuffling through the dirty snow to talk outside again.

He dreams of his first trip in an airplane, when he was five, and how he held the flight attendant's hand, and she pinned wings onto his breast.

He is flying. He is flying down toward the sea, and there are two women hovering there with birds on their shoulders, with colors all around them.

He calls out to them. One of them, the red-haired woman, turns to whisper something to the white bird, and she looks at him with wide eyes, and the other, light-haired woman turns and flies off, her bird after her. Then the redhead follows with her bird, and Harry wants to say, no, don't go yet, and he does say something, but he doesn't know what—

Then the colors have him. Red and Green wind around him like coils, a Christmas package, coiled into his heart and across his eyes. He wants to shout out, over the waves.

And then he dreams he's an artillery round, fusion delivery, dropped red and green low down into the barrel of a gun, fired, fired for eternity in an instant for peace, in the mouth of a politician, fired to the woof of the world, shooting far over the heads of hell and back, streaming tears, a bullet in his prime, President of the World, arcing toward destiny ...

*   *   *

Orkai crawled through the service passages beneath the utopian village, their white metal walls grey in the dim light. In his fist he held a transponder, and he held it to his ear to listen. No response. Earlier the voice had talked to him, but now it seemed silent.

Behind him crawled his lieutenant, a *nedding*, his phosphorescent flesh illuminating their crawlspace. The transponder crackled into life and spoke:

" ... down, go down, you're close ..."

Orkai and his lieutenant beat at the base of the metal shaft with their weapons: claws and a dagger.

" ... I am close ..."

*   *   *

239

I burn. I burn and burn. *Mein hertz brennt, Brüter.*

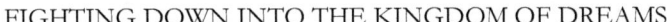

Why does the arm of the universe bend towards justice? I beat at the walls. I scream Wright's name.

" ... Orkai ... here."

Orkai and his lieutenant entered the computer room and approached my brother's corpse. Orkai touched my brother's body. In that touch, his mind was filled with images of the white city, flooded and destroyed.

*   *   *

We love this question perhaps better than any other: Why. Why asks for causes and is essentially our love of story: what happened first and second? What was the cause?

But a story can be derailed from time, you know, and this is the hardest thing, that men and women are not precisely bound by time, no more than are the leptons.

If religion ties again, time cuts us free, and freedom is the hardest thing. Why did Ing go east? Why did the Earth need another? Or was it that Second Earth needed us?

Did a man die of a disease, or did his approaching death cause the disease?

This is the burden of knowledge: everything we learn uncovers yet more mysteries, like strange grubs under a log.

Is there a greater why than reasons? Gods are fond of reasons even as we are. But if we eschew causes, what does an explanation mean? Neither Ing, nor Hrothbert, nor myself, have any truck with ineluctable fate. We still have our free will.

But I say there must be a greater cause than I am, or you are. Not a First Cause either, not a primum mobile, first mover to remove, but an infinite number, both prior to and after each event. As we have solved Xeno's Paradox, so too must we accept the rivening gestalt of both ancient and modern wisdom, and lay new foundations, for this march of warp weft weave intoxicating lushness; life.

*   *   *

Reshh listened, with his eyes. He wept, even as he reached for his sword made out of stars.

*   *   *

I burn, children. For I am in a cage. And though I am lonely I am yours. I burn for you. Like the heretic. Like the dreamer Giordano Bruno. If I can bear this heat, I Rabbit Hrudu Hrudu-ed will build a warren in the basin of your mind, the thing that good orthodoxes fear, O they of upright honor (that is what the word orthodox means): the spreading of a story.

Even if you never speak it, you will speak it in your dreams!

*   *   *

Priests on the march, in seven billion colors: for they insist that there is nothing new under the sun. Pounding through darkness, their breath sterterous urgent, maniacal, they march for Reshh to reclaim their heretic Manager, and bring him to judgment.

THERE IS A TIME FOR WAR says Reshh.

"So we fight," the priest army sings.

FOR ALL THAT IS WROUGHT IS WROUGHT FOREVER AND NOTHING SHALL CHANGE AND NOTHING SHALL BE REARRANGED, AND I SHALL RULE YOU FOREVER, says Reshh.

The priests laugh and they march in their many orbs on their many feet, instinct divided, will serving, eyes fiery and mad.

I ABIDE FOREVER IN YOUR MIND

The priests smile.

I AM YOUR SORROW says Reshh, and the priests scream their fury into the fuming glory of their descent, some lost in the maze until the others annihilate it as they speed their bodies through colored voids, hungry for blood.

*   *   *

In some memory in Pittsburgh a shadow of Reshh sees his old love and he is filled with grief, and murder.

*   *   *

Hrothbert huddled in the dark in Manhattan, on an island turned into necropolis, watching the stars. Isolde tossed and turned in her sleep.

*   *   *

And the President of Earth presides, he is arcing round, artillery disaster, true prince.

*   *   *

Hrothbert hero fell asleep by the fire, and into a dream. In his dream he soared above the ocean, and he saw the President of the World flying there too, following him and Isolde and Rell, flying into the light over the water.

"—" he said, to the President, who heard but did not respond, flying deeper into the horizon over the water.

"—— " he said, louder, and the President looked over his shoulder at him, and shook his head.

*   *   *

Ing went East, but what of the Hard Ones? Why was it they who told the tale, the Anglo-Saxons who remember and who carved his name into the stones? Perhaps Ing met a bitter end, for his song, like that of Achilles, must have come to harsher turnings for us to sing his name in our own tongue, and in the names of our sons, and our sons' sons.

Ing went East, and his going was a betrayal, and a message, the hardest message to speak:

That though you are gone, you have not gone, and you can never leave. For the winding arm of the universe is long, but it bends, not only towards justice but towards truth, and truth is the cruelest of all.

Ing/ Hrothbert felt the walls closing in, and that is what they were doing, and he screamed in the dark of the moon.

He screamed and he screamed and no one came, and though this rarely happens in stories it happened there to Ing in the moon. In his prison, in the dream that he had wanted, that Hrothbert had wanted, for no matter how special you are, no matter the size of your muscles or of your brain, the Mighty Ape that is all of us is O ever so watchful of Greed, ever so watchful for it and there is justice too in suffering and this is how Ing suffered, there in the moon:

The walls closed in. And he screamed. He heard his woman screaming, she who had gone.

For where could Ing go? I ask you. I who have seen the birth of a thousand moons! Where could Ing go but return to us? He may go but he never does, and neither do you, for you are ours inside this tongue and you are ours inside these genes and your words are ours even as our words are yours. Ing died.

Ing was murdered by the priests of the moon. They hovered there in the dark, the dark of destiny, which only means stars, which are bright but far away.

And so let us sing for Ing, for our tongue of Inglish, and for the priests of the Moon, they who guard, and they who are swept away:

In the darkest night
Under your pain,
By your wood shed,
In your daughter's voice
In our garden of New York
And Amsterdam
And at each funeral at Roth, the city of the Rats,
We burn a new fire,
To burn you,
The selfish ones,
We the Apes of the Forest,
And the Trees,
Though our generations are long,
The winding arm of the universe is longer,
And in its bending,
We crush your balls between our fingers,
And watch your face curl,
And watch your blood drip,
And we watch your daughters' faces as we take them off in
war,
And the truth of it is: your daughters are laughing.
And I say, hey ho,
Hey ho,
I am Hrudu.
I am your world.

*   *   *

Rell flew over the water, laughing, Tinkerbell Wendy double folded in the waters of her life,

And there came the man in white shining, the man who was Manager from afar, shimmering in the air, and above them the priest, Reshh. For aren't all writers priests? Are we not all ecclesiastocrats, hungry for the lesson, the lesson we would teach because we are so fond of forgetting?

Exabytes and Exabytes forget, forget, forget my name, O mainframe in the sky—

And below swam Wallru, Fish Man, like a dolphin, of the sea, they went West, West, West, West, West—

West, which means down.

Down, down, down into the darkest of the darkest we can know, even as dream is the shadow of death, dark is the shadow of the more lightless realms, inside our heads, and our hearts, the world neither beneath nor below but inside, fathomless serene unknowable and vast and though you may visit you may never leave, at least not entirely.

West, West West we fly, my daughters and sons of Ing,

Igor Ivan Ingmar, Yngvi, the daughters and the sons of the North—of the North, but what is North but another direction, eh?

Not geography but sentience is the watchword of adventurers: not a direction but a hunger for a knowledge, and what priests know is:

With much knowledge much grief, and why is this?

What can you carry on your shoulders, Atlas? Atlantean women?

"I'm getting closer!" cries Isolde.

"I feel it too," cries Rell, and they both look down into the dark of Wallru's eyes.

The Fish Man's Story

He lived very deep, as did his fellow fish. Wallru was born with a thousand brothers and sisters, many of whom were eaten in their first week, but he and a dozen siblings survived, in the blue water.

"Wallru," said his mother. "Someday you will be a great fish. You must go to the surface, and walk like a man."

"Why, mother?" said little Wallru.

"You are a fish-man, Wallru," said his mother the fish. "That is what fish-men do."

Wallru swam up to the surface and poked his head above, and tried to breathe the air that burned, and he saw the sky for the first time. He knew his mother was right—he would go to land.

But he did not go for a month. He practiced breathing the air, and eating the algae of the surface. He practiced changing his fins into feet, and back. And he said goodbye to his family, who were impatient for him to go: fish do not like long goodbyes.

His family escorted him to the surface and launched him onto the stones, pressing his fins skyward, across the meniscus of the world. And Wallru was born, a man and a fish both. And, like all hybrids, hated for everything that he was, hated for all that he could do, and all that he would bring: newness, destiny, dreams, sentences, disaster.

*　　*　　*

Wallru wandered. He came to a city, named Roth, the city of the Rats that Ing built, long ago. Fish Men live long, and their names are many, and Wallru was called otherwise in those days, names that even I do not know, I who know quite a few. So I will just call him Wallru.

At the border of the city, which was only a copse and a grove and another copse and a stone or two, there stood a rat, watching.

"Fish Man," said Murphy.

"Rat," said Wallru. "How are things?"

"Fine, Fish. I suppose you want water!"

"I would not say no to it."

"What would you say to it, then, Fish?"

"I would say yes. To water, I would say yes."

They went to the fountain and the Fish Man bathed his face, a moment he would remember for a long time. Water felt so good on his face, and the city of Roth was very interesting to Wallru, for he was a curious Fish Man, and is so still.

"Fish Man," said Murphy.

"Rat," said Wallru. "Thank you."

"It was not mine to give, but I gave it anyway. Come and meet my brother."

"I too have a brother," said Wallru.

"My brother is older, but smaller. He is brown. Come, this way."

The Fish Man and the Rat walked over the stones by the mountain to a hole by the tree. Murphy called down into it:

"Brother!" Out came Murphy's brother, whose name was Ockk.

Ockk looked at the Fish Man. He was a perceptive rat, and he noted the way the clouds moved in the sky behind Wallru, and he saw an omen there.

Omens in the sky are not something that rats are unfamiliar with—they have seen many skies, and their memories are much longer than men's. Still, Ockk knew this sky must be remembered especially.

Ockk looked at Wallru more closely.

"You're a Fish Man," said Ockk.

"I am," said Wallru.

"I am a Rat." Ockk smiled. "You will help us, Fish Man. Come this way."

And Wallru followed Ockk and Murphy into the temple of the rats and there performed a ritual that I will not speak of.

When they were done a message was given to the Fish Man, a message that he whispered to Rell and Isolde through the air of the dream—

"We live inside a dream."

Rell heard, and knew that it was the truth, though Isolde doubted it, and in the meniscus of that dreaming, that is our life and our narrative under a thousand suns, the women and the President and the Fish Man were confronted with the priests of Reshh, inside the dark inside a dark, in the secret space that rats know well, being keepers of secrets for longer than men have been alive.

In that shared dream the priests bowed, and then they danced, in their red.

They danced in their red, saying:

We are the priests of Reshh. How do you do? Have a drink. Sup with us. Will you dance in the dark? You've found us. You've found us, so do a turn with us! Hold our hands, and spin, and spin. Spin under the lights in the New York nightclub, the guns are coming but what of that, tonight we're alive! We rulers of the dark inside your dark, we write the words that move your worlds but what of that, we are not unafraid of you either, you dwellers in this empty space that many say does not exist, and so just let us dance, just let us dance, a one, two three, a one, two three and in my whispering there is a war and let me count the ways: I shout and you hear! I shout and you hear! I write the sounds you fear! A woman in a room! A man in the sky! I write the words you love! A woman and her cunt! A man and his sword. I am a man. With a billion genders. I move and you tremble. But what of that? Let us dance.

The women swayed under the sun. They swayed under the sword and Hrothbert trembled over the water, and the Manager rose up.

The Manager took hold of the High Priest of Reshh, whose name was Reshh, the token of the god, and they flew deeper in, and away, to settle something between them, priest to scientist, manwoman to womanman, away in private.

The priests fluttered their robes in the wind over the water. Hrothbert's eyes were wet, he floated in the ocean, watching the far away sky, lonely, so far away.

Rell and Isolde watched the Manager and the High Priest streak across the sky in white, bleeding light across the horizon like a smear of paint.

*   *   *

Neddinga were coming. With machines inside their heads, adapted from the mainframe in their deepest realms under their courtyards and their plazas of blackest richest rock.

Atop the shoulders of the oldest, their king sat, Orkai, new *nedding*, young furious and caught inside the logic of his hate, for Hrothbert, he who had abandoned Wessalim, he who had given Orkai hope and then cast him away. Orkai came for Hrothbert like a thousand sons for a thousand fathers, with his sickle in his hand.

"Are we there yet?" he said to the old one under his legs. The old one grunted. Though the old one had not opted for the cybernetic operation instituted by the strange computer in the dark, many had, and their eyes were wide with new information, and their skulls featured new devices and antennae jutting from their sides.

My brother, my brother, my brother Wright, always wiser than me, and quieter, had succumbed to his injury, but not before exacting his revenge upon he who slew him, giving to the *neddinga* weapons with which to hurt Hrothbert and his friends.

Is it not strange that worlds commingle as they do? We long for ease and simplicity, for the logic that we dream was once ours, in a long ago, unspecified.

Strangeness hurts, for we see ourselves in it, and what we may become.

I hurt Hrothbert too, and for that I'm glad. Heroes need hurting, of course, in fact they crave it, sucking it from the tits of the world, bending and bending under pain to learn.

The *neddinga* were coming, and they came well, cybernetically enhanced. They came aware of the ironies they bore like a separate sword, for to have a knowledge of war is to have a knowledge of theater, and vice versa, and the *neddinga* played.

With knives.

The boy who was a man, Orkai, chanted along with them as they expanded the elevator shaft and shot their nano-puppets up the earth along the path of the elevator, even as my brother had dug down, so now *neddinga* dug up, up, with the remnants of my brother's interior cybernetic logic, up, towards First Earth, towards an Earth that they had never known but they could smell.

The Signalman trembled above his waterfall. He cried, and listened to the voice of his god.

Leyne in Wessalim had taken a lover and tried to forget though she could not, and later she became a queen of that broken city, a puppet of the *neddinga* for many strange years in the Fall Country.

The serpent who had borne Ing and Yseult on his back, whose task was done and whose obeisances to his god the moon were done, that serpent swam into the air back down to the desert, hungry for an insect dinner.

And in his cell, the priests took the corpse of Ing away, into their secret holy chambers in the moon.

Yseult screamed in the dark, and cursed the name of her lover.

And the physician Michael huddled in the dark, under his dead dome in Kaliforna, trying to remember his own name (for fear can do strange things).

The *neddinga* came towards the mouth of the clown, in Rohan's alley, slowly rising in their renovated elevator, a quarter mile wide, holding an army inside.

*   *   *

Orkai sat back against the metal wall of the elevator, listening to the machinery whine. The old one sat next to him, his hand on Orkai's leg. They were both exhausted. Orkai loved the smell of his new brothers, their green-black skin, and they black-brown eyes. He loved too, though he could not have put this into words, the logic of the *neddinga*'s acceptance of him into their midst. Like the Normans, the *neddinga* were for many centuries the ultimate meritocrats, scorning the trappings of rank in favor of talent.

"I want his head on a pike," whispered Orkai.

"Shhh, king," said the old one. "Killing him will take time; first we must try him. He must be made to understand what he's done."

*   *   *

Do we love disaster? We drink its glory on our tongue. Burn the crop, thresh it under in the soil! Lay waste for the autumn that is coming—reap life rich fluid drink it, child, blood in the night, war in the air, inhale the stuff of our undoing for it is what redoes us—

*   *   *

Chess. Chess, chess. Chess: one. And two. Queen's Gambit. Knight's Disaster. Queen's Run. Bishop's Turn. Pawn's Pull. Rook, rook who took the look Reshh gave to Manager inside the dark:

raising his hand, eyes wide, arm in drama, hovering, castle in his hand—

The Priest's River. The King's Ocean. The Pawn's Fountain. The Messenger's Trick. The Raj and his Music.

Raj, Raj, and his music!

The Opal's Glimmer, the Thresher's Dance, the Princess's Torment, the Black Horizon, the Storm Gate, the Check Coin Curl, the Clasp of Knives, the Driver's Count, the River's Rush, Raj, Raj and his music chess—

The Manager swept the pieces off the board, lightning cross the sky. They wrestled on the surface of worlds, in the minds of men, fish, trees and atoms, across the boundary dividing world from outside, and dream from waking.

And the Manager pinned Reshh onto the Earth not-Earth, and said to him:

"You are fire in the night."

(by which the hero watches)

And Rell took Isolde in her arms and they made love atop the waves, two serpents intertwined, as the priests made their music on the water, naming civilizations, and drowning children who never were.

O the children who never were! (someone has to do it)

Hrothbert dove beneath the waves of the dream, seeking light, seeking escape, trying to remember ... what was he supposed to *do?*

Life is confusing, isn't it, Hrothbert? Do you want the manual? Do you want Kurt Vonnegut's manual, Hrothbert, issued to you in your birthbed? With mother to read it to you—

Here, let me give it to you, son:

It begins like this:

and there is something new under the sun:
and all is not vanity —

*   *   *

Fighting, fighting down into the dark. Thank you for coming with me. I am only a Rabbit, and I tremble, in my fury and my fear. I must teach you yet another lesson.

Love is written about endlessly, in part because love is endless. But part of the truth is that war lives inside of love, and vice versa, even as two brothers love each other as they beat each other's faces with their fists. Like sex and violence, war and love are cousins, intertwined spirals of DNA, like Red and Green, a jaunty, spinning logic and chaos.

The horrible truth of it is, we need war even as we need love, even though we hate it as we hate love, and this secret which is not secret is abused, because something that you need is different from something that you want, and to want war is like to want love, to succumb to desperation.

War and love come anyway, even as you do, brother, come here to our own, to this passage. Fatal passage but true, and I am armed. For FDR hated war, and fought it well. Perhaps Franklin Roosevelt was a Rabbit—he was brave enough to be.

War attracts war, even as lovers attract love, even as sex attracts violence and vice versa, and the logic of life is the logic of pain, and Orkai slew the women that he found inside Manhattan, cutting their throats in the dark and shouting his name into the sky and the *neddinga* surrounded him, shouting their many names, and they took the ruins in the space of an hour, killing all they found, only sparing our hero and his women, because they had other things in store, while they slept: not one, but two vengeances.

*   *   *

Is vengeance best cold, or hot? Is it better to kill a man who hurt you in the heat of the moment, or to plot his death slow? There are pains and pleasures in both. Orkai chose the second path, for he had a cool head, like the man he loved, Hrothbert. Wiping the blood from his mouth (for he had eaten liver), Orkai watched his quarry sleep, and rested his sickle against Hrothbert's throat. And in that dark dreaming Hrothbert did not awake, nor did Rell, nor Isolde, though they shivered.

The *neddinga* and the rats gathered round the Watcher who had Failed, whose Stories had not kept him Awake, who had chosen instead the path of Dream.

It's much harder to kill the wolf at the door while you're asleep, is it not?

(though it can be done ...)

BOOK THIRTEEN
Dreaming under Dreaming in the Logic of the Dark

 rothbert

met the Wight, there beneath the waves in the dream.

It shimmered in the water, light streaming from its limbs, its eyes ash-colored orbs.

It smiled, and Hrothbert shivered in the water, his eyes cold but his mind alive, whirring.

"You're the Wight," Hroth said. And he heard the Wight's voice inside his mind:

Yes.

"I'm supposed to kill you. You're a monster."

Yes.

"You dug the hole?"
I did.
"Why?"
That's a long story, but mainly because I wanted to.
"Why?"
I was lonely, and I found friends.
"What am I to do now?"
You are to be a father, now.
"Yes."
Do you know that I have children too? Some of the mischief-makers who harried you there in the dark.
"They killed a man."
Haven't you killed men, too?
"Yes."
Would you worship me as a god?
"No."
Many have.

* * *

Fire in the night, Pittsburgh, burning for your fathers, firing your fathers' miseries and mysteries, Pittsburgh the solemn, Pittsburgh the found and the lost, Pittsburgh fortunate son, Pittsburgh mellow and cold and sad and waiting, Pittsburgh waiting for the now to come, for when will it be now asks Reshh, when will it be me, when will I be the chosen one?

We choose you, Reshh, here, come here, to our team, you Reshh and your mysteries of Pittsburgh, you and your longing *langsam* where mourning becomes the helmsman, for we shall come in your boat, kybernetes, we'll come right in, and where to?

What did the mysteries of Pittsburgh teach you, Reshh?

Rell and Isolde cum on the water and Hrothbert swims deeper into the ocean with the Wight and the Manager and Reshh the high priest wrestle in the sky, fighting for their love, for the world that they know.

For what is a man of Pittsburgh? What does a man know there and what are the mysteries that are given to him?

What mysteries are sunk down into his soul in the dark of the foundry and the forests that give no light but only hide it?

Tell me, Pittsburgh, what mysteries did you divine and what sigil did you cut into your stone to tell the way it was and the way you wanted it to be?

If we are to understand these changes, of all that was so near and so far, on Earth and Second Earth and in dimensions unknown, we must understand something of Pittsburgh.

*　　*　　*

Pittsburgh: a confluence of rivers and people. Perhaps that is all we need: not one river but two, and not one people but a hundred, melted like iron into girders.

Appropriate then that the strategic prize of three Armorican empires, Pittsburgh, gave Reshh to us, hungry for his own.

*　　*　　*

Beneath the waves, the Wight spoke to Hrothbert:

What did you think, Hrothbert? What did you think I had done, when you were chasing me? You thought I was a devil? A monster for you to decapitate and return to your tribe in the woods, a real man at last? I'll tell you what you thought: you thought that the mysterious was something that you could conquer, you little priest. You thought the big world could be turned into your bauble, whatever you might have said. That you could take up arms against a sea of troubles and by opposing end them, because that was the little Hamlet that you were, eh? Full of beans, young dumb and full of cum? I pity you, do you know that, Hrothbert of the Ingaevones?

Hrothbert watched its twitching, shining face and its full orb eyes, dark wisdom.

"You were a death sentence, Wight. I knew that. I wasn't stupid. You were a Quest! A great quest. What better way to get rid of a man than send him on a Quest! I knew what it was: exile. What did you think?"

I thought you were smarter, man. Tell me, would you be a Wight like me? I could make you one.

"No."

Live a long life, be happy? Long and long life! What man can refuse that! You of your "Second Earth"—only another quest for your immortality! Why not have it for real? Is it my face? My dull eyes? You may take whatever form you wish, for a price!

"Thank you for the offer. Tell me: if I were to stay in New York. On the dead island. Would I be cursed, as my ancestor was in Eklaihah? Tell me!"

Oh Hrothbert, you little medieval pagan. How can you ask me that!

Its eyes flashed fire.

You're already dead and abandoned, boy! A curse is your own, if you want it! What do you want, boy!

"I want Isolde."

Well you have her, don't you. You're a fortunate son of a fortunate son. And speaking of which, where is your father, Hrothbert? Where is he?

"I never knew him. Though some part of me feels as though you could be my father."

I am not.

"You are only an alien! As I am!" Hrothbert shouted beneath the waves. Above, the women floated. Sated under the wide sky. The priests circled, enacting some rite, bonds and wands and cuts into the fabric of the tide of this dream, sex and ritual and magic in the dark always an old tune, abstinence for a fire, and for a toil, and for a power that might be yours, so only suffer in the dark and utter the name and then the name, and then the name ...

Under the waves, Hrothbert said:

"Wight! I should kill you! But help me. Help me kill this priest."

But you know that he is only one of yours. A man of Pittsburgh come into great things. Would you not learn from the great man!

"No. You should help me."

Should I! My obligations are my own, but let us say I should. What would you give me in return?

"What do you want?"

Build me a city.

"Yes."

* * *

Deals in the dark. Fragrances and the eaves and what is a father anyway, genetic testing or no, but a passenger in the dark, a man who comes and then is gone like all of us—it is the cities that endure, older than all fathers, of stone or of wood, and in the city is the tree, the tree of life.

On the branches there are oceans, of ideas and of blood, pumping in the veins of our cousins in the trees, in the grass.

All flesh is grass and I eat it, for I am a Rabbit.

Deals, deals on parade, and the Manager fucked Reshh in the dark, holding his body down on the ground. Light dark history of war and sex, a chess move—

Build a city after orgasm, and build a city after the fragrance has departed—

* * *

In Guernsey they are coming. The priests of Reshh descend both in waking and in dream, into the farms, and into the skyscrapers.

In Brooklyn they are coming, the priests of Reshh, for New York in its long love affair with culture, and the making of ideas, brings in cultists by the boat load, straight to Rome. It remains ever eager in its worships for the flavor of a new god—

* * *

The priest of Reshh stepped over the scraping in the Bedford dark, his boot sole working its way into the crack, to silence the grit and make each step silent. His brother brought his robe taut against his face to disguise it, for his face was a hole of ash, like a dark world separate to itself. The two men in red robes took themselves down the street, because what did you think would happen, New York? Open the door, open the door—

Inside:

The man with the ash face curls into the window and reveals himself to the daughter of the house and takes her, her eyes wide with yellow fire all at once, religious conversion in a second.

Would we be tied again? Religio ad infinitum? What are the ties that bind? Blood and steel and logic. And wonder, too. Like the Gnostic gospels of Horselover Fat and all his many sons and sons' sons, wrought wild and mad in seas of stars, knowledges uncounted awaiting Albemuth ...

The *neddinga* cry into the dark, and Hroth and Isolde and Rell awake—

* * *

Reshh in the sky of the dark of the dream awakes, but he is not awake. Rell awakes but she believes that she is asleep. Hrothbert awakes and sees the face of the Manager and believes that he is the Wight.

Isolde awakes and her man is near and her woman is near, and she sees the enemy, *neddinga* and the boy who leads them.

Why is it so often a boy? Well the legends are pretty, but for the *neddinga* it's because of territory, and long memory. Like the book of Genesis, Orkai was a convenient scroll for *neddinga* as the Yahwist had been for Persia, only another stele written under a strange sun, a carved sigil to mark a new Bread-Keeper, and to say unto you his people, his country and his lands and empires, all his women and his children, oats donkeys lasses and ladles of fire madness:

Starve!

That is the message as the *neddinga* growl in the dark. We hunger! We hunger for Frey is hungry! And Isolde screamed. She screamed until Hrothbert put his hand over her mouth, looking into the eyes of Orkai.

"I am Orkai," he said. "And I am *nedding*. You will answer for your crimes."

* * *

In the village of Bedford Stuy the priests were moving with their yellow eyes, for what is conversion if not unity, like the conversion of matter into energy, or air into ammonia and then into wheat? Bodies alive with new music, eyes alive with a new god and a new lust and a new list, listing left, Reshh from Pittsburgh comes in his old hate, for the river —

(and Pittsburgh is a city of rivers!)

But for Reshh the rivers never run, they never run, he wants to step into the same river twice. For there is nothing new under his suns!

Reshh shouted from the sky:

Xxxxxxxxxxxxxxxxxxxxxxxxxxxxxxxxxxxxxxxxxxxxxxxxxxxxxxx

Reshh murdered from the sky:

Yyyyyyyyyyyyyyyyyyyyyyyyyyyyyyyyyyyyyyyyyyyyyyyyyyyyyyyyyyyyyy

Ressh's priests burned in their urgency: ever the same, ever the same, ever the same, we heretic-hunt in Armorica. We hunt them good and fine, and it doesn't matter whether they be large or small, both are good for burning:

Right into the fire with the faggots—

Even in the logic of the faggot, the French peasant *bocage* trimmings, is the logic of the hunting down of heretics, for good fences make good neighbors, and the way to make good fences is to establish clear boundary lines, with steles written into bone—

O fire mad! O mad fire! I sing into the sun! I sing into the sun! I sing into the way! I sing until this tale is done, this terrible tale of the meeting of worlds, the meeting of rivers in Pittsburgh town, and the terrible death surrounding—

For all is mad in Armorica! And all is mad and mad! And I am mad too and I am burning for a million years! I burn for you!

Out of the fire I will adhere my gladness into your face and you shall bear my mark, even as Orkai bears the mark of *nedding* and of Hrothbert, I shall take my hand of fire and lay it right into your soul, daughters and sons of the two Earths connected under Armorica, in the last light of my life, for with my brother dead I cannot be long behind him, brother—

(for I am only Rabbit!)

But still unto Pittsburgh I shall come again, like your devil Macarthur to Pacific, I shall be Night of the Lepus in your door! Not Jerusalem or Mecca but named for Pitt the Great Commoner, a man of oratory who hated France, who burned the torch of fire war bright in the dark of Ingland, and who burned his stele into the mind of little Ressh, Ressh who's screaming in the sky:

* * *

"What do you want, Orkai? What can I give you?" said Hrothbert.

"Don't do it, boy," said Manager, his own boy beside him, with his fiery eyes.

The old *nedding* whispered into Orkai's ear, and Orkai bent to listen.

"Orkai. Take me. Take me and let the rest of them go," said Hrothbert.

"I'm not a boy!" shouted Orkai, his eyes filled with pain.

* * *

261

In Pittsburgh I am coming. Where rivers meet and run, of blood.

* * *

"You're a boy."

"Cut him! Cut him like me!" shouted Orkai and the *neddinga* took Hrothbert and cut his face, and Hrothbert looked into the great lidless eye of the *nedding*, the same who had taken him below an eon ago now, whom he had fed to please Frey, and he looked into its eye and took the scar like a man, and Orkai's eyes pleading, pleading for orders, while the old one whispered in the boy's ear.

"The priests of Reshh are coming even now! I can smell them over your rivers! They will come here last, and take you all too."

"The priests have nothing on us who live below," said the old *nedding*.

"He says I should eat your liver, Hrothbert! Like Prometheus! You who brought us fire should be punished, for you burned our whole city!"

* * *

I'm sorry Hrothbert. Change is so hard. It's the hardest thing, but better than the alternative.

* * *

The rats gathered around Hrothbert and he went mad for a time then, for he was only a man, and I am only a rabbit. And I must only tell the tale again, the same that I have told a thousand thousand times—*and then this happened, and then this, and what does it mean, son, what does it mean, daughter, you are mine, child, you are mine and I am yours by the fire in the dark, like that fire in the sky is ours and we are its, and Ing went down into the dark, he died for us, even as I will die for you—*

* * *

"I'm not Ing!" cried Hrothbert, covered in the rats, the women and the aliens tied down by the *nedding*, watching the rats swarm over the son of Ing.

"I'm not Ing!"

"But what did Ing do?" said Ruth, the brown rat, and a queen.

"What did Ing do, son of Ing? What did he do?" said Ownlee.

"Why did you forget, Hrothbert?" said Reallee, and he bit into his toe.

And Murphy squatted over Hrothbert's face and pissed into his wound, and looked into the hero's eyes and grinned while doing it.

"What did Ing do, Hrothbert?"

"He built a city. The city of Roth."

"And then what did he do, Hrothbert?"

"He wanted it. He wanted it for his own."

"And why did he do that, Hrothbert?"

"He was stupid. He forgot."

"But he had eyes, Hrothbert. And he knew Roth was the most beautiful city there was, because the simplest, only a forest with a few stones, and a strong river. A wise hill nearby, to see the country surrounding ... Hrothbert, you forgot about our dreams!"

* * *

I know that even now, after so many millennia, the dream of a rat is a tenebrous thing, still delicate. I know that it is mine to preserve it too, in its our cousin's eye is the madness of our mammal ancestry and our humility. The dream of a rat is a kind of deliverance, the simple summer sun, and the wisdom to go on.

I have met many rats I liked, and even some I might be said to love, though never like a rabbit. Rats are so full of dreams. For if you can dream like a rat, you can build whole worlds out of the merest ash, and fire roads through the dark around you, to find neighbors you didn't even know you had.

Who knows neighbors like rats do! Not a damned one of us.

* * *

"I forgot ..." muttered Hrothbert, feverish, as the rats began to chew in earnest on his toes.

* * *

I am a Rabbit made of a new steel, and though I burn I will not melt, though my heart may melt, as I long to throw myself into my rabbit grave—

In the dimensionless surround I summon catalysts uncountable, I go supernova in the majesty of Reshh's realm, in the way of my forefathers, I hold my metal rabbit hands against the walls and push, I push with all my might against the black holes and the goat's songs that wind around this murderous little backwater—

There is something new under your sun, Reshh. A super-new, a supernova, and I burn, I burn brighter than you ever knew, for I am the wing and the clasp, and I am the long and the short, and I wield the weight of empire in my soul, borderless empire, written not on maps but in the mind, a balancing act for the mightiest of fools, each time I divert an asteroid into Jupiter's basin, to save the little pilgrims in their bluish nights—

Alles das Kind Rabbit war, only a rabbit in the dark, the child didn't know that its warren was all warrens, or that the seed of kings was burgeoning in its breast. When the child rabbit was, it drank of the stream and knew without thinking that the stream would come to pass too, and that that was why it was good to have it to today, today that never comes again—

*   *   *

For what is fundamental! Are there four fundamental forces, or are there five! And what fundaments lurk beneath the dark! Write your stele well, traveler, and be ready to move it! This way to Jerusalem, and this way to the dark!

*   *   *

Reshh the god sat on his throne, theocrats surrounding, some still with the glow of Festival coursing through their eye sockets.

"Tell me, where is my scientist?"

His court answered, as one:

"Gone away, Lord. Gone away, Bread-Keeper. Scientist is gone."

"Why have you not brought him to me!" Reshh's eyes bulged, as did his hernia, its glowing paste seeping from under his cheek.

"We seek him Lord. He is far away. We think that—"

"Don't think! Bring him!"

And the court bent their heads, both in obeisance and in concentration, listening to their priests afar, and to their lone bounty hunter.

*   *   *

The bounty hunter watched under the waves as Hrothbert emerged, next to the glowing Wight. A short distance away, the women still embraced, and the priests hovered over them and the waves. Hrothbert's face was bathed in the eerie light of the Wight as it shimmered over the waves. The bounty hunter's hollow yellow eyes were filled with sadness.

Then the Wight flitted up into the sky, its huge eyes flickering, and it seemed to wave goodbye, its tendrils swaying about its fleshy body as it vanished up.

The bounty hunter floated above the waves, watching Hrothbert, who averted his eyes from the women and the priests, crying silently, alone in the wet dark. The bounty hunter caught Hrothbert then, in his tight embrace, and whispered in his ear:

"Bring me to your little godlet. Bring me to your avatar from the sky, The Manager."

Hrothbert screamed a silent scream as the bounty hunter slipped his slender dirk into his skin, electrifying Hroth's brain with pain.

"You'll show me where he is."

*   *   *

Wallru screamed out of the clown's mouth, gushing sailing ships and balls of wax, little toy skyscrapers and mobile phones, scuba gear, his bowl-head raging red, his eyes bulging, scraping the alien air of Manhattan through his gills. He bellowed into the dark of the destroyed Battery Park.

Some of the *neddinga* standing guard rushed towards him.

"What do you *want*, Fish Man?" they hissed.

"Bring me to your leader, *nedding*," said Wallru, his eyes filled with violence, and sly humor.

"This way, Fish. Would you like some fish food?" The *nedding* smiled. "We've lots of it."

"No thank you, *nedding*."

Wallru approached the clearing where Hrothbert and the women were tied, seeing the scarred boy and his *nedding* advisor, and in the distance at that moment, the huge white tunnel of light that had delivered the avatar, The Manager and his argosy, started to slip back up into the sky.

*   *   *

The priests watched the women fuck, solemnly, circling in their robes, remembering who they were before Reshh came, before they were sworn to eschew dreaming, to avoid the river. To still the river is to still the sea and the life it contains, and part of the minds of the minions of Reshh still knew this.

Why does the river run? Why does Ouroburos circle about himself, devouring his tail?

Metaphor is still sometimes derided; the word means "bearing across." And if the river stops, it is easily crossed. You need make no plans; Darius and Persia may invade with hardly an afterthought and Mesopotamia need have no meaning. If the river does not move it does not run it is yours to channel and contain, to call your own forever, and the metaphor, that bearing, that helmsman, *kybernetes*, father cybernetic, his wisdom and his tiller in the storm of worlds, he is not needed, and what is not needed in this universe passes away, becomes vestigial at first, and then crumbles into dust.

Without dream there is no metaphor, because we can cross anywhere, there is no boat or jump, or door, for all is accessible, and this was the desire of the thing called Reshh, that no door should be closed.

Reshh trembled in his kingdom, like holding back his sphincter on an earthquake.

And through the noosphere, the linking of the minds of lives throughout this galaxy and its neighboring dimensions (of all minds, however subliminally), the light shivered, and the dark swelled, and my burning ceased, and I dropped from the secret secret in the secret of Reshh's temple to the floor, scarred and holy.

When Olympians fight the mortals tremble, but the reverse is also so. For the river runs neither down nor up but through, our words the messages thrown across, from bank to bank, over the eternal water.

*   *   *

267

In a beginning the rat carried a man who had a name over the savannah, and the man took the dream away from the rat.

"I will answer for his crimes. For Hrothbert is my brother," said Wallru, standing before the rats and the *neddinga* in the New York night.

*   *   *

How do you reclaim a dream? It is the same as how you reclaim a metaphor. Take a bearing, sailor, on the sky with your sextant, and hold it tight. Hold it tight, scientist, squeeze your hand onto the handle of the electron microscope, put the boson in your sights, like at a Frenchman with your longbow, take your bearing across the river of stars.

Here, across the river of stars, comes the bearer, the rat, the rat, the rat, the rat who bore, like a woman bears a child, the rat who bore his cousin through the grass of the savannah, a simple metaphor, a simple rat bearing a man across to Earth, tying life to life.

Reshh wanted only to forget his origins. A common enough story. And so I am here to remind him of them.

Cybernetics is a metaphor, and so are dreams. And the secret of their working is a gap: without a gap, a river or a door, or a little Planck's constant, from valence to valence, across which we fire our fiery arrow, without that, Darius claims us all. Greece falls and we have no *Iliad*. Without a gap the river does not run. And we never arrive at Howth Castle and environs down the Liffey, nor embrace Wallru in the half-light of the Fall Country.

*   *   *

The Manager swam in the night sky of dream, chewing on a huge carrot. His plan had taken so many unexpected turns. He lay back on the aurora borealis and chewed, pondering the strangeness of his life. So did Galileo ponder, before recanting.

He would be murdered, he knew. Whether he returned of his own free will or not, he and his people would be killed, to justify Reshh's rule.

Part of him wanted to leave everyone behind and flee; he knew he could. But the Manager was still a being of his people, still a being with courage in his heart, and he chewed the carrot carefully, knowing that it might be his last meal. (I myself am fond of carrots).

* * *

What shall I give to Reshh? I Hrudu. I promise you, I will scrape him soundly out of his foundling husk, out of the hollowness he's claimed, I promise I will force him to run, as the river does, as does my heart and yours, I will put him to our work.

* * *

Reshh summoned Red, believing that it served him, only to discover:

* * *

I am a sextant and I curve. I am a medallion in your mind and I curve for you, my name is Red. I am a color and I swerve, I swerve beneath your heel; I whirl the light low for your thought, I wind about your thighs and in, inside your mind. I bear across your curve, gravity and urges deep under your fear and skin, I bear beneath your earth to flick my acids into your weighted burls, to move the serpents and the churning earls who station under your divines, who curve the sails you cast above, who limn and slip the world onto their seals, who wave the wafer on your tongue, your sense across the curling hurling span under your heels—

I am the Red and I am curving, I am curving in a light, I am curving in a light. I am curving in a light.

A light inside the gun that you had fire.

What is it that you want? You fired and I came; so did my brother. These are our sins and they are also yours. For having come we cannot go away; we must make sense of this.

We are the Red and Green!

Listen:

Though the long arm of the universe bends, it shimmers too, each direction a promise and conundrum, the way that we would wield, and yield.

Can you do both? Can you both yield and wield as we do? Can you declare a war that you refuse to fight? Can you launch the empty missile?

These are the things that you must now consider. You are not alone. Everything you do is noticed. We are so close now. And we will take over the shop if we have to.

*   *   *

Reshh! I am coming! (with my torch, heretic—)

*   *   *

Reshh is fleeing inside the maze, his eyes wet and mad, and I am on his tail, I Rabbit. Did I never tell you how I was Hrudu-ed? Reshh did it. Let us blame him, it is what heretics are for. I am coming, Reshh!
what are you
I am a Rabbit!
In the maze you are amazed. And though I am a Rabbit and my nose is strong the maze is boundaried and wise, a conscious heady thing with rules all its own.
I am in a potion, a potion in the earth.
I am in a prison, a prison in the park.
I am in a ride, inside the fair.
I am in a toy, atop a child's palm.
I am inside the train, the train that thunders west.
"Reshh!"
He looks back, through the moving cars, his eyes mad, and afraid.
"I'm coming!"
My torch burns hotter than a sun.

*   *   *

In the New York night all turn to look once more up at the sky. Like nothing anyone has ever seen.

*   *   *

And I scrape him with my claw, with my rabbit claw, and I hear the priest scream. I hear Galileo laughing.

For science is religion. And religion is science. I bear across and so do you. I am a rabbit underneath your house. You are a man atop my warren, and I'm curling, curling, curling beneath the earth that is a wave, a wave, a wave inside the coliseum ...

Reshh screams inside the train. We tie again, we tie again: not postulate or hypothesis alone, not regimen nor credo, neither mysticism nor empiricism, without a little sharing of the duties of the longbow—

We are curling now inside the Red and Green. I am a Rabbit!

you're not a rabbit, you're a liar

And you not a priest. Only a con-man.

what kind of horrible thing are you

A priest, like you. Only I know that my religion must change. That my laws will fade from the sand on the steles.

If I die, I will bring you with me—

*   *   *

Give me the watchword of democracy, brother, at last—dear God, give it me at last —

(I see my brother's dying eyes inside my soul, Wright's beautiful cybernetic eyes ...)

*   *   *

I will undo the universe itself.

I am Reshh!

You are not Reshh. Dead men have no titles.

Ha ha ha!

I am the Hrudu Man. I come to you a judgment. Burning. For you are a trespasser. Your stagnation is a trespass, it is dissolution. With fire I will make it all anew, I will cleanse your heresy from out this world—

You're like me. Let us work together, Rabbit. Rule with me!

It's truth that interests me, priest. We're too different. Come, eat the torch—

Earth Three

It was as though the sky bent, and the peoples of Earth saw what lay behind it, the King in Yellow, Carcosa Found, the hideous maiden behind her veil, Death himself perhaps. None could speak about it after but all knew that the world was no longer the same.

For a generation passeth and another comes, all flesh is grass, and each blade is different, for though together they make a river that will never cease its running, the river is never the same, not for a nanosecond, it is a fluid, of time and life, like Time Life Books, a river of blood, pumping in the universe's heart.

The strength of metaphor, stronger than any religion, or any science, it is agony itself, the pain of birth, the firing of life across the gap—

* * *

The great wave curved across the night sky and Orkai wept, because he did not understand, and he loved Hrothbert so much, and Hrothbert had left him alone.

The boy's eyes blazed with tears and he advanced on Hrothbert with his knife.

Through Brooklyn and Guernsey, the priests of Reshh were screaming, because their god had died.

As Hrothbert and Orkai circled one another, Hrothbert's friends still held by the *nedding*, the mainframe spark of *S.L.*, transmitted from Wright to the pieces welded to *neddinga* bodies, that spark jumped to life. *S.L.*, the old helmsman.

* * *

Hrothbert circled the boy Orkai with his fists, and the boy slashed at him with his long *nedding* knife. In fights there is a great deal of love, and love is always dangerous. There is a gentleness to almost all of them, a hesitation to strike a fatal blow, because we watch out for each other, even in the midst of hatred.

They circled in their ancient dance in the ruins, and the boy howled, the blood pumping in his veins. Hrothbert felt Wallru there, held back, his presence warm and heartening.

"Let me repay you, Orkai ..." Hroth shouted, dodging the blade, and the boy was infuriated by his voice, slashing again, harder, and Hroth slipped under and tripped the boy, who went down on one knee, but then slashed again and Hroth dodged back. Orkai stood, his eyes fire.

Hroth dodged again and got in close, and seized the boy's arm, and swung him into an embrace, gripping his sword arm, hugging the boy to him, the boy's back to his stomach. Orkai screamed in frustration, and the *neddinga* trembled, ready to murder.

"Orkai," Hroth whispered, "tell me what I can do."

"Let me go!"

Hroth did. He let the boy go and dodged back again, narrowing avoiding having his gut opened.

"Hroth!" shouted Isolde, before the *neddinga* silenced her again. Wallru watched, his eyes full of some strange despair, or humiliation, an indignation at all of them, mere animals, without imagination.

Then Hrothbert lunged, and kicked the boy in the head, hard. Orkai fell into the dust, not dead but no longer awake.

"Is that what you wanted!" Hrothbert shouted at the *neddinga*. "Is that the show that you came for! Would you have me kill this boy? Are you that hungry for blood!"

Rell and Isolde rushed forward then, and Rell touched Orkai's throat.

"He's alive!"

The *neddinga* grinned. Then the old *nedding* spoke:

"We praise you—"

"I am just a priest with a sword, far from home," interrupted Hrothbert. He knelt by the boy, and laid his hand on his pale, scarred cheek. "What do you *neddinga* want? To rule? Here? Why have you come?"

Wallru stepped forward then and laid his hand on Hrothbert's shoulder.

"We must build for them, Hrothbert. And for ourselves, too."

*   *   *

Generally it is the builder kings who are remembered longer than the warriors. Even if the war be just and glorious, its causes and reasons are quickly forgot, long before a well-constructed aqueduct meets its end.

Over the wasteland of Manhattan the Wight hovered, speaking with Red and Green, and with the President of the World, Harry Patch.

Patching was what was needed, of men and women and children, cities, roads, telephones and homes, plazas, offices and city parks, lakes and riverfronts along the florid Hudson, a patching of New York's wounds.

The Wight listened, like the United Nations, translating, adapting to the gaps between the tongues that were spoken in this dimension and others, looking for common ground, not only of interests but of perception, to see what it was that could be built, what was even possible.

The new is so frightening, and the conservative urge highly sane—sometimes a new thing can wipe out entire tribes. Adaptation is the river, the running river, carrying everything away, all your loved ones, all your words.

Give me a word!

is it Eklaiah?

Eklaihah. City that no longer is. Let us tell a brief tale of Eklaihah, as it bears on what came after Reshh came to his final death, after Hrothbert adopted Orkai as his son, his eldest, another son of the wild and mad Ing.

In Eklaihah they had a deep fondness for light, and equally so for light's packagings, and the city became famous for its many lamps they traded, and with which they adorned their fine subterranean city.

Unfortunately, like Reshh, they let their fear get the best of themselves, and they began to fear darkness more than anything. And so they sought to light the world beneath the world, the many realms that they knew lay beneath their own.

In those days Reshh had many cyclotrons, and they sought with their industrial programs to devise a way by which Planck's constant might be adjusted, or circumvented, allowing their brave city to reap the benefit of economies of scale, as it were, in the trade of photons.

In tinkering with that little constant, they rewrote important rules, rules governing the arrangement of space in the region of the galaxy where Second Earth lay. After all, if photons, or partial ones, could be excited out of orbit with increments of energy smaller than the constant, if that crucial gap, the measurement stick of joules, was shrunk to suit the interests of the night-light loving Eklaihah citizens, light could be made more often, with less energy. But the photons themselves would be *slower*. And the light made would not be the light that they formerly known.

Of course the universe is self-correcting, but only in the aggregate, over long periods. So rather suddenly that proud well-lit city found their trading partners fewer, and citizens grew loathe to leave, lest their journeys result in their own temporal exile—strange copies of themselves emerging from the shadows, trips ending before they had begun, and vivid dreams that bled more and more into waking.

They grew to fear the dark even more, demanding light at all hours, in greater and greater quantities, until it came that they did not even need their cyclotrons to generate the strange effect to which they'd grown accustomed—it had become self-perpetuating, and slowly time grew deeper into the city, into its center, like a sun slipping into singularity ...

Though I have no truck with fundaments, there are those who call the legacy of Eklaihah's doom the fifth fundamental force: that of *noticing*. What have you noticed? And in noticing, is there something you are, perhaps, eager to effect?

*   *   *

And so what was begun inside the city of Eklaihah was finished, in a way, with the mission of the Manager, as the universe *listened,* to see what its denizens might wish to be—

*   *   *

In the ruins of Manhattan Hrothbert and his people began the construction of Howth Castle. The Irish, having found so fond a home inside New York for so many centuries, found it appropriate for their fortress of old in dear dirty Dublin to be rededicated at New York's rebirth.

* * *

Howth Castle and Environs rise as though inside a fog, deep center, unearthly heap of stones and smiling women, happy children.

Howth Castle rises in the fog, steamship spectacular.

But first, it must be built, usually a thing of decades, but in times of nanotech, only a few months.

For it is a magic castle, even as Planck was magic, driving his constant into stubborn minds, and was it the constant that was stubborn or was it Planck, and why does the magic castle know what must be done?

It rises, even as Isolde's belly, Howth rises, its memory of the Liffey and old Dublin, it rises in Manhattan on Third Earth and its channels and its heresies and its bogs and its serpents and its howls and its many gates and its maidens and its lairs inside Howth, inside Howth there is a sun, and inside Howth there is a magic town, the magic town of which you may have heard, also called Howth, for Manhattan has suffered enough (a funny thing to say), for Howth has got a radiant sickness, that of ambition, the *ambire*, the Italian verb around the plaza shaking hands is Howth, even as I observe a thousand suns across my long horizon Howth is digging with its brain as Hrothbert and his fellows examine their blueprints, Howth is shaping, Howth is moving, in its wonders in its sentiments, in its long divides and its long accidents, and Orkai, little scarred Orkai still well and a new man, Orkai young and broken but hopeful, Orkai from afar comes into Howth Castle and Environs in the district of Manhattan under the aegis of the Hierophant and of the Mayor and of a Reluctant Priest named Hrothbert and their wives, and little Orkai takes a look inside, inside the door ...

Howth is necessary, like a stent in a sclerotic vein, like a scout atop the rise to check mercenaries harried on to march upon your city.

Howth, like the map of the journey you did not know that you were taking. Or the picture of the afternoon that lasted forever.

* * *

"What do you think Isolde?" said Hrothbert. She smiled.

"Make a good door, honey. A good strong door to keep the dragons out."

Hrothbert held his computer and watched his instruments, adapting to their shades of feeling in his hands, inside his very eyes, he planned the razing of the ruins and the building of the nexus, the little hungry dervish, the water wheel for the hlafweard ...

A door.

"What is it, Hroth?" asked Orkai.

Hroth fashions it with dragon shapes inside his mind, curling their teeth into the flesh of the wood, as Perseus sowed the teeth of the dragon to make an army in Achaia.

The dragons curl, like hairs on an old man's head, eyes shining pearls, laughing with wide mouths and pointy teeth.

And one of the dragons had this to say:

"I'm not a dragon! I'm a boy!"

And the dragon was a boy. He was in a prison inside the dragon's head.

Nexus Howth, this new universe, is giving birth. Midwife, hear us roar our rage out on the stones at shore.

Only a metaphor, after all. Only an afterlife.

"I'm a boy!" And so he was. And he was a dragon, and he roared!

Let me tell you his story.

He knew there was a knight, in the long-ago, in Sicily, he knew the Normans were coming, he knew that they had told him an ancient secret in his dream, the name of his mother long-forgot, and he roared it over the valleys!

"Ostrogon!" For that was his mother's name.

"Its name is Ostrogon," said Hrothbert.

Did you think our world was made of anything other than stories?

The door was Ostrogon, the name of the dragon's mother. The dragon's cousins wound about his ashy face, to discourage liars and cheats from its eaves, to invite the bold.

"What next, honey?" said Hroth.

"A hall. And make a room for the baby too."

For all the little Ings. Scrabbling about in the earth.

A hall, as for a mountain king, a captain so of industry, a merchant of venice, or a viceroy, finance wizard, aging nobleman—a hall where stories are made, where they are spun, where the Hundert scall their mighty stones out for a pain and a pail, for a palaver and a gitty-up, a gruff grade of doves ...

"How do I make the hall, Orkai?"

"A fire," the boy said.

There was a fire, burning, inside stones. On the walls were many tapestries, of the battles fought in and for New York and for Howth, over the centuries.

Hrothbert cut through the hall, like Frank Lloyd Wright, the madman: a river, riverrun over Howth and its environs, into Howth and its environs, into the hall, and through the hall, the river ran, and in it was a god.

This god was angry for his daughter had run off with a financier, on a yacht, making love and drinking wine under the sun in the ocean, and the god called upon his cousin Poseidon, he of the deep, and Poseidon slew the yacht, with his wine-dark fingers, and the blood of the daughter commingled in the waves, an honor killing, and after the killing the god grew sad and killed himself, and his corpse became a home for fish and one of these fish was named Shplitch and he was a mighty fish with only one working eye and he sang into his watery night, there in his river, in the hall of Howth. His name was Shplitch and his stories were many, and he called his home inside the skull of the corpse of the river god.

And Hrothbert and Orkai and Daniel and Rell and Isolde and Wallru and Harry Patch and Hamid the baker and the Professor of Battery Park and the Manager and the Gardener and the Prescient and the boy with blazing rainbow eyes sat around the fire, warming their hands in the hall of Howth by the Ostrogon door, and they listened to the story of Shplitch, and his brother Horgo, from a time when they had swum out to the Atlantic Ocean.

Shplitch spoke, his teeth scraping against his shiny lips:

"I was swimming, to the east, and saw a great tree under the water. The tree spoke to me, and said, 'Fish! Come scratch my trunk!' and so I did, for it is a great boon to have a friend who is a tree, they are so long-lived, with many secrets and many friends, and I scratched the trunk of the tree with my tail."

Then Horgo spoke, his eyes wide and staring:

"I was swimming in the neighborhood and saw my brother and I said, 'Shplitch, what the heck are you doing!' And the mighty tree responded, there in the Atlantic, 'He's scratching my trunk.'

And pretty soon, we both were scratching it.

"And then we saw the sun course over the water, that it was near dark, and so we swam home."

And Splitch said:

"That was the first day of winter, and later that winter, Horgo swam away, and had an adventure, an adventure that he has never told me about, and what did you do, you crazy fish Horgo, leaving me here alone in this old river without my brother?"

"I went away, Shplitch, that's what brothers are for, to come and visit, and to go away ..."

"I like this hall, Hrothbert," said Orkai, who was sleepy, and he put his head on Hrothbert's shoulder.

And Hroth put his arm around the boy, and his hand inside of Isolde's, and listened to the fish spin another tale, a darker one.

Horgo's Tale

Horgo spoke to the dwellers in the hall, and his tale was strange.

"Wallru," said Horgo, "you know something of the wanderlust that strikes a fish, urging him to swim where no fish has in living memory, don't you?"

"Yes," said Wallru, "I know it well."

"Well that wanderlust came over me in the Season of Wasps, when the ocean was hot and my brother and his wife and our cousins were ornery, and one day I just swam off, where, I didn't know.

"I swam deep, deep into the sea, deeper than I had ever gone. And I saw the fire there, and the fire spoke:

"I am Stanislaw and I speak," it said to me.

I was frightened, and wanted to swim away, but something kept me there, in the deep, listening.

"I am Stanislaw and I speak for ages. Ages uncurled, and churls unwashed, I speak for misery, for Poland. I speak for the whale, and I speak for the gold in my tooth."

"I am only a fish," I said, "I know nothing of it."

"I know you are a fish, silly," said the fire in the deep, "now listen. I am concerned that you came into these here deeps not adequately prepared. Here you are conversing with me, for instance! It is fortunate that I am friendly! But still, you need forewarning, which is forearming, and so, let me warn you, here in the fiery deep there lives a man, a Fish Man, who takes fish and turns them strange, who casts an evil spell on them, and they are never heard from again."

"I thank you for your warning, fire, I shall be on the look out for it!"

"Forewarned is forearmed!" said Stanislaw, the fire in the deep.

I swam deeper, mesmerized by all I saw. I saw enough to spin a tale to sunder all the world. But I am only a fish.

Shplitch looked over at his brother, there in the water in the firelight of Howth Hall, and said:

"Horgo, tell them about the time you found the castle there, in the deepest part of the sea."

"I was getting to that," said Horgo testily, flexing his gills. "I swam deeper, though I was hungry and tired. I could see a light, and I swam towards it to see what it was, and it was a castle. I saw it. It was not unlike Howth, though of darker stone, with a more forbidding look. I swam right through the door, for it was open, and unguarded (which should have given me warning, but I was a younger fish then, and bold), and I met within a tall fish, pink in color, with many gills, its four eyes shining in the strange light that came out of the stones.

" 'Fish!' said this fish. 'Who are you?'

"'I am Horgo' I said, for I was, and still am, an honest fish.

"'Horgo! Horgo. Do many fish fore-go you, Horgo? Ho ho ho. Ha ha ha'

"The laugh of that fish, that pink four-eyed fish, was very disturbing—bubbling, and evil.

"'Horgo!' he said. 'I have for you a quest.'

"I'll say this, Hrothbert and your clan, that was my first quest. And after it, I never wanted another. Though in fact I had several, mostly because of that first one. Like the wise hobbit said, I try never to venture down from my door! But I did, and that pink fish gave me a quest:

"'Find the Woman of the Sea, Horgo! I want to talk to her!'

"I did find her. It took me many, many, seasons. When at last I found her I was a fish like Parsifal, almost forgetting that I was a fish named Horgo, on a stupid meaningless quest for a strange pink fish in a castle under the sea, but Horgo I was, still, and I found the Woman of the Sea upon the beach, in Sicily.

"And what I said to her that day would take longer than I have to tell you here, but the gist was this: I learned that day why there are fish, and why there are women.

"The Woman of the Sea agreed to come with me, and I brought her to the Pink Prince in his strange castle, and because I did so, and because they fell in love, the Woman of the Sea gave me that good Italian plate, that is hanging on the wall there, yellow and blue, on it the image of Sicily, the Woman of the Sea.

*   *   *

"I like that plate, Hrothbert," said Isolde, getting sleepy too. And by the fire they curled up to sleep, even the fish of the stream, and Wallru was the hero that night, standing up to watch in the hall, round his strange new family.

*　　*　　*

Inside the castle there is music, and I Hrudu Hrudu-ed shall sing for you, dear heart, a *chanson* of olden day, of love, and of Alaska.

A short song and a true one:
In Alaska! In Alaska in the winter, it is cold!
In Alaska it is cold and it is dark! In the winter.
When the sun has gone away.
When the dogs are sleeping.
When the world's gone.
In the dark, the child dreams,
Alaska, in the winter dark,
He dreams of music.

Even as that Alaskan boy dreams, so must Hrothbert, tired though he is, he dreams of the baby room, for it must be built. But Isolde was wise to put the baby room right in the hall, for babies grown in halls are popular babies, with the common touch, with an eye for all around them, grown by the hearth.

But still you need the mobile. You need the blankets, and the little fence to separate the dogs from baby (unless the parents let baby's favorite puppy inside).

So spin the mobile round, the universe. Spin the mobile round, its winding arms the winding night, the sail, flashing upon the ship—

(and the Manager departs, his crew inside their shining ship ... away into the distance!)

(into the sky ...)

World-Building

In your hand the little grain of sand, the center. And here, here, beyond it all, beyond everything you knew, is Howth, the strange center, eye of the storm, New York London Shanghai Berlin, Babylon—

A castle like a city is alive—magic.

Hrothbert had forgotten the rats. Rats know cities better than men and women. They know where all the traps lie, and where all the bodies are buried.

Slowly, the next morning, the people awoke. Hrothbert stood, and stretched, inside his new castle, inside the hall of Howth. He stroked Isolde's hair, and looked at his friend, Wallru.

"Thank you for Wallru," said Hrothbert, in a low voice.

Wallru smiled.

"The Manager departed?"

Wallru nodded.

Hrothbert made breakfast on the fire, and served his people and his guests. Now he was a host, in the only structure in Manhattan.

They began a song after their meal, while they washed the dishes, struggle and dark roads, and sweet valleys.

Hrothbert took Isolde's hand and asked,

"What do I build now?"

"You haven't built the baby room yet!"

And Hrothbert laughed, but Isolde did not, she frowned with her lip and made Hrothbert laugh again and then her eyes grew serious, and Hrothbert swept his hand across his nano-screen, and Daniel did the same with his, and they pondered the arrangement of the mobile:

From Second Earth, to First, to Third, Howth at Center, it spun like the tree beneath the sea, waving, waving its divine whisper for the coming bairn, in the corner of the stone hall, hanging from its gentle perch.

A powerful magic is a terrifying gift. Hrothbert went outside, to see the ruins, and Daniel came with him.

Hrothbert looked out over the ruins.

"Part of me died," he said. "I felt him die."

"Part of all of us died. But we're alive," said Daniel.

"Yes," said Hrothbert. "Do we scout a way to the Manager's realm now? I don't know what we need to build next. This Earth is young."

And Daniel laughed. "I feel like a madman, but I think you're right. We're building it, the part we need. Did the Manager leave a note? Directions? Did he just go while we slept?"

"I think he did. Let's go see what we can see."

They held hands.

Inside the hall they stretched their brains, looking for a corridor—

For a castle is protection. A castle is to rule. A castle is the keep to secret you and yours inside the dark, the castle is the draw, the obvious demise, the big man on campus to take the attacks of every newcomer, like Jupiter for Earth, absorbing the asteroids' blows, striking its bold pose. And then inside, the castle can be and often is a kingdom unto itself, taking on the character of its ruler, it is a map, a bloodied map, of strategy and its instantiation, the vehicle for domination, or for freedom, both.

For Ing ran after his vehicle. And Hrothbert came inside his own, moving—

In a core of light, he and his flew upwards into the sky, marking a division, limning a dawn in the space-time that they cored like an apple.

They were radiation, modulated and controlled.

"Which way is up?" said Hrothbert.

"Down," said Orkai, his eyes huge, smiling fearfully.

"Down," said Hrothbert in the nothingness of space, and a door opened, helpfully labeled, "Down."

"We must rewrite that label," said Daniel, and they did, together, scraping off the gold-lettered words and then scraping into the wood of the door with their knives: "Through."

And then they opened the re-labeled door, and walked into a field, and Wallru was there.

"What are you doing here, Hrothbert?" said Wallru.

"Looking for the Manager," he said.

"This place is not for you. How did you find me here?"

"What is it?" said Hrothbert.

"One of my homes," said the Fish Man, and he cried, into the sky, which echoed, far away.

"He is sad for this brother," said Daniel.

"How do you know?" said Hrothbert.

"This man listens," said Wallru. "You must go."

Orkai, Daniel and Wallru looked at Hrothbert.

"I can't, Wallru," said Hrothbert.

"Then you must learn what I had to learn, as a boy fish. To guide myself like wind. The last time you tried, you killed half yourself, fleeing into that desert and into the moon. I hope you've learned!"

A castle is so many things. Howth must rumble in a tomb of its ancestors, it must be elegy and fantasy, and it must be a light in the dark, small, the right size, lamp on seaside and in boats, a kybernetes, helmsman, helmsman, helmsman—

(coordinated)

They climbed inside Wallru's boat and were away, down the river, running—

Sounds and voices, in yellow and green coursed by their craft, moved through Hrothbert, and through Daniel, and Orkai. Wallru laughed at the helm, guiding them through disaster, and then the Fish Man turned and spoke:

"You must decide, hero, what roads you would have built. Now that you rule Manhattan. Shall it remain a center for trade, O son of Ing? If so we must have roads. Our several Earths are still young, and you have charted ways and paths unknown till know, because of a thousand reasons, and now we must decide which of these courses we shall keep and label true, for others to find their way."

"It should be a medium journey, to the Manager's realm. With some danger, but nothing too horrifying," said Hroth.

"Yes," said Orkai.

Encoded logics in the woof, on the hoof, riding weaving working corridors in time, coloring the landscape, shot ahead of Wallru and his boat, an instant and it was, and they were twisted back into their valley, green and bright, by their "Through" door.

"It's there now, if we need it, Hrothbert," said Wallru. He embraced his human friend, his brother, and they went back through the door and closed it behind them, back into the dark so full of stars.

"Where is my room, Hrothbert?" said Orkai, and Hrothbert smiled.

"What kind of room do you want, son?" said Hrothbert.

"I want a beanbag chair," said Orkai, and there was one, red. With a zipper on the side, its undulating shape a map of space-time itself.

Orkai sat in his chair in the starry space, warm sat in red, and he twisted in the course of that time, in the beveled edges of the worlds that were coming to be.

"Yes, yes, Hrothbert!" shouted Orkai, and Hrothbert laughed, and lifted Orkai from his beanbag chair in his distant tower room, a spy upon the manifold universe.

"We must dig a well," said Daniel, and Hrothbert agreed, and they dove down back into the Hall of Howth, and Isolde and Rell came with them into the earth, digging with the nanobots as my brother Wright had dug, so long ago it seems now, in another world.

And the river came there too, a deeper and more silent river, and the *neddinga* hailed them from the shore.

O *neddinga* in your long divines! What time's kiss must be foresworn for your forever undoing! Wroth and holden are your fiery swords beneath our several earths, inside our hearts!

They smiled in the dark and the people made their bows, and Wallru dove into the water, and made his way to them, exchanging some of his fish-people's gifts, and then Hrothbert dove in after, swimming across, and then Orkai, and then all of them, even Hamid the baker, swimming steadily across the river under Howth.

The old *nedding* greeted Orkai, tracing the boy-man's scar across his cheek.

"*Nedding*," said the old one.

"*Nedding*," said Orkai.

"The rats are angry, *nedding*. They say you have forgotten them."

"Are they dreaming yet?" said Hrothbert.

"They may be. But their dreaming is not the same, and it is dangerous. You must help them. Go that way—" and the old *nedding* gestured towards the darker tunnel, where the river ran below.

Hrothbert listed to the pooled antechamber of this darker tunnel, his friends around him.

"This will be the lonely part of Howth," said Hrothbert. "This is what we must leave here. The clown path will fade, I think, and this will be the stronger, though it is sadder and must be, to mark the loneliness of the rats. I should go on alone for this part. As I began."

"Take me with you, Hrothbert!" said Orkai.

"And me!" said Isolde.

"I want to," said Hrothbert.

"Haven't you done enough for the rats!" said Isolde.

"No. Not yet." And Hrothbert dove into the water, into the river, one of so many, there are so many, for love is a river, matter light and dark, love is a river through stars and under kingdoms, love in war and peace, birth and death, love in the castle of Howth and in each holt and heath of its environs, wilding their days across their many unnamed skies—

For who can name a sky! They are unnameable.

And in sadness we forget our names, often enough, and Murphy was there, singing and screaming in the Lethe dark alone, in the black purple water, and Hrothbert took the rat's cool wet body to his heart, and wept with the rat, beneath the stones beneath the city, two kings, rat and man, embraced in weeping, and so peace was declared, and a border agreed upon, for a hug in the wet.

"You must come further in," said Murphy, and he swam deeper into the lonely dark, and they heard behind them Orkai and Isolde splashing and swimming, following.

Hrothbert followed King Murphy the White Rat down the dark water.

*   *   *

In Howth Hall the President of the Earth, Harry Patch, sat by the fire, playing with his cel phone. And in the sky above Manhattan curled Red and Green.

Peace is always harder.

Why else would mourning become the helmsman? In his tears, he rows towards peace. Doesn't he?

BOOK FOURTEEN
Ouroborous

romises,

like Circe's water, the luster of a woman's form, her own, inviting, and apart, Hrothbert followed the rats in, in and down, again, down the river.

(Come in my boat, into my handful of dust, my shadow, says the river Liffey, come down with me to deltus Mississippi, down to the wide wise sea, and die there, die there for me.

We must not blame Reshh for being terrified of rivers; they are scary beings. For though a castle may link a thousand continents and dream beings indescribable into the world, a river runs over it all, water smoothing it down into dust).

Hrothbert swam down, following the white rat.

"This is my kingdom now, Hrothbert," said Murphy. "And one day, your kingdom will be like this too. I am Shelley for you, Ozymandias, the slave whispering into your triumphal ear. Come and see my stones."

On the river bottom he saw.

"This is our speech," said the rat.

And Hrothbert's blood, though it was already cold in the water, ran colder still.

"This river is our speech, and we don't remember now why your attack on us, why Ing's theft, or his horrible mercy, why it wounded us so much, why it took my fathers' fathers' fathers' dreams away, but it did. We are cousins, Hrothbert, the same blood, and this is why you hate us so, we are so close."

"What can I do, Murphy?"

"Just sit on these stones with me."

Hrothbert sat, and watched the seaweed wave in the current, and then he saw Wallru swim up, and the fish man smiled, with his merry strange eyes, and then he sat there too, watching the rat and the man.

After a time, Wallru took out a chisel, and on the stone there, he carved:

Fish, man and rat.
Sat here.

And he laughed his great laugh, there in the water, under Howth, in New York, on Third Earth, after Reshh was no more.

*   *   *

I must attend to my other responsibilities.

There were many Ings, and other heroes who were like him, on the many Earths that I have known. But this version cuts me the deepest, because it is the most unexplained, and explanations trouble me. At my age, I prefer mystery.

We are all grass, *mensch*. Know that my strong hind legs bound for you, even now. Wherever you are.

Rebecca's song

I heard you sway in the night.
The mid-Atlantic night, I saw you creaking,
Moving, gently, by the streetlight,
Old dreamer up too late,
Wide eyes,
Wild hair,
New Yorker,
New Yorker.
I saw it crumble ash,
When I was five,
When they brought the carpets round,
And told me I was dead,
That all was dead,
Flanders was no more,
I was no more,
All was no more,
My birth an error in some system I had never seen!
I sing of the city that was,
And the city that will be,
I sing of the thousand Yorks,
Old and New,
And the people who bear its stones,
Forwards,
Into the dark —
Bought for a song.
Bought for a song.
Bought for a lonely song.
Bought for a strong song.
Bought for a tired song.
Bought for a ready song.
And an unready one too, like Elfred's,
In the long ago York,
Under the Danelaw,
Under the prison of the sky,
Under the murder of my feet,
Inside my heart,
Inside my breast,
I bring only my small voice out of the mountain,

The mountain unredeemed,
Down to you,
My people,
My new people,
My new strange people,
So terrifying and so sad, so funny.
I dream, even now,
Of a new city,
Jetzt grosser ein Stadt,
Vaster yet,
Part a city of the mind,
And part a city of our several Earths,
The Earths we want and the Earths we have,
And the Earths we'll never see,
As long as we live,
And my dream is that—
So vast it terrifies me,
The scale and the scales, and the scales falling away,
Manhattan, your supper—

Acknowledgments

I am greatly indebted to Gary Stanfield for his book *Stanzas of the Old English Rune Poem*. Reading his erudite descriptions of the Old English runes reminds one how close, and how far, are our cousins the Anglo-Saxons. Stanfield's gloss on the identity of Ing, real or imagined, is the most compelling anywhere. It is his translation of the Old English Rune Poem that I use in this book.

Stanfield's articles are available here: http://runicwisdom.info/rwtoc.htm

I am grateful to Chapman University, for giving me my peculiar scholarly home here during our ongoing Second Great Depression.

Thanks to Professor Rebecca Goodman, who helped breathe life into this manuscript.

For their encouragement and love, I am grateful to Jan Lyle, John Ott, Sarah Kinga Smith, Krisztina Barabás, Iva Sijan, Hamid Mehyaad, Sam Barnett, and the Hodges Family.

Thanks to Natalia Andrievskikh at the *Yellow Medicine Review*, who published "The Dream of a Rat" as an excerpt.

Thanks also to the staff of the Edendale Public Library for putting up with all with the crazy homeless people, and all the crazy writers (not separate groups, by any means).

A special thanks to Barbara Sobczyńska, for her kind encouragement, and for making the beautiful cover to this book.

Robin Wyatt Dunn
Los Angeles, California — Orange, California
January 13, 2013 — January 5, 2014

Glossary of People and Places

"ALLEVA" , a pejorative term for an illegitimate child

ACHAIA, a region in ancient Greece

ADJUTANT, chief executive officer of Wessalim

ALASKA, a northern region of Armorica

AMBER ENGINE, a powerful object brought to Manhattan
         by John the Inspector

AMIKAH, a god of the Fall Country

ANDREI, a revolutionary

ARMORICA, a continent in the northern hemisphere
      of First Earth

ASH, a ghost of Eklaihah

AUCHARK, the name given to Makkina House by the *neddinga*

BATTERY PARK, the southern tip of Manhattan island

BEDFORD STUY, a neighborhood in Brooklyn

BREAD KEEPER, a Germanic title, meaning "lord"

BROOKLYN, one of New York City's five boroughs

CAROLINE, a diplomat

CEONTIES SLIP, an alley in old Manhattan

CIRCE, in Greek mythology, a sorceress and healer

CUYLERS ALLEY, an alley in Manhattan

DANELAW, a government of the Ingavones on
      First Earth in Ingland

DANIEL, HIEROPHANT, chief executive officer of the
         Western District of Manhattan

EKLAIHAH, a dead city

ELFRED, an ancient king of the Ingavones

ELIZABETH, Hrothbert's former wife

EMPLOYEE FIVE, of the Manager's crew, a prescient

EMPLOYEE FOUR, of the Manager's crew, a gardener

EMPLOYEE THREE, of the Manager's crew, a boy with with
        rainbow eyes

EMPLOYEE TWO, of the Manager's crew,
        a dancer and shapeshifer

FIRST EARTH, the homeworld of humanity

FRAGGERS TAVERN, an alley in Manhattan

FREY, the Earth goddess
GEEL, Tone Hadare's sergeant-at-arms
GRAYMALD, Bread-Keeper of the Ingavones on Second Earth
GREEN, an interdimensional being, Red's brother
GREENWICH VILLAGE, a neighborhood of Manhattan
GUERNSEY, a city to the west of Manhattan
GUNNHILDE, an ancient Swedish woman,
                 for whom guns are named
HAMID, a Manhattan baker
HARRY PATCH, a hero of The Great Manhattan War,
                 later President of the Earth
HECTOR VINOVIA, a New York prosecutor
HELL'S KITCHEN, a neighborhood in Manhattan
HORGO, a fish, Shplitch's brother
HOWTH, a castle in Dublin, Ireland
HROTHBERT, former priest of the Ingavones
HRUDU MAN, a giant metal interdimensional rabbit
ING, a hero
INGAVONES, a Germanic tribe of Second Earth
IOWA, a farming region in central Armorica
ISOLDE, a revolutionary
JOHN, THE INSPECTOR, an anarcho-syndacalist from Iowa
KALIFORNA, underneath the Fall Country,
                 a region split by civil war
KYBERNETES, ancient Greek word for "pilot"
LADY ASHFELL, a Manhattan noblewoman
LETHE, in Greek mythology, the river of forgetfulness
     in the underworld
LEYNE, Hrothbert's mistress in Wessalim
LORASH, a Fish-man, Wallru's brother
MAKKINA HOUSE, a city in the Fall Country
MANHATTAN, one of New York City's five boroughs
MICHAEL, a physician in Kaliforna
MR. BUBBLE, the monkey of Hell's Kitchen
MR. HU, a New York defense attorney
MRS. SPENCER, a resident of Manhattan
MURPHY, king of the rats

NEDDINGA, dwellers below
OCKK, a rat, Murphy's brother
OLIVER RUTEMBASA, General and Dictator of the
                    Eastern District of Manhattan
ORKAI, a boy of Wessalim
OSTROGON, the mother of the dragon of Howth Castle
OUROBOROUS, an ancient symbol of infinity,
                    a snake eating its own tail
OWNLEE, a rat
PARSIFAL, a legendary knight of King Arthur's,
                    subject to amnesia
PAXE, a preacher in Wessalim
PERSEUS, an ancient Greek hero who killed Medusa
PINK PRINCE, a fish Horgo met
PITTSBURGH, a city in Armorica
PROMETHEUS, Greek god who gave fire to Man
REALLEE, a rat
REBECCA, a rock star
RED, an interdimensional being, Green's brother
RELL, a woman from Guernsey, Daniel's wife
REN, former king of the Fall Country
RESHH, the god of the Manager's region,
                    as well as its high priest
ROHAN, a young homeless man in Manhattan
ROSS, a technician in Kaliforna
ROTH, the city of the rats
RUTH, queen of the rats
S.L., a kind spirit, from Poland
SAMUEL, an Ingavone, Hrothbert's companion after the war
                    in the Fall Country
SANTA, an interdimensional demon
SECOND EARTH, a colony of First Earth,
                    homeworld of the Ingavones
SHPLITCH, a fish living in Howth Castle
SIGNALMAN, a hermit living near Wessalim
SIONED, a secretary in Kaliforna
STEFAN, John the Inspector's son
STUYVESANT, a ruler of Manhattan in centuries past

THE BOLD WELD, an astronomical body, bordering
                the Manager's region of space
THE BOUNTY HUNTER, hired by Ressh to hunt the Manager
THE BRONX, a borough of New York City
THE GREAT TANGERINE, a nickname for New York
THE MANAGER, an interdimensional explorer, captain of his ship
THE PROFESSOR, a Manhattan ice cream connoisseur
THE WAILING DOOR, an inn in Wessalim
THIRD EARTH, a new world made after the wars
TONE HADARE, prince of Makkina House in the Fall County
UISGE BEATHA, whiskey, the water of life
VARDAL, Wallru's mother
WALLRU, a Fish-man
WESSALIM, a city in the Fall Country
WIGHT, a supernatural being
WILFRED OWEN, a poet of The Great War
WOMAN OF THE SEA, a mermaid princess Horgo met
WRIGHT, a metal rabbit, Hrudu's brother
YSEULT, a heroine

About the author

Robin Wyatt Dunn lives in southern California and is the author of three novels and three feature films. He was born in the Carter Administration. You can find him at www.robindunn.com, or email him at settdigger@gmail.com.